IT'S TIME TO TAKE
CARE OF THEMSELVES.

"Sweet child," Miss Addie said. "I don't want to leave you children home alone, but I can't sleep at some-one else's house. Not at my age."

"It's okay," I said. "We'll be all right tonight. And tomorrow night, if Old Finn still isn't home."

"We will?" Nightingale said.

"I have my bow and arrow," Baby chirped. "I could kill a burglar."

"You see," I said to Nightingale. "If Baby isn't worried, we shouldn't be worried either. We'll lock the doors, sleep here by ourselves. If trouble comes, we'll run down to Miss Addie's place."

"You're sure?" Miss Addie stood up slowly, held steady to her chair before she took a couple small steps from the table.

"Sure," I lied. Even if I wasn't, Miss Addie was already heading toward the door. We were on our own, whether we were ready now or not.

OTHER BOOKS YOU MAY ENJOY

KEEPING
SAFE
the
STARS

SHEILA
O'CONNOR

PUFFIN BOOKS
An Imprint of Penguin Group (USA)

PUFFIN BOOKS
Published by the Penguin Group
Penguin Group (USA) LLC
375 Hudson Street
New York, New York 10014

USA • Canada • UK • Ireland • Australia
New Zealand • India • South Africa • China

penguin.com
A Penguin Random House Company

First published in the United States of America by G. P. Putnam's Sons,
a division of Penguin Young Readers Group, 2012
Published by Puffin Books, an imprint of Penguin Young Readers Group, 2014

THE LIBRARY OF CONGRESS HAS CATALOGED THE G. P. PUTNAM'S SONS EDITION AS FOLLOWS:

O'Connor, Sheila.
Keeping safe the Stars / Sheila O'Connor.
p. cm.
Summary: In rural Minnesota in 1974, thirteen-year-old Pride Star, raised to be independent,
must accept help from friends and neighbors to care for eleven-year-old Nightingale and six-
year-old Baby when her grandfather is hospitalized with a brain infection.
[1. Self-reliance—Fiction. 2. Sick—Fiction. 3. Family life—Minnesota—Fiction.
4. Neighborliness—Fiction. 5. Orphans—Fiction. 6. Old age—Fiction.
7. Minnesota—History—20th century—Fiction.] I. Title.
PZ7.O22264Kee 2012
[Fic]—dc23
2011038846
ISBN 978-0-399-25459-8 (hc)

Puffin Books ISBN 978-0-14-242758-3

Printed in the United States of America

1 3 5 7 9 10 8 6 4 2

For
Bobby and Georgia O'Connor,
who taught us all what it means to be a family

and
Mikaela, Dylan, and Tim Frederick,
because everything begins and ends with you.

1

WAIT

It was Old Finn who sent us down the wood path to Miss Addie's. First he kissed us each good-bye and told us not to worry, then he said to stay put in Miss Addie's tiny trailer until he came home from St. John's.

Which is exactly what we did—me and Nightingale and Baby—we sat there at Miss Addie's cutting photographs from movie magazines, building paper towns, and stringing necklaces from noodles. We waited and we worried, even though Old Finn had told us that we shouldn't.

When darkness finally came, I opened Miss Addie's tattered phone book and hunted down the number for St. John's Hospital in town. "It's been too long," I said. "Old Finn only went in for a fever."

"He must be sick," Miss Addie said, concerned. "Your grandpa can't abide a doctor, so for him to drive into St. John's . . ."

Nightingale set down her noodle necklace; I saw my own

fear cross her silent face. I knew what she was thinking—she was thinking same as me—*What if something bad had happened to Old Finn?* Old Finn was our only known family, the last one left to love us. If we lost him, we'd end up all alone. At eighty-three, Miss Addie was too old to raise three kids.

"Maybe we should wait," Nightingale said.

"No," I said. "By now, Old Finn ought to be home." Somehow facing down our troubles was always up to me. Baby was just six and Nightingale too timid. Old Finn always said it was the burden of the oldest to see the worst before everybody else, to be on the watch for trouble so the younger Stars stayed safe.

I put my finger in the dial and started with the three. 3-6-7. Everyone was watching; I couldn't hear a single breath. "But, Pride . . . ," Nightingale started like she wanted me to stop. Her serious black eyes were full of worry.

"Perhaps I should be the one to speak," Miss Addie offered weakly. She stood up from her chair and shuffled toward the phone.

"Okay," I said. I knew St. John's would tell a grown-up more about a fever, even if Miss Addie wasn't half as self-reliant as the Stars. Most days it was us who tended to Miss Addie.

We all sat there still as stone while we watched Miss

Addie listen. "Oh dear," she finally said, and I heard in her hushed voice the news was bad. Baby snuggled close against my chest. "Well, yes, I'm the next of kin," Miss Addie answered, flustered. "Let me leave my number." *Next of kin* meant "family," but Miss Addie wasn't that. I couldn't believe Miss Addie had just lied. "All right," she said. "Thank you for your help."

She hung the heavy phone back on its hook, took a few long breaths like she was weighing how much trouble she ought to tell three kids. "I'm afraid," she said, a nervous warble rising in her voice. She fiddled with her wig of snowy ringlets. "Old Finn has some kind of infection. Some trouble with his brain."

"His brain?" Nightingale gasped. Old Finn's brain was full of history and Latin, algebra and physics, geography and ancient Greece. He had a head packed full of knowledge, some he tried to teach to us. Square roots, symphonies, and sonnets. "Old Finn can't lose his brain."

"Not lose." Miss Addie tried to say it cheerful, but still she worked her wrinkled hands into a knot. "Hopefully his trouble will just pass."

"But when's he coming back to Eden?" Baby asked. "Before we go to sleep?"

"Probably not," I said, because I knew the answer without Miss Addie even saying. I rubbed my hand over Baby's soft brown bristles. Baby kept his head shaved like Old

Finn, wore matching Wrangler jeans, cowboy boots they both bought at Newport Saddle. He'd been a miniature Old Finn ever since we moved to Eden.

"I imagine I'll have to keep you children here," Miss Addie said like she wasn't really certain.

"Here?" Baby's eyes grew huge. Miss Addie only had one narrow bed. There wasn't any place for us to sleep. The tiny trailer floor was covered with our crafts.

"But we're Old Finn's next of kin," Nightingale said, matter-of-fact. She was tucked up in the rocker, her knees up to her neck, her ruffled nightgown draped over her thin legs, her long black braids brushing her bare feet. "Why didn't you tell the truth?"

"Oh dear." Miss Addie shrugged, ashamed. "I didn't know what else to say." She shook her head like she wished she hadn't lied. "But when it comes down to you children, your grandpa doesn't want me passing information."

I thought about the visits from the county, how Old Finn worried every time that school woman came to check our lessons. Or how in Goodwell he'd walk away from questions he didn't like. *It's not anybody's business how we live at Eden*, Old Finn always said.

"Miss Addie's right," I said to Nightingale. "Old Finn wouldn't want a soul to know he's sick, or that we're left at Eden on our own. Even for one night."

"Maybe more," Miss Addie said as gently as she could. "We can't be certain what the future holds."

2

SELF-RELIANCE

Old Finn always joked he inherited Miss Addie—a retired, eccentric actress—as if she were some kind of keepsake his bachelor uncle, William Martin, left behind when he died and willed Eden to Old Finn. I only knew she'd been living on this land for years and years, long before Old Finn came from California; and when he made his home on William Martin's forty acres, Miss Addie just stayed put. Miss Addie and her craft projects and costumes, magazines and records, her little black-and-white TV, mounds of clutter that filled up most of the trailer.

"I'm afraid I wasn't set for company," Miss Addie fussed when she woke up the next morning. She looked ancient in her housedress, shrunk down to bone with sags of pale, paper skin. I missed her layers of makeup, her strings of beads and bangles, the lively flowered muumuus she wore during the day. "I've only got a smidgen left of milk. One small dish of Wheaties."

"That's okay," I said. After a night on Miss Addie's scratchy carpet, one flimsy sheet spread over us all, I was ready to head home. "We have plenty at the cabin." I sat up, gave Nightingale a nudge. I didn't want Miss Addie to feel bad about the food; she'd already divided her last can of mushroom soup for supper. Filled us up on stale saltines. "Come on, Baby." I shook his little shoulder. "It's morning now; we need to head on home."

"Home?" Baby rubbed his eyes.

Nightingale pulled the sheet up to her chin. "Home without Old Finn?"

"You sure you children can fix breakfast for yourselves?" Miss Addie asked.

"I'm thirteen," I said. "Been thirteen for three weeks. And Nightingale's on her way to twelve. Plus breakfast is my job." We all had jobs at Eden; Old Finn had been preaching self-reliance since the first day that we came. Nearly two years straight of self-reliance lessons. Independence. Even though I'd been standing steady on my own two feet since the day I learned to walk. Still it was Old Finn's self-reliance that taught me how to fix a toilet, change a fuse, brew potato soup for supper, weed the garden, and chop wood. It's why we had our school at his table instead of going into Goodwell like everybody else. After all that training, I didn't need Miss Addie's Wheaties to get by. "And until Old Finn gets done with his fever, we're going to have to practice independence, rise to the occasion."

Rise to the occasion was Old Finn's famous phrase—it meant tackling a problem whether you wanted to or not.

"I'll rise!" Baby jumped up to his feet. "I'll fry up the sausage. Spread jelly on the toast. Shoot a squirrel for supper."

I laughed at that last part; Baby always had a dream to hunt.

"Miss Addie, why don't you come with us to the cabin?" Nightingale urged. Miss Addie hardly ever left her trailer. Like Old Finn, she was happiest at home. "You can be our family for today."

"Oh dear." Miss Addie sighed. "It's such a long walk on that wood path, and Lady Jane will frighten if I leave." Right now, Miss Addie's golden tabby was curled up in her lap, but mostly Lady Jane stalked mice in the meadow or dozed lazy on the hood of Old Finn's truck.

"Lady Jane won't mind it for one day," Nightingale argued. I could tell she didn't want to go back to our cabin without a grown-up along, even one as frail as Miss Addie. Nightingale wasn't ready to face Eden all alone.

It was sad and strange to cross the dewy meadow, to know the cabin would be empty, that Old Finn would be gone. Atticus and Scout grazed peaceful in the pasture, but Old Finn's shadow, Woody Guthrie, moped sad-eyed in the yard. "Oh no," I moaned. In the worry of the night, Woody Guthrie had gone without his supper. Summers, Old Finn let the horses eat free off the land, but Woody Guthrie needed to be fed.

I called Woody Guthrie's name, gave a couple claps. Nightingale and Baby called him, too, but he just stayed there, staring; his spotted hound-dog head hung between his paws; his floppy ears draped on the ground like he didn't want to move an inch with Old Finn gone.

I ran ahead, left Nightingale and Baby to meander with Miss Addie; Miss Addie never moved too fast. Inside the silent cabin, Old Finn's coffee mug sat empty on the table; his dusty work boots stood beside the door. I grabbed Woody Guthrie's bowl and filled it with the last crumbs of broken kibble. Like Miss Addie's milk and Wheaties, Woody Guthrie's food was nearly gone.

I opened up the pantry. Old Finn's scribbled grocery list was taped up to the door. Friday was his shopping day in Goodwell, but when Friday came he'd barely left his bed. I added Miss Addie's milk and Wheaties, Woody Guthrie's Alpo.

I grabbed the eggs from the refrigerator, put a pat of butter in the pan, set the plates out on the table, poured Baby his milk. I was doing *first things first*, the way Old Finn always taught me. First I'd feed my family, then I'd ride to town for groceries. Groceries and a visit to St. John's.

3

MAKING DO

I'm riding in on Atticus," I said. I ran the water on our dishes, scrubbed the film of fried egg from our plates. "I'll leave him at the Junk and Stuff with Thor, just the way I've done it with Old Finn." Now and then, Old Finn and I would set off for a ride, a time for just the two of us to talk. And Thor's place was the closest you could get a horse to town.

"Alone?" Miss Addie rubbed her neck. I was glad she'd painted makeup on her face, clipped on her emerald earrings, put on a bright green muumuu; she didn't look quite so fragile anymore. "But it's another mile at least from the Junk and Stuff to town. You'd have to walk that highway."

"I can do all that, Miss Addie," I said. "I've got to shop for groceries. Old Finn couldn't go on Friday, and you need your milk and Wheaties; Woody Guthrie's kibble is all gone."

"I'll go, too," Nightingale offered.

"You will?" I asked. Like Old Finn and Miss Addie, Nightingale hardly ever wanted to leave Eden. "You've got to put on town clothes."

"I know." She frowned. Nightingale dressed in nightgowns the way other kids wore jeans. Flannel in the winter; cotton in the summer. Ruffled sleeves and fancy collars all year round. And she was always in bare feet. She'd been that way since we were little; it's how Mama landed on that nickname: Nightingale. It was the word Nightingale gave the sleep gowns Mama sewed. "I want another nightingale," she'd beg. And Nightingale stuck.

When we moved in with Old Finn, he didn't make a stink about the nightgowns, so long as Nightingale put on clothes for town. It's why she went to Goodwell only for the library and ice cream, a visit to the doctor now and then.

"Me, too!" Baby said. "I'm going into Goodwell."

"I can't take you, Baby. Not today." I didn't want Baby with me at St. John's, not until I saw Old Finn myself. "You stay here with Miss Addie."

"Yes." Miss Addie patted his small hand. "I need a friend here, Baby."

While Nightingale climbed up to our loft to dig through clothes, I sat at the table to work with Old Finn's list. Some things he'd written, like liverwurst and rump roast, razor blades and Borax, could wait till he was well. Miss Addie knew exactly what she needed: Velveeta, macaroni,

Wheaties, Wonder Bread, and milk. Seven different kinds of Campbell's soup. Oscar Mayer bologna. Gingersnaps and fresh saltines.

"I'm not sure what to buy," I told Miss Addie. "Old Finn makes the list; I just help him cook."

"It's easiest to think about the week," Miss Addie said. "Buy foods you can repeat, like macaroni. That's the way I do and I get by."

"Food we can repeat?" I said to Baby.

"Chocolate cake!" he clapped.

"That does sound delicious," Miss Addie added.

I opened up Old Finn's Goodwell Baptist cookbook and found the recipe I used for chocolate cake. We had everything I'd need except for eggs; I'd fried the last of them for breakfast. "We're all out of eggs," I said. "But I can buy those at the Junk and Stuff from Thor."

"First we ought to figure out the money, Pride," Nightingale called down from the loft. "We'll need it to buy groceries."

I hadn't thought about the money; I only knew we needed food to eat. It was Nightingale who had the gift for numbers. Letters, too. Of all of us, she took to Old Finn's schooling best. While I was tending to the horses or working in the woodshop with Old Finn, Nightingale balanced Old Finn's ledger, helped figure out the bills. She knew how money worked and where it went.

"Old Finn keeps ten dollars in the coffee can," she said. "But ten dollars won't go far."

I looked over at Miss Addie. Grown-ups had money. She could pay for food, just like she paid for movie magazines.

"I'm afraid I didn't earn much as an actress," Miss Addie said. "I write my list; your grandpa buys my groceries." I could tell she was embarrassed to have Old Finn buy her food. "But I never ask for much."

"You don't have any money?" Baby said. "Not a penny in your piggy bank?" Baby's piggy bank of pennies was a washed-clean tobacco tin.

"Just my two JFK half-dollars I've saved as souvenirs. But I'd hate to spend my souvenirs for soup." Miss Addie kept her JFKs hidden in her closet in a tiny velvet box with *Lovecraft Jewelry* written on the top. Sometimes she'd take them out to give a look or remember JFK. I wasn't spending Miss Addie's souvenirs; I'd buy her groceries same as Old Finn did.

"We have ten at least," I said. "That ought to be enough."

I climbed up on the counter, opened up the highest cupboard where Old Finn's secret coffee can was kept. Money for emergencies. One ten-dollar bill was folded up inside. "I'll just buy the little that we need. We've got potatoes in the pantry. Applesauce. Canned peaches we can eat."

"That's the spirit," Miss Addie said. "And I can go

without the gingersnaps and crackers. Velveeta, too. I can eat my macaroni with a little dab of butter."

"Butter?" Baby said. "I used the last for toast."

Butter, I wrote down on my list. *Milk. Eggs. Bread.* We could live awhile on sugar sandwiches and eggs.

4

PRIDE'S FIRST LIE

Woody Guthrie wanted to go with us, but halfway down the driveway I forced him to turn home. I had plans that didn't include a dog.

I rode up tall on Atticus the way Old Finn always did, while Nightingale trailed behind on Scout. At thirteen, I was a foot too tall to ride right on a pony, and Old Finn promised by the time I turned fourteen, I'd have a quarter horse like Atticus to ride. Nightingale was on the small side of eleven; she could ride another couple years on Scout. And Nightingale never rode Scout much outside of Eden; mostly it was me who liked the long rides with Old Finn.

When we reached the Junk & Stuff, I slid down off the saddle and opened up Thor's rusted corral gate. Maybe once there'd been horses on his land, but now it wasn't much more than a patch of weeds beside a weathered barn. "You girls come without Old Finn?" Thor asked. He was one of the only almost-friends Old Finn had in Goodwell. Thor and Nosy Nellie, the woman who sold Old Finn's wooden birds at the Northwood Nook in town.

"Yeah," I said. "We're riding in for groceries."

"Groceries?" Thor took off his seed cap and ran his hand over his bald head. In his dirty blue-jean bibs and ragged flannel shirt, Thor looked like a skinny scarecrow stuck out in some field. His face was long and blank, his nose too big, his crooked smile full of yellowed teeth. "Don't your grandpa drive into Goodwell for the groceries?"

"The truck's run into trouble," I lied. I'd spent the long ride getting ready for that story, thinking to myself just how I'd say it, letting Nightingale know it was ahead. A lie that wasn't any different from Miss Addie's *next of kin*. But the second that I said it, I had the sinking feeling Thor could see it in my eyes, the place Old Finn always said a lie would show.

"That so?" Thor gave a glance at Nightingale. "And what's this one's name again?" I was glad she'd traded in her gown for my old cutoff jeans. My cutoffs and a faded cotton T-shirt Mama used to wear. Clothes so big they bagged around her tiny body, but Nightingale never wanted to buy clothes of her own.

"Elise," I said. We always used our given names in town. Baby's name was Baxter; my real name was Kathleen, but at Eden, safe with family, we all preferred the nicknames Mama gave us long ago.

"Well, her braids are almost dragging in the dirt," Thor

joked, but Nightingale didn't give back a laugh. They weren't dragging in the dirt, but they hung long, just beyond her waist; maybe in a few more years they'd drag down to the dirt. "Wish I had a head of hair like that," Thor said with a wink. The only hair Thor had was a little band of white between his ears.

"She's been growing out her hair since she was six," I answered to be friendly. Nightingale hardly had a word for anyone but family, family and Miss Addie and that bee-hived hairdo lady at the library who helped her pick out books. "And she's eleven now, so that's five long years of hair."

I took the tack off the horses, hung it on the fence, pulled the hose over to the trough, and turned it on. I'd done this same routine enough times with Old Finn, and every time, Thor just stood by like a scarecrow and watched. People on his land didn't bother Thor.

"So that's the trick," Thor said with a wink. "Think five years would grow this hair of mine?"

"Probably not," I said, embarrassed. Thor hardly had hair enough to grow.

"Well, all that hair can't take the place of shoes." Thor nodded down toward Nightingale's feet.

"She's got shoes there in her sack," I said. Nightingale wasn't going barefoot to St. John's.

Thor sank his hands into the pockets of his rumpled overalls; every time I saw Thor he was dressed in blue-jean bibs. Same way Nightingale wore gowns, and Old Finn wore his Wranglers and plaid shirts. I liked pastel summer T-shirts with butterflies and peace signs, turtlenecks in winter, bell-bottoms all year round, but I didn't stick to one look every day. "You can't walk a mile back here hauling groceries. Not along that highway."

The second that he said it I realized he was right. Just Woody Guthrie's kibble was too much to haul home. I looked around the yard for a thing to help us carry. The Junk & Stuff was little more than Thor's small house, a chicken coop, that weathered barn, and a big dirt yard where the flea market set up every other Saturday in summer. It's why he always let us leave the horses here; there was nothing on his land the two could hurt.

"What about your wheelbarrow?" I pointed to the rusted wheelbarrow propped against the coop. "You think that we could take it into Goodwell?"

"You'll wheel that a mile on the highway?" Thor said, surprised. "Then turn around and wheel it back this way?"

"I will," I said. "I'm strong enough for that. And then I'll buy a dozen eggs to boot."

He gave a little laugh. *A dozen eggs to boot* was Old Finn's phrase. "Well, listen here," he said. "If your grandpa's truck is down, I can drive you to the Need-More. Got to get some groceries there myself. I'm safe enough." Thor chuckled. "You know I drive the school bus for Goodwell."

"No thanks," I said. Even if he let us leave our horses and

17

even if he was Old Finn's almost-friend, I didn't want Thor to know we were at Eden all alone. Or that Old Finn was sick now at St. John's. And St. John's was the place we needed most to be. "We need to walk in on our own so Elise can earn her badge. Girl Scouts," I said, like that should be enough. I don't know how that new lie crossed my mind. Neither of us had ever been a Girl Scout, but last year Nightingale had bought a Junior Girl Scout Handbook for a nickel from a woman at the Junk & Stuff, and this summer the three of us had worked to earn some badges, even Baby, who didn't count as a girl.

"Girl Scouts?" Thor said. "They got scouts grocery shopping now?"

"Homemaker badge," I said to sound official. I wasn't even sure that badge was in the book. Nightingale nudged me with her elbow.

"Well, then." Thor nodded. "You tell your grandpa that I offered."

"I will," I promised. "I'll tell him that you did."

5

DOER; DREAMER; DARER

You lied twice," Nightingale said, alarmed. I looked back toward the Junk & Stuff; Thor was still in that same spot, watching the two of us cross his land out to the highway. "And he didn't believe the part about the badge. He knew that was a lie." Nightingale hated lies—even little white ones. Old Finn said she was a stickler for truth.

"Couldn't be helped," I said. I steered the wheelbarrow down into the ditch. Old Finn never let us walk along the shoulder. "You know Old Finn doesn't want folks in his business. And he won't want anyone to know he left us out at Eden all alone. Not anybody. He won't want the county to get called."

Old Finn disliked the county, same way he disliked all government, the war in Vietnam, and Richard Nixon. It's why the FBI kept a file on Old Finn, followed him around in California, kept track of the history he taught, the books he wrote, the meetings he attended, the help he gave to young men who didn't want to go to war. He told us it was all those people watching that made him give up on the world and move to Eden, take up his peaceful carving, tend his land, live a life with animals alone. He didn't want another word written in that file.

What the government gives, he told us in our lessons, *the government can take.* And every time he said it, we knew that he meant us.

"But we should just keep quiet," Nightingale argued. "Quiet would be better than a lie."

"Sometimes quiet doesn't work, Night," I said. "Not everyone gets by without a word."

Old Finn always said the sixteen months between us might as well have been the world. Nightingale and I were so night and day we hardly even looked like sisters. She was small and silent, dark eyed and dark haired just like Daddy, book smart and private like Old Finn. I was tall and talkative, gray eyed with dirt-brown hair, sturdy and strong-minded just like Mama, quick to act, fast to make decisions. Mama used to say I came to earth a doer. Nightingale a dreamer. Baby came to earth a darer—it's why he tried to fly and why he had twelve stitches in his chin.

Still, different as the Stars were, all of us were part of the same heart—Mama's heart—and even gone, her love kept us a family. No matter what, we hardly ever fought. I didn't want to fight with Nightingale now.

The two of us trudged along in silence, the sun beating

on our shoulders, the ditch weeds slapping at our skin. Hard as I tried, I couldn't keep the wheelbarrow from catching in the ruts. Hot blisters rose up on my palms.

"Thor won't ever know," I finally said to break the silence. I didn't want Old Finn to see us in a fight.

"It's still a lie," Nightingale insisted.

"It doesn't matter now," I said with a sigh. The Texaco was up ahead, and after that the Cat's Pajamas, an antiques store where tourists liked to shop. Goodwell Pie Place. Butler's Bait and Tackle with the giant walleye hanging out in front. "We're almost to Old Finn. He'll be the one to tell us what to do."

St. John's smelled just like the dentist's—floor wax and disinfectant and old lady perfume.

"Michael Finnegan," I asked at the front desk. The clerk didn't look much older than thirteen—fourteen, maybe fifteen—but she had that perky-bright-blond-ponytailed look from teen-girl magazines. Plus frosty lips and painted nails and a starchy, pink-striped dress. I wished I had my own job at St. John's so I could be here with Old Finn, earn money for our family, and wear a fancy name pin just like *Suzy*. Pink and perky Suzy. Only mine would say *Kathleen*.

She flipped through a roll of cards, then wrote a number on a little slip of paper. "Just so you know," she said, "I'm not sure he's having visitors today. Stop by at the nurses' station first."

"No visitors?" But we had to see Old Finn. Self-reliant as we were, we still needed Old Finn to say what ought to happen next, how long we'd be at Eden on our own.

"I don't know." Suzy shrugged. "Sometimes, they're just too sick."

"Too sick?" Nightingale asked.

"He's not," I said. I didn't want Nightingale scared.

Suzy looked beyond us toward the glassy entrance where we'd left the rusted wheelbarrow parked right out in front. "Is there a reason for that thing?" She wrinkled up her perfect, perky nose. Mine was wide and flat and speckled brown from too much sun. "Are you gardening in Goodwell?"

"Buying groceries for my family," I said proudly. Buying groceries was a job just as much as sitting at a lobby desk flipping through some names. I only wished I had a uniform to wear.

"Okay," she scoffed. "But the wheelbarrow's weird."

6

OLD FINN

Old Finn's nurse wouldn't let us in his room. Instead she walked us down the hallway, opened up the door a little crack, and let us have a glimpse of Old Finn dead asleep, his mouth open in an O, his whiskered face dropped over to the side. For the first time in my life Old Finn looked *old*, broken-down in a way he'd never been. Old Finn chainsawed trees, hoisted bales of hay, put a new roof on the work shop. He still galloped Baby three times through the meadow before we went to sleep. Old Finn was strong enough to do the same with Nightingale and me, but we were just too big for games of horse.

"What are all those things?" I whispered. I could see Old Finn must have needed rest.

"What things?" she asked.

I pointed to the tubes and wires snaking from Old Finn, the machines beside his bed. Old Finn wouldn't want to be connected to machines.

"Just medicine." She glanced at Old Finn's chart. "Are

you girls related to Mr. Finnegan?" She looked at us suspiciously, narrowed her eyes at Nightingale dressed in Mama's baggy shirt.

Bernice, her name tag said, but she had the same bright-white blond hair as perky Suzy, the same frosty pink smeared over her lips.

"He's our grandpa," Nightingale answered like she'd already forgotten to keep our business to ourselves. She stared in at Old Finn, her hand pressed against her chest as if she had it on his heart.

"But why is he so sick with just a fever?" I didn't understand how Old Finn went from well, to sick in bed with just a fever, to wired up in some strange hospital in just a few days' time. It made me think of Mama leaving us one morning, and by afternoon the sheriff was standing in the driveway saying she was dead. I didn't want to lose Old Finn like that.

"Is your mother with you girls by any chance?" Bernice asked me. "Or will she be in today? We'd like to speak with family."

"She might," I lied. Nightingale stepped hard on my foot. I hoped up there in heaven Mama would forgive me.

"And is your mother Addie Lee?" Bernice glanced at a note in Old Finn's chart. "Addie Lee?" she said again. "She's listed as the next of kin."

"Mmm-hmmm," I said. I couldn't take that lie much

further than a hum. Miss Addie was too old to be our mother; if we brought her to St. John's, the nurse would see that for herself.

"We've phoned your home but we haven't got an answer," Bernice said. Not our house, we didn't even own a phone; it must have been Miss Addie's that she meant. And Miss Addie was at our cabin now.

"But when will he be well?" Nightingale's big black eyes were wet with worry.

The nurse hung Old Finn's chart back on a hook, opened up her desk drawer, and handed us two quarters. "Here," she said. "Why don't you run along? The hospital's no place to waste a day. You girls go buy yourselves an ice cream at the Butternut. Your grandpa needs to rest."

"We'll watch him rest," I said. Old Finn would never leave us sick all by ourselves. Last winter, when I had scarlet fever, he hardly left my side.

"Not today," she said. "A hospital is no place for you children."

"Can we come again tomorrow?" I said. "Do you think he'll be awake?"

"I'm afraid that I can't say," Bernice said kindly. "But tell your mother the staff would like to see her. To put a plan in place. We'd like to work with family if we could."

"We're family," I said. She could tell me whatever she'd tell Mama.

"I know." She smiled. "But we'd prefer your mother would come in."

"He's really sick," Nightingale blurted when we stepped into the lobby. "Really, really sick."

"Just for today," I said to cheer her up. "Tomorrow he'll be better."

"The nurse didn't tell us that." Nightingale looked so small and orphaned standing in that lobby, like a stray in long black braids and Mama's faded shirt. A single tear washed a path along her cheek. Both of us were dusty from the ditch. "And, Pride," she creaked, "Miss Addie isn't Mama."

"I know," I said. I didn't want Suzy in her uniform to hear about my lies. I put my arm over Nightingale's shoulder, nudged her through the door and out onto the sidewalk. "I didn't say that she was. I only gave a hum."

"But what if Mama heard you?"

"She didn't," I said. I used to think Mama watched me every day, that even up in heaven she could see inside my soul. But the longer she was gone the less I could believe it.

"But God did," Nightingale said. "And what if all your lies make Old Finn worse?"

Nightingale had a fairy-tale brain; it's why she thought her nightgowns were real dresses. Most days she disappeared into the make-believe of stories, book after book, but she didn't think of those as lies.

"They won't," I said. "God doesn't work that way." I didn't really know how God worked, but no good god would make Old Finn get worse.

"But now they want to meet with Mama," Nightingale said. "And Miss Addie is too old."

"I know," I said again. I grabbed the wheelbarrow handles and steered it toward the street. "Don't worry, Night, I'll get it figured out."

7

IMPEACH

I didn't have the answer to the fever or how long we'd be alone at Eden or how I'd get someone who looked like Mama to go into St. John's, but I could buy our groceries at the Need-More, check things off the list while Nightingale added all the numbers in her head. And I felt better being busy, better working for my family than standing on that sidewalk watching Nightingale fret. I filled the cart with all Miss Addie's groceries, including her Velveeta so she wouldn't go without, plus milk and butter, Wonder Bread and Alpo, four cans of SpaghettiOs and Sugar Smacks for us. Baby always begged Old Finn for Sugar Smacks.

When we finished with the groceries, we had twenty-seven cents left of Old Finn's money and Bernice's ice-cream quarters just waiting to be spent.

"What about the Butternut?" I said. We needed something happy to get our minds off Old Finn, how broken-down he'd been in that small bed, all those strange machines, the way Bernice wouldn't say when he'd be well. "Let's buy ourselves a treat."

"We should save." Nightingale slipped the coins into her pocket. "Just in case we need more money up ahead."

"We'll save the twenty-seven cents," I said. "But we ought to get the ice cream Bernice wanted us to buy."

When we stepped into the cool of the Butternut Café, I saw right away it buzzed with some big news. The radio beside the register was on, and both the summer tourists and locals leaned in that direction just to listen.

"I can't believe our country's come to this," the waitress said. She splashed a stream of coffee into a cup.

"You're telling me." An old man shook his head. "I voted for him twice."

"My kids can't even watch cartoons," one woman added. "I wish just once they'd shut this garbage off."

I knew then they were talking about Nixon. The trouble with the president was always on TV, boring daytime hearings that interrupted Miss Addie's favorite shows. Old Finn didn't own a TV, but I sometimes watched the Nixon troubles on Miss Addie's little black-and-white. I didn't understand what Nixon did exactly, but Old Finn said he lied to save his skin. Tricky Dick, he called him. And Old Finn said he ought to be in prison like every other crook.

"He's going to be impeached," somebody else said. "That's how it looks this morning."

"Impeached?" I said to Nightingale; she always knew strange words. It made me think he'd be cut up like a peach, set out on a platter, or diced into a jar. Or else a sword would be stuck straight through his chest. "Doesn't that mean something with a sword?" I asked.

"A sword?" Nightingale squinted. She laughed for the first time since we'd left the house that morning. "That's impaled, Pride."

Nightingale made us eat our ice cream on the curb, same place we always ate when we came in with Old Finn. The two of them couldn't bear a place packed full of people.

"What's that mean, impeached?" I asked again. I was glad to find another subject besides Old Finn in that bed. I ran my tongue along the ribbons of thick fudge. Fudge swirl for me; banana nut for Nightingale. Baby liked plain strawberry and Old Finn licorice ice. It made me sad to eat a cone without Baby or Old Finn.

"I think it means he's going to get in trouble. Old Finn always said he'd get what he deserved."

"What's that?" I asked. I didn't know enough to know what he deserved. It was Nightingale who asked Old Finn all the questions about Nixon.

"It means he could lose the job of president for lying. All those lies, they're finally catching up."

• • •

When we wheeled up to the Junk & Stuff, Thor was on his front step sorting through a box of broken doorknobs—glass and brass and silver. He didn't look too worried about Nixon.

"You must have some strength," Thor said to me. He nodded toward the groceries, Woody Guthrie's bag of food. "That's quite a load you're steering."

My muscles burned, I had blisters on my palms, but I was proud I'd made it back from Goodwell. I could carry Baby, split wood, build a fire by myself. Saddle Atticus without an ounce of trouble. Now I could get our groceries, keep food in our bellies until Old Finn got well.

"I got those eggs," he said. He reached over toward the porch, lifted the gray carton from the railing.

"The eggs!" I turned to Nightingale. "You forgot to save money for the eggs. I can't bake the cake without them."

"We got twenty-seven cents." She reached into her pocket.

"The eggs'll cost us forty." I pointed to a tattered cardboard sign tacked up on the coop.

"Twenty-seven cents would suit me fine." Thor pulled the rumpled red bandana from his back pocket, dabbed it at the backside of his neck.

"I'll bring the rest tomorrow," I said. Old Finn didn't believe in charity. He told us taking always ended up as owing, that people gave to get, that in the end there wasn't a lender you could trust. I didn't want to owe money to Thor.

"You just repay me with that cake. Next time you come this way I'll take a slice." He lifted up the Alpo. "You girls can't get all this food home on a horse. You earned your badge, why don't you let me drive the groceries to your place. Give your grandpa a hand with that bum truck."

Nightingale stabbed me with her elbow.

"No, sir," I said. "We haven't earned it yet. We still got to get the food back by ourselves." If Thor drove us out to Eden he'd see Old Finn was gone.

"Then you're gonna need some stronger sacks," he said. "I got some old seed sacks in the barn. That paper won't hold out."

Thor helped us tie the seed sacks to our saddles, then loaded up our bags. "I can see," he said, "you girls got your grandpa's independence—he always has to take things on his terms. Apple didn't fall far from the tree." He gave Atticus's neck a gentle pat.

"I guess." Mama used to say the same about Old Finn. *My father takes life only on his terms.*

Thor laughed. "Hard to think two girls can be so head-strong."

I couldn't tell if he meant it good or bad. I nudged my heels into Atticus's sides; I was ready for the privacy of Eden. "We'll get your seed sacks back."

"Don't hurt none to lend a hand to neighbors," he said.

"Just this May, your grandpa helped me mend that broken fence. Put a new roof on my place."

"I know," I said. "He was happy to help out." Old Finn gave. It was taking help from others he didn't like.

"Me, too," Thor said. "That's why folks are here."

8

READY NOW OR NOT

Mama wasn't speaking to Old Finn when Daddy died of cancer. She didn't invite him to Serenity for Daddy's funeral or send a picture two weeks later when Baby was first born. Mama said it was because Old Finn didn't understand interdependence or why she and Daddy moved us to a commune, a living-all-together place in the mountains of New Mexico. Later, Old Finn told me it was the leader of Serenity, Daniel Walker, he didn't like. Old Finn said Daniel Walker wasn't fit to lead a dog, and smart people like our parents should have seen that for themselves.

I think Old Finn was right because four years after we'd scattered Daddy's ashes, Daniel Walker accidentally crashed the peace van he was driving, killing everybody in it in an instant, even Mama, and leaving us alone with no one in the world. By then, we didn't even have an address for Old Finn.

That's why the sheriff took us from Serenity and put us in the shelter, a crowded old motel run by the county, a crabby place that mostly kept rough kids. A place where Nightingale cried herself to sleep, and the big boys bullied Baby, shoved him down the stairs, took away his toys. A place where Mrs. Traynor lined the children up for lice checks, and Miss Hawkins threatened to shave off all our hair, even Nightingale's long braids she'd been growing like a garden. A place where some mean girl broke my locket, and Miss Hawkins said I knew less than a nit, all because I told her it was Nightingale's human right to keep her braids. And everyone made jokes about Serenity, called us Commune Kids and Flower Power Freaks. And no one cared that Mama was just gone.

And then one day Old Finn arrived from Goodwell, a man big as a bear, with thick, strong arms, Mama's wide, smooth face, kind gray eyes identical to Mama's, and short white hair shaved down to bristles on his head. He got down on his knees, squeezed the three of us so hard he almost took my breath, and he promised us he'd get us from the county, go through the court, jump through all their legal hoops, work through their red tape, and as soon as that was finished he was taking home the Stars.

Which is exactly what he did. And three weeks after Mama died we had a new home here at Eden.

I knew we owed our good life to Old Finn. It was Old Finn who got us from the county, who always said his job was keeping safe the Stars. So if I had to tell a few white lies or ride horseback miles through the heat or wheel groceries home from Goodwell, I didn't mind so much because I knew it's what Old Finn would want. He'd want to keep the Stars out of a shelter or sent away to fosters, the kind of horrible things that happened when a guardian was gone. A lesson we learned well when we lost Mama.

"We're going to need some quiet." I thumped a wooden spoon against the table; we'd held lots of family meetings, but always with Old Finn.

"Pride," Nightingale argued. "Quit acting like the boss."

Acting like the boss was in my blood; Mama always joked I'd been born bossy, but Nightingale hated to be bossed. "Okay." I shrugged and tore a sheet of paper from the teaching tablet Old Finn used for school. "You go ahead and start." I handed Nightingale our shoe box of old crayons. "You make a list of how we'll all survive."

Nightingale pulled out a purple crayon, then she stared down at the paper like she wanted her first sentence to be perfect, just the way she did when we had to write a composition for Old Finn.

"Go ahead," Baby said. He was born impatient.

Finally, Nightingale printed out a number one.

1. Say a hundred prayers a day for Old Finn's brain.
2. Stop with all the lying. (PRIDE!)
3. Get back to our lessons.

I couldn't believe Nightingale wrote that; if it were up to me we'd take these few days off. Kids weren't even meant to be in school in the summer, but Old Finn made us have our lessons all year long.

4. Earn the money to pay Thor his thirteen cents. And more if we need groceries.

"That's good," I said. "But we can get the thirteen cents from Baby."

"Take my pennies?" Baby fussed. "But I don't want to give those up."

"It's just thirteen," I said to Baby. "Thirteen pennies isn't much. But a hundred prayers a day?" I looked at Nightingale. "Who's going to say all those?"

"I thought we could divide. Thirty-three apiece. Thirty-four for me. Or twenty-five if Miss Addie wants to join."

"Of course." Miss Addie nodded. "I will pray." She was drooping at the table, dozing on and off. The long day spent at our cabin had worn Miss Addie out.

Nightingale passed the shoe box on to Baby. He was just learning how to print, so instead he made a drawing. He drew the three of us holding hands under a rainbow with Woody Guthrie sleeping at our feet (just the way that he was right now) and Miss Addie in her ringlet wig standing near her trailer. And up above the rainbow, he drew a man that had to be Old Finn. Old Finn or God, but it was Nightingale who mostly thought of God.

"This is what I want," Baby said. "I want my family safe. And for me to get my thirteen pennies back. I've only saved to forty-six so far."

"You'll get them back." I kissed his bristled head. "I promise you that, Baby. And I'm going to keep you safe."

"You go now." Baby passed the crayon box to Miss Addie.

"I don't know," she stammered. "I'm not really family." Up until last night, Miss Addie was a friend, an old actress who occupied a little patch of Eden, and I had a hunch she didn't want to be much more.

"We need you in our family," Nightingale said. "You're the only grown-up we've got."

"Isn't that a sorry state?" Miss Addie fiddled with her earring. "I don't think your grandpa meant to leave you here with me."

"He said we ought to wait there at your trailer," Baby said.

I squeezed her hand; I didn't want Miss Addie giving up on us. "And so far we've done just fine."

"Let's hope." Miss Addie sighed like she wasn't quite so sure. She sifted through the crayon box until she landed on the color that matched the rose red of her lipstick and her nails.

I don't know, she wrote in shaky cursive, then she stopped.

She set the crayon down on the paper. "I don't know where I'll sleep," she said. "I already miss my trailer. Lady Jane must be meowing at my door." Lady Jane was probably mousing in the barn or curled up in the hay. "I'm afraid I can't stay here."

"You want to leave?" Nightingale said like she hoped it wasn't so.

"Sweet child," Miss Addie said. "I don't want to leave you children home alone, but I can't sleep at someone else's house. Not at my age."

"It's okay," I said. "We'll be all right tonight. And tomorrow night, if Old Finn still isn't home."

"We will?" Nightingale said.

"I have my bow and arrow," Baby chirped. "I could kill a burglar."

"You see," I said to Nightingale. "If Baby isn't worried, we shouldn't be worried either. We'll lock the doors, sleep here by ourselves. If trouble comes, we'll run down to Miss Addie's place."

"You're sure?" Miss Addie stood up slowly, held steady to her chair before she took a couple small steps from the table.

"Sure," I lied. Even if I wasn't, Miss Addie was already heading toward the door. We were on our own, whether we were ready now or not.

9

WISH YOU WERE HERE

The three of us didn't sleep up in our loft. Instead we left on every light inside the cabin and climbed into Old Finn's bed where the smell of hard work was still clinging to his sheets. Minty soap and sawdust, garden dirt and grass, summer sweat from the hours he spent tending Eden. At the bottom of the bed, Woody Guthrie was snoring on my feet; even Woody Guthrie wouldn't stand guard.

At every little creak we'd startle, huddle closer. Just the sound of branches scratching at the screen gave us all a scare. Finally, Nightingale said we'd feel safer saying prayers, our twenty-five apiece for Old Finn's brain, but I didn't even make it up to five. I couldn't keep my mind on praying; I still had the problem with the hospital to solve. That nurse, Bernice, expected to meet Mama.

When Nightingale and Baby had the heavy breath of sleep, I climbed out of Old Finn's bed, went out to the sofa to sit there by myself. I couldn't think with all that sleepy breathing going on. By tomorrow, someone needed to be Mama. Someone would have to go into the hospital to talk about Old Finn.

I need someone to be you, I thought to Mama.

That's you, she said to me. *You're my spitting image.* Old Finn always said I looked like Mama; Mama said it, too, but I couldn't see myself growing up to be as pretty as she was. Maybe one day my freckles would fade like Mama's did, and my teeth wouldn't look so big, or my legs and arms too long for my body. Maybe my thick brown hair wouldn't tangle into frizz. But that day seemed a long time off right now.

I try, I said. *I'm tall like you now, Mama.* I knew Mama's voice was only in my memory, but it helped my heart to imagine she could hear. *I even have your big, long feet. I'm size seven now.*

My pride and joy, Mama said. *I can always count on you, Pride.* I pictured Mama setting Baby in my lap the way she used to do when she was busy fixing supper.

You can, I said. *Though I wish that you were here.*

When I woke up the next morning, Mama's visit was almost like a dream. The sun was shining in the window; Woody Guthrie was whining at the door.

I'm down at Miss Addie's, I wrote to Nightingale and Baby. Both of them were still in bed asleep. *We've got Sugar Smacks for breakfast.* I set the box out on the table with two bowls and two spoons. Tomorrow, I'd fry up eggs or pancakes, but I still had a chocolate cake to bake before my trip to town.

Outside, I raced across the dewy meadow, past Atticus and Scout, and Lady Jane already stalking bugs in the tall grass. Through the windows of the trailer, I could hear Miss Addie's small TV; Miss Addie always kept her TV loud.

"Pride?" Miss Addie looked surprised when she opened up the door. "Is everything all right, child?" A nervous rattle trembled in her words.

"We made it through the night," I said.

"Oh, good," Miss Addie said like she'd forgotten that she'd left us. Or maybe she'd forgotten Old Finn was in St. John's.

"This business with the president." She hobbled toward her TV and shut it off. "I'm sad to say I lived to see a thing like this."

"I know," I said, but I didn't care about Nixon. Washington, D.C., was too far away to matter to me now. All that really mattered was Old Finn.

"Your grandpa will be happy to see that man impeached."

"I'll tell him when I see him. I'm riding in today."

"Again?" Miss Addie frowned. "All the way to Goodwell on that horse?"

"Thing is," I said, "I can't go as myself. I'm going to need a costume. Some makeup for the trip."

"Makeup!" Miss Addie said, excited. She was always

after me to put makeup on my face, to pat on the crusty powder that covered her old skin, but I didn't want to be orange skinned like Miss Addie. "You're growing up, dear Pride!"

"Maybe some," I said, if makeup made me older. "I just need to look as old as Mama." We still hadn't told Miss Addie that the hospital thought that she was Mama. Nightingale said my lie might set off a nervous spell, wear down Miss Addie's anxious heart. "The hospital, they want Mama to come in."

Miss Addie blinked, confused. "They don't know your mama's gone?" she asked as gently as she could.

"No," I said. "And I didn't want to tell them we were out here on our own, because Old Finn wouldn't want that. So instead I have to go as Mama."

"You?" Miss Addie shook her head. "I have a gift for makeup from the days I was an actress. I could paint you up to twenty, but I'm afraid your mama would be thirty now at least."

"I know," I said. "But maybe with your wig? That long black one I used to wear for dress-up?"

"My Cleopatra wig? From summer stock in Grand Marais?"

"Yes," I said. "That's it." I loved Miss Addie's stories of summer stock in Grand Marais, the place Miss Addie used to be a star. "You always said that wig made me look older."

"Yes." Miss Addie smiled. "I remember that it did."

I waited at the table while she rummaged through her closet. When she came back to the kitchen she had the long black wig, plus the old green box of makeup she let us use for plays. Our first Eden winter I'd spent hours directing fairy-tale plays. Miss Addie did our makeup and our costumes, Nightingale wrote our scripts, Baby colored in our programs, put out all the props. I'd worn the Cleopatra wig for *Snow White* and *Sleeping Beauty*. Nightingale never minded my big roles; she was happier to write than stand onstage.

"You think that this will work?" I asked.

Miss Addie unscrewed her jar of peachy face cream and rubbed a wet glob of Revlon makeup on my cheek. "I'm sure it's worth a try, Pride," she said sweetly. But I could see in her old eyes she wasn't sure herself.

10

MAKE-BELIEVE

When Miss Addie finished with her painting, my eyelids were bright blue, my lashes black and crusty, my skin a sickly shade of tan. A little mole was painted near my nose. My lips were red; Miss Addie's clip-on earrings pinched against my lobes.

Miss Addie tugged the wig onto my head and hid my loose hair underneath it. The inside netting scratched against my scalp. I'd forgotten how Miss Addie's wigs always made my head itch.

"You got an outfit at your place?" Miss Addie asked. I was too tall now to fit into her costumes. The only costume shoes I could fit into were a pair of plastic high-heeled slippers with feathers on the top.

"I think," I said. There was a cedar box of Mama's things tucked back in Old Finn's alcove. Maybe I could wear a dress of hers.

"Well, now," she said with a smile. She puffed a final

pat of powder on my nose. "You may just pass for thirty after all."

Baby shrieked when I walked into the cabin, and Nightingale let her book drop to her lap.

"Pride?" Baby gasped. "How come you look like that?"

"It's makeup for a play," I said. "Like I wore for *Sleeping Beauty*."

"But it isn't *Sleeping Beauty*."

"I'm just getting ready, in case we put it on again," I said. Baby was too young to understand me dressed as Mama.

Nightingale sighed like she'd already guessed my plan. "That isn't going to work," she said. "You can't be Mama, Pride."

"Mama?" Baby frowned. "Pride doesn't look like Mama."

"That's right," I said. I tried to hide the disappointment in my voice. I didn't need to look like Mama to make believe I was; I just needed to look a whole lot older than thirteen. "But you know what?" I poured a bowl of Sugar Smacks and sat down at the table. "Last night at our meeting, we never got to my part of the list."

"That's true," Baby said. He couldn't take his eyes off my face, the long black wig, the little painted mole.

"And I said all of Nightingale's prayers before I went to sleep. Said a few this morning, too." I was lying, but Nightingale wouldn't know.

Nightingale cleared the morning dishes from the table,

walked over to the sink, and got started on the washing. Nightingale rarely did the dishes.

"I only have one thing," I said to Nightingale. "And I let you have four."

She flipped off the noisy faucet and turned to look at me. "Okay," she said. "What's yours?"

"However long Old Finn's fever lasts," I said, "we're going to have to stay on the same side. Stick together as the Stars. The way Mama always said."

"Did Mama really say *stick together as the Stars*?" Baby never tired of the same stories about Mama; this one I'd told a hundred times.

"She did," I said. "When Daddy died. And lots of other times. Whenever Nightingale and I would start to bicker, she'd say—*The Stars have to stick together, stay on the same side.*"

Nightingale ran her rag over the bowl; she knew that it was true. She'd heard Mama say it plenty.

"We have to stay a family first," I said. "Do the best we can while Old Finn's gone. Even if we don't agree. It's what Old Finn would want. Mama, too."

"I'm on your side, Pride." Baby jumped up from his seat, ran over to my chair, and pressed his head into my chest. "I like the wig. Even if it makes you look a little like a witch."

Nightingale laughed and I laughed, too. Maybe I did look a little like a witch.

"Okay," Nightingale said. "We'll stay on the same side.

But I don't want to end up in trouble like the president. Because once you start to lie . . ." She stopped and stared into the sink. "And you know, just pretending to be Mama, well, that's a kind of lie, Pride."

"Or else it's make-believe," I said. "You love make-believe."

"No," Nightingale said. "This is definitely different."

"Well, if it's a lie," I said, "it ought to be my last."

11

HOOT

When I rode up to the Junk & Stuff, Thor's saggy eyes widened in surprise. "That's some kind of getup there, Kathleen." He pointed at my wig. I was glad Mama's paisley minidress was hidden in my knapsack. I still hadn't settled on a story to tell Thor. "You headed for a masquerade?"

I gave a little nod. A masquerade was the perfect explanation. And I hadn't really lied. "So you knew that it was me?" I said, a little disappointed. Maybe I didn't look thirty after all.

"More or less." Thor hooked his thumbs under the straps of his stained overalls. "But, I bet it was the horse. I always recognize your grandpa's horse."

"Oh, right." I slapped my forehead. Who else would be on Atticus?

"Why don't you let me tend that horse today?" Thor said when I got down off the saddle. "You got your masquerade.

I'll see to the tack, get the fellow water. Your grandpa's truck still down?"

"Uh-huh," I said, which didn't count as a yes. "I got the seed sacks that you lent me. And the thirteen cents we owe." I pulled Baby's pennies from my pocket and handed them to Thor. "Here's your money for the eggs."

"Your grandpa make you pay?" Thor dropped the pennies into his pocket without bothering to count. "I know he won't take credit. But thirteen cents was hardly worth the trip."

"Nope," I said. "We paid you back ourselves."

In the greasy bathroom of the Texaco in Goodwell, I tried to hold my breath so I didn't smell the stink. I switched into Mama's dress, quick painted on another coat of lipstick, then walked out past the gas pumps in the direction of St. John's. Every couple steps I lost my balance in Miss Addie's stupid slippers.

"Hey, babe, what's the rush?" somebody shouted. Over at the Lucky Strike a group of teen boys leaned against a car. "How about those feathered shoes?"

I pulled my shoulders back and hurried down the street, but the whistles and the jeers followed until I'd gotten past the Pie Place. I didn't want to look as old as Mama if boys were going to joke.

"Hey," Suzy said when I walked into St. John's. She was standing at the counter staring at my wig. "I know you.

You're the wheelbarrow girl!" Suddenly my cheeks burned pink; humiliation stung my grimy face. If Suzy saw me through my outfit, Bernice would know me, too.

"No," I said.

"You sure are. You were in here with your sister."

"No." I shook my head. I didn't want to say another word.

"Well, it isn't Halloween," she said, laughing. "You don't need a costume now."

I stumbled to the bathroom and stared into the mirror. Miss Addie's crusty makeup made everybody laugh. I yanked a wad of towels out of the holder, ran them under water, scrubbed the layers off my face. Black streaks bled under my eyes. Women came and went, but I didn't care. I stuffed the wig into my backpack with Miss Addie's plastic slippers and my tin with Old Finn's cake. Then I stepped inside a stall and shimmied out of Mama's dress.

"Hey?" somebody said. I peeked out through the stall crack; it was Suzy in her candy-striper jumper, her perfect blond hair pulled tight in two high pigtails. She'd never wear her mama's clothes to town. "I didn't mean to hurt your feelings."

"You didn't." I just wanted her to leave.

"I hope you won't report me." She sat down on the sink. "I can't get any more reports."

"I won't," I said. I knew better than to snitch; if you snitched at the shelter the older girls stuck you with a straight pin or dug their nails into your skin until you bled. Besides I didn't have anyone to tell. I was too embarrassed to tell Nightingale I hadn't passed as Mama. That I'd been dumb to wear those feathered slippers and that wig. I was glad she wasn't here to see it.

"Your patient any better?" Suzy asked.

"I hope," I said. "I brought a piece of cake."

"Cake?" She smirked. She turned and looked into the mirror, tightened up her pigtails, smoothed the wrinkles from her jumper. Those boys outside the Lucky Strike wouldn't have laughed at Suzy. "Got to go," she said over her shoulder. "I'm sure he'll think your costume is a hoot!"

12

GONE

All that and it was a different nurse working the front desk on Old Finn's floor. Kind Bernice was nowhere to be found. I didn't need to come as Mama after all.

"May I help you, hon?" a big-boned woman asked.

"I'm here for Michael Finnegan." I hoped Old Finn would be awake today, and if he was, I hoped he wouldn't mind the stain of orange left on my face, the rings of gray underneath my eyes. "Do you know if he's awake?"

"Michael Finnegan?" she asked like I'd come to the wrong place.

"He's my grandpa. And he's in here with a fever. Some trouble with his brain." His slice of cake was waiting in my knapsack; I'd come all this way to sit here at his side.

"Oh dear," she said. "Mr. Finnegan was transferred to Duluth. St. Mary's Hospital."

"Duluth?" My heart dropped to my knees. Why would St. John's move Old Finn to Duluth? Old Finn hated cities; he wouldn't get well in Duluth.

"They have specialists in Duluth," she said. "Doctors there will know about his brain. I'm afraid we're just too small for certain cases." She slid her pen behind her ear. "The next of kin was notified this morning."

"She was?" I swallowed hard. I was Old Finn's next of kin, but I wasn't even listed.

"Yes," she said. "Dr. Atchinson phoned Miss Addie Lee. It says right here she was notified." The doctor must have called after I left Miss Addie's trailer, maybe while I was on my way to town. "Is that your mother, dear?"

"No," I said. I didn't want Miss Addie to be Mama. I wanted Mama to be Mama, to be here with me now.

She looked over the paper. "There isn't any other family listed here. Is there someone else's name we should pass on to St. Mary's? Your parents' names perhaps?"

"No," I said.

"Okay," she said as if my answer didn't make sense. "So you don't want your parents listed?"

"No," I said. "I just want to see him."

"He's gone," she said again like I didn't understand. I knew he was, but that didn't change the deep want in my heart. "You'll have to visit in Duluth. St. Mary's is the best place for him now."

"But he won't get well in a city. He hates the city. It's

why he moved to Goodwell—so he didn't have to see the city anymore. It's too much time with people."

She glanced down at her watch, shuffled through her papers. "You should head on home now," she said.

"But how long will he be gone?"

"All these questions," she said. "You're going to have to ask your mother, dear."

"You've changed," Thor joked when I walked up toward the barn. I'd changed, but it wasn't just my clothes. The hope I had was all gone from my heart. "What happened to that wig? The masquerade all done?"

"I guess." I was too beaten down to care about the lies I'd told this morning. I had to find a way to get to see Old Finn. "You ever go into Duluth?"

Once, we'd gone to Duluth in Old Finn's truck, but I didn't know how to get there by myself.

"Sure," Thor said. "Can't say I like it much. Why you ask, Kathleen?"

"Just wondering," I said.

"That so?" He gave a little tug on his black seed cap, ran his hand beneath his big hooked nose.

I shrugged. "Just thought I'd like to go, look at the big lake. Maybe take the Greyhound for a trip?" I'd seen the Greyhound bus parked outside the Lucky Strike; maybe one could take me to Duluth. I didn't know any other way to get into that city by myself.

"Greyhound? Your grandpa won't get on a Greyhound bus."

"Maybe not," I said. "But can you take the Greyhound to Duluth? I mean does one go there from Goodwell?"

Thor crossed his arms over his chest and leaned back against the railing. "Things all right out at your place?"

"Fine," I said. That wasn't quite a lie; so far we were self-sufficient. We'd made it through the night; we had food enough to keep us fed.

"Well, if there's something that you need." He put his hand down on my shoulder. "If I were you, I wouldn't run off to Duluth."

"I won't," I lied. Thor's hand on my shoulder almost made me cry. I reached into my bag; Old Finn's tin of cake was waiting there. Thor ought to have it now. I still had a near-whole cake on the countertop at home and I didn't even want to eat a bite.

"Here," I said. "It's just a single slice, but it's devil's food. I baked it up myself."

"Well, glory be," Thor said. "Thirteen cents and cake? You sure do like to make good on your debts. But while you're here, I got a slab of bacon for your grandpa. Bought too much at the butcher. Tell him it's my thank-you for the roof."

13

SELF-RELIANCE

When I got back to the cabin, Nightingale and Baby were waiting in the driveway. Woody Guthrie was sleeping in the shade; Lady Jane was curled into a ball on Baby's lap.

"What about Old Finn?" Baby asked. A coat of gravel covered Baby's Wranglers; his hands were mapped with dirt. By tonight he'd need a bath or a dip down in the pond. Maybe I could hose him down with Atticus and Scout.

"Did you finally get to see him?" Nightingale set her crochet project in her lap. Nightingale was always crafting some new thing—knitting, stitching, weaving. I didn't have the patience to move a needle back and forth. "Is his fever any better?"

"Thor sent home some bacon." I held up the paper package. "So I'll fry it for our lunch. Bacon with French toast. Save the SpaghettiOs for supper." I wasn't in a hurry to tell the truth about Old Finn. It seemed possible to stay alone with Old Finn just in Goodwell, but harder now that he was in Duluth. So far away and sickly he couldn't offer any help. Plus we'd need a lot more money now. Money for tickets to Duluth. Electricity and groceries in case we'd be left alone for long.

"But what about Old Finn?" Nightingale repeated. When Nightingale went hunting for an answer she was slow to stop. "Did you get to see him, Pride?"

"Not today," I said.

"So that nurse knew you weren't Mama," Nightingale said like she wanted to be right.

"That wasn't it," I said. I didn't want to think about the costume or the way that Suzy laughed. "I couldn't see him because Old Finn wasn't there. They've moved him to Duluth."

"Duluth?" Nightingale gasped. "You mean Old Finn is gone?"

"Not so far," I said, even though it was. "We can get there on the Greyhound."

"You mean he isn't coming home today?" Baby said.

"Not today," I said. "But soon. He's going to get well faster in Duluth."

"Did someone say that, Pride?" Nightingale asked, suspicious. "Or did you just make that up?"

"It's what the nurse told me," I said. I didn't like Nightingale on the lookout for a lie. "But for now, we ought to think about the money. We're going to need to earn some if we're getting to Duluth."

"Money!" Baby clapped. "So then I'll get my pennies back?"

"You will." I smiled.

"But how will we get money?" Nightingale asked.

I'd wondered that same question the long ride home from Thor's. One thing we'd never done is have a job for pay. "I think we have to sell something," I said. "The way other folks stick signs along the highway for maple syrup or fresh raspberries. Even eggs like Thor."

"We don't have chickens, Pride," Nightingale said like I was stupid. I knew we didn't have chickens.

"I know," I huffed. "Those were just examples." I looked over to the pasture. Scout stood at the fence waiting patiently for Atticus. She'd stay put until he was back there at her side. The two of them couldn't bear to be apart. "Maybe pony rides?" I said. "Like that carnival those kids put on in Goodwell? That one in some backyard? They had pony rides and games."

"That was for a charity," Nightingale said. "Muscular dystrophy. They did it from a kit. And we can't be a charity."

"Well, still," I said.

"Pony rides and popcorn!" Baby jumped up from the dirt. "That'll be our business. And we'll sell souvenirs the way they do at Deerland."

"We don't have souvenirs," Nightingale said. She looked over at the pasture. "But maybe we could sell some rides on Scout."

"We'll make the souvenirs," I said. "Like those." I pointed to Nightingale's crocheting. She already had a stash of pot holders and bookmarks, lanyard necklaces. I'd made a couple God's eyes out of yarn and sticks. Baby painted rocks.

"But who would come?" Nightingale said. "That carnival was in the backyard of a house right in downtown Goodwell. And Deerland and the Junk and Stuff are just off the highway. No one ever comes out to our place."

I shrugged. I didn't have every answer yet. "We'll have to get the tourists. Put out signs with arrows so they can find their way to Eden."

"The tourists Old Finn hates?" Nightingale raised her eyebrows.

"That's who goes to Deerland. And that's who buys the maple syrup from the farms." Every summer, tourists crowded Goodwell, people from the city who vacationed at the lake cabins in northern Minnesota, noisy families who flocked to the resorts. Some of them bought Old Finn's wooden birds from the Northwood Nook in town. But Old Finn never let them visit Eden.

"He wouldn't want those folks coming to our cabin," Nightingale said.

"I know." There wasn't any sense to argue otherwise; Old Finn's opinions were too strong. "But at least it's self-reliance. And Old Finn would be happy about that."

14

KEEPSAKES

After lunch we painted up four signs, made stakes out of the broken picket-fence slats we dug out of the barn. Then I stacked them in Baby's wagon and walked the three long miles back toward town. Hot as it was, I was happier to walk there in the heat than have to ride Atticus to Thor's place once again. Thor would mean a batch of brand-new questions, another heap of lies I'd have to tell.

PONY RIDES AND POPCORN!!! I stood back and admired Nightingale's big, bright painted letters. Nightingale's artwork would get folks out to our place; she'd made our business look happier than Deerland.

When I finally got back to the house, Nightingale had washed a load of laundry and designed the perfect popcorn cone out of paper and some tape. "We'll use these for serving," she said. Nightingale always thought ahead. Out back, Baby was leaping from the swing, practicing his flying, even with the stitches in his chin.

"Mama's darer," I joked.

Nightingale shook her head. "I can't keep him off it, Pride."

"Baby," I called out the back window. "You weren't made to fly. And you can't break another bone with Old Finn in Duluth. I'm not taking you to Goodwell for more stitches."

"His stitches!" Nightingale said. "Isn't he supposed to get them out this week?"

I glanced at Old Finn's calendar. "Looks like it's tomorrow," I said. "*Three thirty, Dr. Madden.* That's all Old Finn has written for the week."

"Maybe it can wait," Nightingale said. "Until Old Finn gets home?"

"Maybe so." I didn't know how long stitches stayed, but when I got a job at St. John's Hospital like Suzy, I could learn about those things. "I'll go down to Miss Addie's, call the office, ask if we can wait."

"You'd call the office, Pride?" Nightingale frowned. "Wouldn't they wonder why a kid would make that call?"

"Did you see that girl named Suzy? Working at St. John's? The one dressed like a candy cane?"

"You mean the candy striper who said the wheelbarrow was weird?" Nightingale scowled; she didn't like her either, and she didn't even know what Suzy had said today. How she'd called me a hoot.

"Candy striper?" I asked.

"That's what they call the girls who volunteer. It's why they're dressed like peppermints."

"How old did you think that candy striper was?"

Nightingale shrugged. "I don't know, fifteen?"

"Right," I said. "And I'm almost fourteen. So I can call the doctor. Take Baby in tomorrow by myself."

"You're only just thirteen." Nightingale flipped one black braid over her shoulder.

"That's on the way to fourteen," I said. "Which means I'm almost fifteen. In another year, I'll be working at St. John's. I can take Baby to the doctor."

Nightingale shook her head, rolled another popcorn cone, and taped the long end closed. "I don't know, Pride. Sometimes you're just too sure."

I grabbed the dry clothes from the line, carried Old Finn's basket to his room. There was still a stack of clean clothes left out on his dresser, same place they'd been the days that he was sick. Old Finn's headache must have hurt him horribly; he never let his clean clothes gather dust. He was always army tidy, the one good thing he said he picked up in the service. And now we hadn't even made his bed. His old brown quilt had fallen to the floor; Woody Guthrie's dirty paw prints were stamped across the sheets.

I smoothed the quilt back on the bed, folded Old Finn's clothes, sorted out his socks, shoved his checkered boxers into a drawer. It felt wrong to be in charge of Old Finn's clothes; Old Finn liked to handle his own wash. I opened up his sock drawer, stuck a handful in, but then I stopped. I'd never had a glimpse of Old Finn's sock drawer. It was like a tiny secret chest of private keepsakes: a pocket watch, faded snapshots of Mama as a girl, another one of Mama on a cable car with me. There was a necklace and some medals. Strange coins from other countries. A woman's ring. And tucked tight against the side, a stack of tissue-paper letters bound by a thin red rubber band. Maybe letters Mama wrote when she was young?

I pulled them from the drawer and held them in my hand. A sweet perfume drifted from the paper. The one on top came all the way from France. Had Mama been to France and I didn't know it? I felt like I'd discovered some deep secret, some part of Old Finn's past I wasn't meant to see. I hid the letters in the waistband of my jeans, pulled my T-shirt down and loose so Nightingale wouldn't suspect. I knew she'd say to leave them in the drawer, but I just couldn't. Snooping was a weakness I couldn't stop. I liked to imagine private things people hid down in their hearts. I'd snuck so many peeks into Nightingale's diary looking for the secret things she'd never tell me, but most days were just the ordinary things that happened at our house.

"Where you going?" Nightingale asked as I hurried through the kitchen.

"I'm going to say howdy to Miss Addie," I lied. "Make sure that she's okay. Maybe give a call to Baby's doctor."

"But what about our dinner?" Nightingale said. "Shouldn't you get it started?" The day had stretched so long I'd lost track of time. Two trips to town, a cake baked, Old Finn in Duluth, a brand-new business started—and I still had to get the family fed. When Old Finn was home, we always ate at five.

"We can run a little late," I said. "It won't take me long tonight." SpaghettiOs were quick to cook; it's why Old Finn refused to buy them. He didn't like suppers that came out of a can.

"Why you going to Miss Addie's?" Nightingale gave me her slow, suspicious stare.

"Just checking in," I said. "But I'll get the supper fixed."

15

DEAR MICK

I didn't go to Miss Addie's trailer; instead I ran past Baby on the swing, headed down the wood path, then took my shortcut to the clearing where I sometimes went to think. A little secret dream spot protected by tall pines with a patch of sunlight warming through the trees. It was the perfect private place to steal a look at Old Finn's letters. I pulled the stack of letters from my jeans, dropped down on the stump. One quick tug, and the worn rubber band just snapped in half. I slipped it into my pocket; I'd have to find a perfect match before Old Finn got home.

I opened up the thin blue sheet of paper; it was an envelope and letter all in one.

Dear Mick, it said. *Mick*? But Old Finn's name was Michael. And Mama only ever said Old Finn. Not even "your grandpa" or "my dad."

September 2, 1972

Dear Mick,

France is absolutely everything I had dreamed and more.

I'm finally here in Avignon after a crazy week in Paris. Seven days of great museums, artists on the streets, that fabulous thick coffee with a froth of steamy milk. Imagining Monet, Picasso or Matisse once painting there in Paris. Sometimes I think I can't live back in Duluth, but of course come May I will. I wish so much we'd had the chance to see Europe together, but my students have been wonderful, full of curiosity, devouring the work of all the masters. We only managed two days in the Louvre; I could have stayed forever. I could hardly bear to see all that beauty in one place. Someday we're going to come here, darling, and you'll be able to see it all yourself. Not the broken Europe you knew back in the war. But how it blooms in peace. Flowers on the boulevards. Flowers in the window boxes. Something lovely growing everywhere.

Today we're heading to the country for a watercolor class. Maybe I'll paint you a small picture, so you can see the grass really does glow gold. I want to get this to the post before we catch the train.

I think of you all alone in Eden, but of course I know you like to be alone. Still there's so much of the world that

we could see. Good things that would help you have some
hope. Humanity is better than you think.

How's that sound, Gloomy Gus?

Your love is here with me. And mine with you at Eden.

Justine

Justine? A woman who called Old Finn her darling? A woman who took Old Finn's love all the way to France?

I looked back at the page. *September 2, 1972.* Was this Justine living in Duluth? She said she'd be back there come that May; that May would have come and gone last year. But if she was in Duluth why didn't we know her now? Why didn't she ever visit here at Eden?

"Pride!" Baby screamed, excited. I tried to stuff the letters back into my jeans, but without the rubber band the stack wouldn't stay together.

"Pride!" Baby called again. "Our first customer is here!"

"Okay," I said. I ran back up the path, snuck into Old Finn's dusty shop. His toolbox was open on the table, his chisels left beside a delicate small cardinal. White curls of wood collected on the floor. If Old Finn were here I'd be working right beside him, building another little birdhouse we'd string up in the tree. My crooked birdhouses hung all over Eden. I didn't have his patience for the carving—the best I'd ever done was a lopsided wooden heart I'd carved Old Finn for Christmas—but still Old Finn said I had a knack with nails and a hammer. Sureness with a saw. This summer I was starting on a stool.

"Pride!" Baby called again.

I set the letters in his toolbox, latched it closed so they'd stay my private secret. When our first customer was finished, I'd come back for Justine.

16

PONY RIDES AND POPCORN

Our first customer was a worn, ragged mother with three rambunctious boys—all of them Baby's age or younger, all of them whining loud at once and darting through her legs. I was happy Old Finn wasn't home to hear it; he couldn't abide a whine.

"And they call this a vacation?" The woman snarled at me. "Maybe for my husband. All he does is fish." She slapped the youngest off her leg. "Pajama party?" she said to Nightingale, but Nightingale ignored her. She'd been wearing gowns so long the jokes had grown old.

"I fish," Baby said. He stuck his pudgy hands into the front pockets of his Wranglers, rocked back on his cowboy boots the way that Old Finn would. Even with a face covered thick in freckles, missing teeth, stubby little legs, Baby liked to think he was a man.

"Well, good for you," the woman snapped. She

rummaged through her purse and pulled out a cigarette case. Then she stuck one in her mouth, clicked a silver lighter, exhaled a cloud of smoke straight into my face. "I guess you have a daddy who cares about his kids."

"My daddy's dead," Baby said. Daddy being dead was a fact since before Baby had been born. Saying it didn't seem to make him sad. "Old Finn takes me fishing."

Nightingale sent a worried look my way; Old Finn wouldn't want us telling our private history to strangers, especially not a tourist smoking in our yard. *The less folks know, the better* was the way he lived his life. He always said you couldn't be certain who was asking or what a person might do with your private information once they had it.

I put a hard hand on Baby's shoulder, squeezed it tight so he knew now to be quiet.

"Oh my," the woman said. Flecks of dried red lipstick clung to her top teeth. "Well, I'm sorry to hear that." Suddenly, she stopped and gave us a long stare, studied us the way Bernice had done our first day at St. John's. Maybe it was Daddy's being dead or Baby's strip of stitches or Nightingale's going barefoot in that nightgown with her black eyes and small face, but I could tell she thought that we were odd. If strangers were coming to the cabin, Nightingale might have to wear clothes like other kids.

The woman blew another stream of smoke. "You hear that, boys?" she said. "These poor kids don't even have a daddy. Tell them that you're sorry." She slapped another off her leg, yanked the oldest by the arm. "Do what I say, Tommy. Or you're going in the car."

"Let go!" Tommy shouted. I couldn't believe a boy as old as Baby hung from his mother's dress. Or kicked her in the ankle. Or whined like he was two. "I'm not saying that I'm sorry."

"It's okay," I said. I didn't need a bratty boy to say that he was sorry about Daddy.

"Did you come here for a ride?" Nightingale asked sternly. I could tell she wanted this woman off our land.

"I'm ready to do anything. You try four days in a cabin with these kids. The beach is filled with weeds. No wonder they're at each other's throats. And there's not a thing to do in Goodwell. Next vacation, I'm going to New York. Alone!"

I grabbed an apple off the tree, coaxed Scout in from the far end of the pasture, and saddled her for business. She wouldn't like these wild boys any better than we did, but she was calm enough to lead around the yard.

"How much?" the woman said.

"Quarter each," Nightingale said. "And we got a cone of popcorn for a dime." We hadn't popped it yet, but popcorn didn't take long.

"Quarter each," the woman said with a laugh. "I guess I can afford that. I can tell you're not in this to get rich."

· · ·

The whole time the boys were getting rides on Scout, the woman perched on Baby's swing and smoked, ashed her cigarettes right in Old Finn's grass, ground them out, and left her lipsticked butts right where Baby played. And every time I tried to tell each dirty boy his turn was over, he'd pitch such a terrible fuss, she'd order me to let him ride a little longer. Longer still. I walked circles through the yard so she could smoke.

"Okay," I finally said. "This was lots more than a quarter." She should have paid a dollar for each boy. And it was late; I needed to start supper. Justine's letters were waiting in the woodshop.

"No," Tommy whined. "They got more time. I want my equal turn."

"They didn't," I said. I reached up to help him off the saddle, but he kicked me in the stomach so hard I accidentally dropped him to the grass. Money or no money, I couldn't keep this business up. All this, and we'd only made seventy-five cents.

"Ow," he howled. "She hurt me."

"What?" the mother glared. "What'd you do to Tommy?"

"She threw me on the ground," he sobbed. "She broke my leg. She did."

"I didn't." I hadn't done a thing but get him off Scout; he hadn't fallen far. "I dropped him 'cause he kicked me in the stomach."

"Can you stand up?" she said to Tommy. When she

pulled him to his feet, he limped like Lady Jane with a burr caught in her paw.

"I broke my ankle, Mommy!"

Baby put his hands on his hips, squared his shoulders the way he did when he was mad. He didn't like these tourists either. No wonder Old Finn lived a hermit life. "You can't break your ankle getting down from Scout," he said. "I can jump down from a tree. I jump off my swing when it's almost to the sky."

"Aren't you the smarty-pants?" the woman hissed. She lifted Tommy, hugged him like a baby. "Where's your mother? I want to speak with her right now."

"Not home," I said. This woman was so mean she'd probably call the county, tell them we were out here all alone.

"Well, she better have insurance. My husband is a lawyer. You can bet you'll get the bill."

I looked at Nightingale. Insurance? I didn't know what this woman meant. And we didn't have any money for her bill.

"Let's go," the youngest whined. "I'm hungry. You promised we'd get candy." He yanked hard on her dress.

None of us said a word about the popcorn.

"Get my purse!" she ordered. It was sitting at the swing with all her cigarettes. When the youngest finally ran back with her bag, I waited for our money, but instead she fished in and grabbed her keys.

"It's seventy-five cents." Nightingale held out her empty

hand. "That's how much you owe us for those rides." Somehow having customers made Nightingale braver. "A dollar now because all the rides took longer. They really each got two."

"I'm sure you must be kidding?" The woman sneered. "I'm not paying you. You'll be paying me. And plenty when I'm done!"

17

NOT TELLING

After that first customer, a couple new ones came, all tourists, but none of them as rude as that mean woman. They didn't litter Baby's swing with cigarette butts or order me to give their children extra time. When the last one drove away, we'd sold five more rides and seven bags of popcorn. We were worn out and starving, but we'd already earned $1.95.

"We ought to have a Closed sign," Nightingale said. The horses were brushed down; we were all done for the night. She stretched out in the grass and stared up at the sky. Ants crawled over her bare legs and Nightingale let them; she didn't have the heart to harm a thing. "I'll paint one in the morning. We can hang it from the apple tree on the far end of the driveway. That way folks will see it when they come."

"That's good!" I said. "I'm ready for a rest."

"But first we have to eat." Baby rubbed his hungry belly. "I can't wait much longer, Pride."

I didn't want to move an inch off that grass, but I knew Baby still had to be fed. "All right, all right." I sighed to show I was exhausted. "I'll go in and heat the can. It's SpaghettiOs again."

"But we ate that last night, Pride," Baby said. It wasn't quite a whine, but it came close. I was the one who'd gone all the way to Goodwell once today, then walked back to the highway with a wagon full of signs. Baby hadn't been kicked hard in the stomach or worn a stupid wig to pass for Mama or spent the last two hours leading Scout around the yard. If anyone could whine, it should be me.

"But you always beg for TV foods from those commercials. Sugar Smacks and Twinkies. Frosted Pop-Tarts. Oreos. SpaghettiOs."

"But I didn't like them, Pride," Baby complained. "I want Lucky Charms with the secret prize inside."

"We don't have Lucky Charms. We've got SpaghettiOs or peanut butter toast. Carrots and zucchini out in Old Finn's garden. Tomatoes. Potatoes in the pantry." Baby hated vegetables.

"What about fried chicken?" Baby said. "And Old Finn's Sunday biscuits. Yesterday was Sunday, but we didn't get our Sunday dinner, Pride."

Sundays Old Finn always made a special dinner. But I

77

couldn't mix his biscuits or fry chicken by myself. For some things, I still needed Old Finn beside me in the kitchen. "We can eat our chocolate cake," I said. "That'll be our treat."

Baby looked away, and from the side I could see his lower lip puff out in a pout. "But that lady was so mean," he said under his breath.

"What?" In all of the commotion, I'd already forgotten that mean lady had been here.

"And she didn't even pay us for the rides." I heard the tears clog up Baby's throat. Baby never ever cried, not even when he had to get the stitches or cut his hand deep on Old Finn's army knife. "Did Mama ever act that way to us?"

"No," I said. "Not ever." Baby was so young he didn't remember Mama like we did. "And the other folks were fine," I said. We spent so much time at Eden, we weren't used to anybody mean. Old Finn never even raised his voice. In one day, I'd had snotty Suzy and that woman, but now Suzy didn't seem bad. I reached over and rubbed Baby's little back. "They were nice enough."

"Not really nice," Nightingale added. All the kids had laughed at her pajamas except the ones too young to talk.

I kissed Baby on the head the way Old Finn did before we went to sleep. "Some folks are mean," I said. "Like the kids were at the shelter. But we're the Stars, we're tough enough to take it."

"You sound just like Old Finn." Nightingale let a lady-bug land on her small wrist. "He always wants us tough."

"I don't want to live without Old Finn," Baby said.

"Me either." I was already worn out from being oldest. And I still had to fix our supper, make sure Baby got a bath. "Old Finn home is what everybody wants."

"What about Miss Addie?" Nightingale asked when we sat down for supper.

"Miss Addie?" Miss Addie always ate off by herself, except on chicken Sundays when Old Finn walked a plate down to her trailer. "You think she needs some supper?" Miss Addie had her macaroni and Velveeta. "I'd have to heat up more SpaghettiOs." The one can that I heated had hardly fed us three. I'd already given Nightingale and Baby all the meatballs so they'd have enough to eat.

"I wasn't thinking of her supper," Nightingale said. "I was thinking of the pony rides and popcorn. Do you think we ought to tell her we had strangers at our place?"

Nightingale already knew the answer to that question. Of course we ought to tell her, but Miss Addie wouldn't allow us to run a business here at Eden. "She won't want those tourists on our land."

"I know." Nightingale pushed the soupy rings around the bowl.

"And right now," I said, "it's the only business that we have. And we need to earn some money."

"I know." Nightingale nodded.

"So we can buy a chicken," Baby added. "And stuffing. And green beans cooked in bacon. And Lucky Charms when Pride goes back to the Need-More."

"So?" I said to Nightingale. "Is not telling just the same as lying?" It was Nightingale who had *not lying* on her list. A lie or two didn't worry me that much.

Nightingale rested her head against her hand, just the way she did when Old Finn posed a puzzle we couldn't solve. "Not saying is a secret," she finally said. "And a secret's not a lie."

"But what about the president?" I said. "So we don't end up impeached. Were his secrets or did he tell real lies?"

Nightingale laughed. "I think impeached is only for the president."

"Well then," I said, "I don't think that we should worry. And bothering Miss Addie with our business might only hurt her nerves."

Nightingale nibbled at her meatball. "I guess," she finally said. "We don't have to say for now."

18

AN EVENING TREAT

Let's take Miss Addie cake," Nightingale announced when our SpaghettiOs were finished. I wondered if the secret already hurt her conscience. It was awfully late to carry down dessert.

"Okay," I said, "but Baby needs a bath." And I still wanted to get back to Justine's letters.

"I can take a bath tomorrow," Baby said. He was always trying to work his way out of a bath.

"We don't have to stay there at the trailer," Nightingale said. "But I know she'd like to see us." Nightingale and Miss Addie were two peas in a pod.

We looked like a parade marching through the meadow, Baby at the head with a pitcher of Kool-Aid, Nightingale carrying the cake, me bringing up the rear with Miss Addie's wig and slippers, the emerald earrings safe in my left hand. So many things had happened in one day it hardly seemed only this morning that Miss Addie had smeared makeup on my face.

Those boys out on the street. Suzy in the bathroom calling me a hoot. Old Finn sent to Duluth. A brand-new business started. Letters from Justine. I hoped tomorrow things would go back to slow and steady, the way they were when Old Finn was in charge.

"My dears," Miss Addie said when she opened up the door. "I haven't heard from you since morning. I thought for sure one of you would stop by."

"I'm sorry," Nightingale said. "We've just been so busy."

"Busy with crocheting?" Miss Addie asked as if needlework could eat up a whole day.

"Only some," Nightingale confessed. "I didn't get too far."

"Crocheting's not a race." Miss Addie smiled at the cake in Nightingale's hands. "Oh my child, I love an evening treat!"

She shuffled to the cupboard, handed me a stack of mismatched fancy dishes. Sometimes at the Junk & Stuff Old Finn found a teacup with a saucer or a fancy silver fork, and brought it home with Miss Addie's magazines. Miss Addie did love dishes, even though we were the only company to serve.

"How was the costume, Pride?" Miss Addie asked like she only just remembered.

I slid the biggest slice onto her plate. I could make another one tomorrow; we'd have chocolate cake all week. Now that we had Thor's eggs, all of the ingredients were here. "I changed my mind," I said.

"You did?" Miss Addie frowned. "After all our work this morning? You looked so lovely, dear." Only in Miss Addie's eyes, but I didn't say it. "But what about those nurses at St. John's? The ones who had you worried?"

I was glad Nightingale had her nose in the TV; I didn't want her saying she'd warned me I was wrong.

"They sent Old Finn to Duluth," I said. Miss Addie should have known that. They spoke to her today.

"Oh dear," she fussed. "Duluth's so far away."

"They said he'd get well faster. Didn't they call this morning and tell you that same thing?"

"This morning?" Miss Addie blinked. "Oh yes," she said. "A doctor called with something." She took a piece of paper from her pocket and handed it to me. "Here." It was a number in Miss Addie's wobbled writing. That, and a word in shaky cursive I couldn't read. *Enceph*—— something. "What's this?" I said.

"I don't know," she said, confused. "I think it's the number to St. Mary's."

"It's long. And I've never seen a phone number like this here."

"That's long distance, Pride," Miss Addie said.

"Unfortunately it costs money to make a phone call to Duluth. You'll have to pay." She slumped down in her seat. "Do you know when someone's coming?"

"Coming?" I repeated. I wasn't sure what she was asking. Had Miss Addie heard the cars?

"To help us get along here. At least until Old Finn . . ."

"No," I said, "we're fine. We don't need any help."

"But my medicine is gone. I discovered that today. And Old Finn is the person who keeps track."

"Your medicine?" Nightingale asked, worried. Suddenly she snapped off the TV, walked over to the table, and sat down at her plate.

"He always picks it up at Wagner Drug." Miss Addie pinched the loose skin on her neck. "I need it for my blood."

"We'll get it in the morning," Nightingale promised. "First thing when we wake up. It's too late to go to town tonight."

"You will?" Miss Addie smiled weakly.

"*I will*," I said. Nightingale made the promise, but she wouldn't be the one riding Atticus to Thor's, then walking into town. I'd be the one riding into Goodwell twice. "But could you wait until three thirty? Because Baby sees the doctor then. And after that, I can go to Wagner Drug."

"Three thirty?" Miss Addie said. "I'm not certain that I should. Perhaps Wagner's would be willing to deliver?"

"No," I said. "We're not calling Wagner Drug to ask for

help." I stuck the slip of paper in my pocket; I didn't want Miss Addie calling anyone and telling them our truth. Plus medicine cost money. "I'll take care of it myself."

"I'm sorry," Miss Addie said like she'd been scolded. "I don't need the medicine before tomorrow night."

19

TWO SOLITARY SOULS

Old Finn wasn't the only one who believed in self-reliance; Mama taught it every time she counted on my help. Plus the commune constitution made kids and grown-ups equal, so just living at Serenity gave me lots of practice solving problems for myself.

"Don't worry," I told Nightingale. "I'll get Miss Addie's medicine somehow. We got a dollar and ninety-five cents, and more we'll earn tomorrow." Baby's fresh bath body was sprawled between us in the sheets. I'd tucked him in so late, he'd gone to sleep in seconds.

"I hope," Nightingale murmured. She sighed a slow, loud yawn. "Aren't you out of steam?"

"Not yet," I said. I'd been racing past *what-next* since Old Finn got his fever, and no matter what last happened, some new problem waited to be solved. I had too much on my mind to fall asleep. I closed my eyes and tried to say the prayers. *Dear God, please get rid of that infection. Dear God, please get rid of that infection. Dear God, please make Old Finn well.* I counted on my fingers. Twenty-five was taking way too long. Plus I wasn't sure who listened to my prayers— was God only make-believe or was there really a good God caring for Old Finn? Out of all of us, Nightingale was the only one who had a sense of God. Baby didn't much wonder, and Old Finn didn't want to say. Still, he never took us to a church.

"Nightingale," I finally whispered. "Will God really make him well?"

Woody Guthrie gave a grunt, stretched out his long dog legs until all four of them were pointing toward the ceiling. I wondered if Woody Guthrie thought of God.

"Nightingale?" I said again.

I slipped out of bed and looked out Old Finn's window at the night. I didn't want to think alone on God. God made me think of death and heaven, and how someday I'd lose everyone I loved. Outside, the moonlight washed the backyard blue. Justine's letters were waiting in the woodshop. Justine's *Dear Mick* would take my mind off God. I dashed out the back door, ran across the grass like some dark spirit was behind me. But it wasn't night that scared me; it was the emptiness of Eden.

I took the letters to the loft, snapped on the little cowboy nightlight Old Finn bought for Baby, stretched out on my stomach, and unfolded the next envelope. It was another piece of tissue paper that opened to a page.

September 20, 1972

Dear Mick,

So today we're on the train to Nice. The Cote d'Azur is lovely, the same azure as your beloved Eden sky. Remember that night we sat out on your porch and watched that gorgeous sunset, and you said the sky was really just the ocean upside down?

I couldn't imagine Old Finn saying that. Maybe Justine's letter was meant for someone else. I looked back at the address. Mick Finnegan. It had to be Old Finn.

Those are the silly things I think of.

It sounded silly. Old Finn could name the stars; he knew they weren't fish.

I must confess, all this lovely quiet has made me reconsider your offer of a summer spent at Eden. I don't know who would tend my garden in Duluth, but I can see the magic of painting at your cabin—the perfect peace, your animals, the steady sky and sun. Pines and birch and the wash of sunrise pink just beyond the hills. And to know you'd be nearby, carving in your woodshop. I'm beginning to believe two solitary souls could build a life together.

I am working on that little watercolor that I promised, small enough to mail to your place. It's impossible to get the colors perfect. I see now that's why the painters did so many studies.

If you look at that Monet book I bought for you last Christmas, you'll see the blue I mean. Find <u>Fort of Antibes</u>. That's it. Azure. The color of your summer sky.

The Monet book? I remembered Old Finn teaching that in art. The time he made us take a close look at a painting, see all the blues and pinks and greens in a single tiny square. Was that a lesson from Justine? Did she know Old Finn taught us at the table?

It is good to know your Addie's on the mend. My grandmother had a series of small strokes, and I can't say she fared as well. But that's a story for another time. I can hardly keep the pen to paper with the rocking of the train.

Be well, my love.
Write. I look forward to your letters.
Justine

• • •

A series of small strokes? Old Finn never mentioned that. One of the actors on Miss Addie's *Edge of Night* had a stroke and died. Did Miss Addie almost die? Was that why she needed medicine? To stay well from a stroke?

I laid the letter on the bed, closed my eyes to think, but somehow my thoughts seemed to blur like rain. Miss Addie and azure. The sky the same as sea. Happiness for two solitary souls.

20

SUGAR SMACKS AND COFFEE

Pride!" Baby screamed. I heard his little feet pound across the floor. He opened the back door, screamed my name again. "PRIDE!"

"I'm just up here, Baby. In the loft."

Justine's last letter was open on the bed. What was that word? *Azure?* I pulled the stack together, hid it in the crack between the mattress and the wall.

"I fed Woody Guthrie," Baby shouted. "You want us to have Sugar Smacks for breakfast?" I knew he'd wait there at the ladder until I surrendered and crawled down. "'Cause we should start; we have to set up shop. Sell our souvenirs." A good night's sleep and Baby was all ready to do business. "Nightingale's going to print the prices now!"

"Okay," I croaked. I could hardly find my voice. My body felt so worn my butt ached to the bone. I rolled over on my side, tucked my hands under my cheek. Another hour, then I'd get out of bed.

"Pride!" Baby said. "Come on! Someone's driving in."

"A customer already?" I jumped up from the bed, quick changed into a pair of shorts and T-shirt. I wasn't greeting folks in my pajamas. Then I heard the slam of the front screen, followed by the chatter of Baby's gabbing with someone on the porch.

By the time I got down from the ladder, both Nightingale and Baby were already outside. The two of them were talking to a man and his small daughter, or mostly to the man; the little red-haired girl was high up in his arms, her pixie face hidden in his neck like she was shy. Something in the man reminded me of Daddy—not his red mop of shaggy curls or the rusty stretch of whiskers on his face or his wire-rimmed round glasses—but something in the way he held that little girl, tight, the way Daddy used to hold me in his arms.

The man had left his bright orange van parked crooked in our driveway with half-peeled protest stickers plastered on the back. Peace Now. Impeach Tricky Dick. People Before Profits. It looked like something from Serenity, not Goodwell.

"Hey," he said, waving, when I stepped out on the porch.

Woody Guthrie gave a little growl. I leaned low and ruffled up his ears.

"Hey," I said, embarrassed. My morning hair was still in tangles; my teeth weren't even brushed.

"They're looking for some food," Baby said. "Like breakfast."

"Not a pony ride or popcorn?" I asked, confused.

"I got to say we're starving." The man gave me a big smile. "Sage and I, and popcorn won't quite do it. And I'm desperate for a coffee. Saw your signs out on the highway, thought we'd take a look."

"We've got Sugar Smacks," Nightingale offered flatly. I could tell she didn't see Daddy in this man. But here she was selling off our breakfast.

"And I can make some coffee," I said.

"Everything's a quarter each," Nightingale said. "Sugar Smacks and coffee. Pony rides. The popcorn is a dime."

"Sounds good." He scratched his rusty whiskers. More than coffee, he needed a razor and a bath. Both of them would look better in clean clothes. The little girl wore a wrinkled peasant dress dragging past her knees and her legs were nearly brown from too much dirt. It was the way Baby looked before I made him take a bath. "The only horse Sage ever rode was rocking." He gave a great big laugh. "You got one of those?"

"Hercules," Baby said. "He's a great big rocking horse on springs. I've still got him in the barn, but I don't use him. We could pull it out."

"That still would cost a quarter," Nightingale added.

"You kids drive a hard bargain." He gave a smile to Nightingale, but she didn't smile back.

"So altogether you owe us a dollar." Nightingale held her hand out. When it came to money, she didn't seem so shy. And after that mean lady, Nightingale always got our money first.

He reached into his pocket and pulled out a worn wallet, faded at the edges just like Daddy's. For years, Mama kept Daddy's wallet in her drawer—Daddy's wallet with pictures of Nightingale and me. Now it was in the box of Mama's things up in the alcove. "Here." He handed Nightingale a dollar. "I'm Nash," he said. "This is my daughter, Sage." The two of them looked alike with their red hair, just the way Nightingale and Daddy were both dark.

Nightingale closed the money in her fist, but she didn't offer up a name.

"I'm Baxter," Baby blurted to be friendly. "But I just go by Baby."

"Baby?" Nash smiled wide at Baby. "I like that name a lot."

"And I'm learning how to read! Old Finn teaches at the table."

"You are?" Nash said. Sage turned to look at Baby. It was the first she'd pulled her face out of Nash's neck. "Maybe you can give a hand to Sage."

"How old is she?" Baby asked. "'Cause I'm already six."

Sage looked too young to read; I didn't learn to read until I was almost nine, and even then, I didn't read all that much, but Nightingale taught herself to read at four. At

Serenity, kids got to study what they wanted. Mostly I picked fishing or baking, tending to the ponies or playing duck-duck with the young ones in the yard.

Daniel Walker called our learning free school, but Old Finn called it no school, which is why he made us have our school lessons all year round. Old Finn said we'd missed a lot of ground.

"She's five," Nash said. "A little on the shy side." He reached up and gave a sweet rub to her curls.

"Nightingale's shy," Baby said.

"I'm not." Nightingale blushed.

"If you can stay awhile," Baby said, "we'll have our souvenir shop all set up."

"Souvenirs?" Nash raised his eyebrows. "Pony rides and popcorn? Breakfast on the fly? You kids are sure industrious. Who's the boss?"

"I am," I said. I didn't want him asking questions about Mama or Old Finn.

"She's not," Baby said. "Pride's not the only boss. I'm the one who thought up the souvenirs. There's Nightingale and me working this business."

"Pride?" Nash asked, confused.

I stepped forward and squeezed Baby's little shoulder. He'd already said too much. Young as he was, he still needed to keep quiet. At least he should have said Kathleen and Elise. Pride and Nightingale weren't names for the world.

"That's me," I said.

95

"But she's still not the boss." Baby shook his shoulder; he couldn't bear to be held down.

"Nice name," Nash said. "Pride? Don't think I've ever heard it."

"She was Mama's pride and joy," Baby said. "And I was Mama's baby."

"I'm not surprised." Nash nodded. "I say the same to Sage. My pride and joy. My dad said it to me."

"He did?" Baby said. "I never knew my d—" I squeezed his shoulder harder. I didn't want him saying Daddy died. He should have learned his lesson yesterday.

"So that means you must be Nightingale?" Nash tried another smile, but Nightingale just gave him a dull stare, the way she was with any sort of stranger. "I'm guessing you must sing. Or someone hoped you would."

"It's just for her pajamas," Baby said. "Nightingales. It's all she likes to wear."

I grabbed him by the elbow, cupped my hand over his mouth. "You come in and get the Sugar Smacks," I scolded. "I'll put on the coffee."

Baby wriggled free, pulled my hand away. "I want to get out Hercules for Sage," he said. "Come on." He gave Sage's foot a friendly tug. "You can help me move it." At Eden, Baby never had a kid his age to play with—he only ever had the two of us.

Nash lowered Sage down to the ground, and right away she took off with Baby toward the barn.

"She's sure not shy with him," Nash said, surprised. "He ought to run for president. He's got a lot of charm. And we could use a new one that's not Nixon."

"I know," I said. "And Nixon is impeached." I was proud to use the word.

"I'm hoping that he will be," Nash said.

"You want sugar in your coffee?" Nightingale asked. Old Finn drank his with extra sugar.

"Black," Nash said. "Black as oil is best."

21

FRIENDLY QUESTIONS

Nash and Sage felt more like company than customers, maybe because right away Nash treated us as friends. He said he was a writer for a travel magazine out of Chicago, a sometimes freelance writer really, who had pitched a piece on northern Minnesota, a land he'd always hoped to see, so he and Sage set out on a quest, hunting down the best of the back roads of northern Minnesota—something more than Paul Bunyan Land or bait shops.

"And not the usual tourist traps." He laughed.

While he and Sage ate cereal, we listened to his stories— how Sage's mother was in school to be a lawyer so she'd stayed home in Chicago to study for a test; how he and Sage had spent a night in a Finnish farmer's barn that doubled as a chapel, and how Sunday morning church folks stumbled on the two of them still snoozing in the straw. He said they'd already visited the Hockey Hall of Fame, but that baseball had been his sport when he was young. He asked us if we played, and Baby brought out the new blue mitt and the baseball Old Finn bought him for his birthday; then Nash and Baby tossed it back and forth between them, Nash catching that hard ball with his bare hands.

When their baseball toss was finished, Sage and Baby ran off to ride on Hercules again, and Nash stayed put on our front porch steps still making conversation, asking friendly questions, more than I could answer, and most I had to answer with good lies. Through all of this, Nightingale listened, silent, from a distance, refilling Nash's cup for a quarter every time.

I told him that we lived here with Mama and Old Finn, which really could have happened if Mama moved us up to Eden the way that Old Finn wanted after Daddy died. I said Mama was an artist who learned to paint in France. Especially the sky and grass. And she studied lots of painters like Picasso. The longer that we talked, the easier it was to mix truth in with my lies.

When he asked about Old Finn, I said he was a carver and a history professor who'd moved all the way to Eden to find peace. It made me glad to brag about Old Finn. And when Nash asked if he could see Old Finn's wooden carvings, I told him they were sold at the Northwood Nook in town. Old Finn had statues on the shelves out in his woodshop, but I knew he'd never let a stranger step inside.

"Your mom's paintings at the Northwood Nook?" Nash asked.

My heart stalled for a second; I didn't want him asking Nosy Nellie about Mama. "No," I said. "Mama's paintings are in Paris."

"Paris?" Nash said, surprised.

"In some of the museums," I said. "Paris has a lot."

"So I've heard," he said. "Then your mom paints in the cabin?"

"No," I said. "She paints out in the fields. Farther down the wood path."

"And you kids just run this business by yourselves?" Nash asked. "Because it's a whole lot more ambitious than your average Kool-Aid stand. And it sure puts my sixth-grade paper route to shame."

"We're doing it for charity." I didn't want to say we had to buy Miss Addie's medicine, plus three tickets to Duluth.

"Charity!" He smiled. "Well, good for you. What charity?"

I looked at Nightingale. "Multiple?" I tried. "Multiple discov—"

"Muscular dystrophy," Nightingale interrupted. She flashed me a mean look.

"Ah," Nash said. "Muscular dystrophy. Worthy cause. I've seen those backyard MD carnivals put on in Chicago. Don't they send you kids some kind of kit?"

"We're not working from a kit," I said. "We invented it ourselves."

"But you run the thing all summer?" I could see he

was impressed. "Aren't those MD carnivals usually just a day?"

"We're not sure how long," I said.

"You must make a fair amount. You're already earning money off me and it's still morning."

"More coffee?" Nightingale interrupted. She took the cup from Nash and handed it to me. "You get it, Pride," she ordered and pointed toward the cabin. I didn't like Nightingale bossing me around.

When I stepped into the cabin, Nightingale followed at my feet. "That man asks too many questions! And you're telling all those lies!" Nightingale meant it as a whisper, but it came out as a hiss.

"They're just stories, Night. I didn't say anything I shouldn't. I couldn't let him know we're out here all alone or earning money for our tickets."

"You can't lie about a charity. People do those for good deeds. It's wrong to make him think we're going to give away the money."

"Come on," I said. "He's just passing through. And the longer he listens, the more money he spends. We still need Miss Addie's medicine. Our tickets to Duluth. And Baby wants a chicken dinner—he won't last on SpaghettiOs for long."

"Pride?" Nightingale rolled her eyes. "That can't make it right. And Mama as an artist?" Nightingale stared at me. "How'd you make up France?"

"Just thought of it, I guess." I wasn't going to tell her now I'd snooped through Old Finn's things.

Nightingale sighed a long, sad breath.

"What?" I said. "It's just a couple stories."

"Lies," Nightingale corrected. "And you promised at our meeting that you'd stop. But now you've told so many."

"Why didn't you try to stop me? You know when I get started on a story." I stared into her black eyes. Sometimes I saw the worst of myself there. I didn't have an ounce of Nightingale's goodness.

"What now?" she said.

"He'll leave any minute," I said. "They'll go. And that'll be the last."

"We're all out of coffee," I said when we stepped out on the porch. "And we got to go to town. Baby's got those stitches to get out."

"Sure enough," Nash said, but he didn't make a move to leave. Over in the side yard Sage and Baby were bouncing wild on Baby's old spring horse. I wished I could be Baby's simple age again.

Finally, Nash walked over to his van and opened the back door. Inside it looked like someone's messy bedroom, clothes thrown over a big mattress, pillows, piles of magazines. Nash scrounged around and pulled out a big black camera. "I'd like to take a picture," he said. "Show this scene to Sage's mother. She'd want to see our girl on that spring horse."

"A quarter each," Nightingale said.

"A quarter for a picture?" Nash said, surprised.

"A dime is fine," I said. I couldn't see charging Nash for a picture of his daughter. I wished Mama were alive to see Baby on that horse.

We walked with Nash toward the barn, stood beside him while he snapped pictures of Sage and Baby riding tandem on the horse, Sage in front, Baby's little freckled face peeking out behind her shoulder.

"So is that the real live pony?" He pointed toward the side corral where Scout and Atticus had wandered in for water. "The one kids pay to ride?"

"That's Scout," Baby shouted. "I can ride her bareback. Atticus belongs to just Old Finn."

"Ah, literary." Nash took a couple pictures of the horses. "*To Kill a Mockingbird*. Someone must like books."

"Nightingale," Baby said. "She can't get her nose out of a book. Old Finn either. He has shelves and shelves of books."

"And where's Old Finn this morning?" Nash asked. I'd already said Old Finn had gone to Goodwell; I didn't know why Nash was asking Baby now.

Baby froze and looked at me. For once he knew better than to blurt.

"He went to town for groceries," I repeated.

Nash nodded. "Think that I could get one shot of you girls with that real pony? Or maybe all of you? Could Sage and Baby sit up on its back?"

"I'll do it." Baby jumped down from Hercules. "Someday I'm riding in a rodeo."

"I bet you will," Nash said with a laugh.

Baby ran to the corral, climbed between the fence slats. He dragged the empty milk crate to Scout's side, grabbed hold of her mane, and hoisted his stubby body up onto her back. I opened up the gate and stepped inside.

"If I set Sage down in front," Nash asked, "do you think that you could hold her?"

"Sure," I nodded. Even Old Finn would understand a picture for a mother; one photo of our family for someone in Chicago wasn't going to hurt.

Nash set Sage up with Baby, then I stood to one side of Scout and held firm to Sage's waist. "It's okay," I whispered when she stiffened in my arms.

"Come on, Night," Baby called. "Get here in the picture. You stand on the other side of Scout."

Nightingale stood still for a second. "Night," I begged. "Come on."

"Hurry," Baby screamed.

Finally Nightingale came into the corral, barefoot in her nightgown the way she always was, taking careful steps to miss the horse turds. Both of us held tight to Sage's waist. "Great!" Nash said. He looked at us through his camera, snapped our photo from one spot, then the next. "Pony rides and popcorn," he said. "You kids could be my story. Minnesota off the beaten track."

22

OFF THE BEATEN TRACK

Us?" I gulped.

"We'd be in a magazine?" Baby shrieked. "Like Miss Addie's movie stars?"

"Could be," Nash grinned.

"You mean you'd write a story about us?" I asked. "Our business would be famous?" At least we'd be famous in Chicago—far enough from Goodwell that Old Finn would never know. The county people either. "Like the Jackson Five or the Osmonds?" Those singing kids were always on the covers of the magazines at Need-More. Now it would be us.

"Not the Jackson Five exactly," Nash said. "It's a travel magazine. We're not talking about *Time*."

A look of horror darkened Nightingale's face. "No," she said. "We don't want our picture or our story in a magazine."

"I do," Baby argued.

"It'd be off in Chicago?" I asked Nash just to be sure.

"Well, I haven't written it yet." Nash laughed. "I'm not even certain of the angle. But if I were a tourist here for novelties, this is one place in northern Minnesota I'd sure stop. Pony rides and popcorn, Sugar Smacks and coffee, three kids running their own business and all for a good cause."

"Don't forget we're selling souvenirs," Baby added.

Nash laughed again. Baby was so cute, Nash would probably write the whole story about Baby. "One more run around the yard," he said to Sage. "And then we ought to leave." He lifted her from Scout, and then he lifted Baby. "Wait," he said before they took off for their race. "Let me just get one more for the road."

Baby posed with his arm flung over Sage's shoulder, black stitches like a path along his chin, his missing two front teeth. Already I could see him on the cover in his cowboy boots and Wranglers. I wished Mama were alive to see us on the stands.

"Old Finn likes his privacy," Nightingale said to Nash. He did, but Old Finn would never have to know.

"If I decide to write it, and my editor approves it, I'll need your mom's okay. I can ask Old Finn as well, if she thinks that would be necessary."

"It's okay," I said. "Just go ahead and write it if you want.

But can we get a copy here? Three so we can have them for our keepsakes?" We'd have our magazine the way Miss Addie had the clippings from her plays.

Nash laughed. "I can see you really are the boss." He pulled a tiny spiral notebook from the pocket of his jeans. "I need a name and number to reach your mom. That way I'll have it for permissions."

"Justine," I said. I didn't want Mama to be Addie Lee again. Then I rattled off a number that started 653, because 653 was a made-up number not anywhere near Goodwell.

"Justine?" He held the pen over the paper, waited for the rest of Mama's name.

"Justine Matisse," I said. It was an artist's name I remembered from the letter.

"Matisse as in the painter?"

"Yep," I said. "Exactly."

"So your last name is Matisse?" He wrote it down, then slid the notebook back into his pocket. "Well, no wonder she likes France."

"Pride!" Nightingale scolded the second Nash and Sage were gone. Her cheeks were pink, her fists clenched white with rage. "All those lies. And now we're in a magazine."

"Not yet," I said. "It isn't even written."

"We'll be in the Need-More with the groceries!" Baby cheered. "And Wagner Drug. We'll be right there on the newsstand like Miss Addie's magazine. And they'll read about our pony rides and popcorn. And Scout. And me and Sage on Hercules. Maybe my new baseball mitt will be in the story, too!"

"They'll read we're earning for a charity," Nightingale said. "And that Mama's name is Justine Matisse. Justine? Mama's name is Bridget." She glared at me. "Look at what you've done, Pride. You've caused all kinds of harm."

"Not harm," I said. My cheeks were burning, too. I didn't want to harm my family; it was my job to keep us safe with Old Finn gone. "I'm just good at telling stories, thinking up fast answers for the questions strangers ask. Same way you're good at math. And geography. And learning. And Baby's good at hunting and jumping off the swing and making people happy. I can make up stories, so I do."

"Pride," Nightingale huffed. "We can't be famous and a secret all at once. And Old Finn would never want our story—"

"It won't be us exactly. It's only sort of us. Half us and half people I made up. And we won't be famous really. Nash said so himself. It's just a little story. In Chicago."

Nightingale stormed up toward the cabin. "A little story full of lies," she said. "And all of them are yours."

23

HELTER-SKELTER

The three of us were quiet setting up our souvenir shop. I built two simple shelves from bricks and boards. Baby lined his painted rocks up in a row. Nightingale arranged her crochet crosses, her bookmarks, the cotton hot-pads she wove on her small loom. I mixed a pitcher of Kool-Aid, baked a batch of oatmeal cookies we could sell. All that setup kept us busy, but still my head felt hot, my stomach swirled with shame. Nightingale was right; I shouldn't have told so many lies to Nash.

"I'm sorry," I finally said to Nightingale. Baby had gone off to find more trinkets for our shelves.

Nightingale straightened out her row of bookmarks. "Are you going to put your God's eyes out here, Pride? Sell them for a dime at least?"

"I guess." I didn't want to think about God's eyes. "Did you hear me say I'm sorry?"

"I did," she said, but I could tell she didn't forgive me. Especially for lying about Mama. "Whatever extra that we earn, it needs to go to charity."

"Okay," I said.

"At least he can't get Mama to say yes," Nightingale said, relieved. "So our story won't be in his magazine. Old Finn will never see it. Or anybody else."

"True," I said, but I felt a little sad. I still wanted our family on the newsstand, this good business that we made, even if we weren't quite the Jackson Five. "Poor Baby will be mighty disappointed." I set the rooster cookie jar up on the top shelf. I could sell my cookies, even if they weren't as fancy as Nightingale's crafts. "And Nash was nice at least. Nothing like the tourists." I didn't want to end the subject with Nightingale mad.

"Nice?" Nightingale wrinkled up her nose. "You can't trust a stranger, Pride. Not anybody. Old Finn's told us that a hundred times. And there you were, trusting him too much. He could tell the county."

"Tell them what?" I said. "I told him we had Mama and Old Finn."

"That man could've been a spy, someone trying to get new information to put in Old Finn's file."

I'd forgotten Old Finn's file; Nightingale understood that trouble with the government better than I did. "I didn't say a word about the war or that Old Finn was against it.

And I don't think pony rides and popcorn could be trouble for Old Finn."

"You don't know who's watching," Nightingale warned. Someday Nightingale would grow up to be a hermit exactly like Old Finn—all alone at Eden with her books.

"You never should have let him take our pictures," Nightingale said. "Or told him all those things."

"I know, I know," I said, ashamed. I just wanted Nightingale to stop. I hated when she stepped into being older, or showed me I'd been stupid when I was supposed to be in charge. I felt better as the boss. "He was just so friendly," I said. "Tossing the baseball, telling stories. Drinking coffee on our porch."

"I saw that," Nightingale snipped. "And he left without paying for those pictures after all."

We didn't have another customer that morning, and by noon a mass of storm clouds moved fast across the fields. "Hey," I called. "It's rain." Nightingale and Baby were inside at the table, making a book of brand-new reading words Nightingale thought Baby ought to learn. *Bat. Cat. Rat. Hat.* I grabbed Woody Guthrie by the collar, yanked him through the door. Then I went back for the rooster jar of cookies, grabbed a bunch of Baby's painted rocks. Nightingale's lacy crosses lifted in the wind like little kites.

We all ran helter-skelter to save the souvenirs—

Nightingale chasing down her crosses, Baby dumping a load of rocks into his shirt. I scooped up the God's eyes and the hot-pads, the bookmarks, the key chain lanyard Baby had dug out of the junk drawer. By the time we'd got it all inside, and Atticus and Scout were already in their lean-to, a rush of rain was coming down in sheets.

"That's it for our business." Nightingale frowned. "No one's going to come here in the rain."

"Or hail!" Baby said. Tiny balls of white ice blanketed the grass; I opened the back door and set out a soup pan the way we always did with hail. Then the three of us curled up on the couch, the afghan stretched between us like it was winter in the cabin. The whole house smelled like cinnamon and sugar. I set the rooster jar down in the middle, held it while Nightingale and Baby grabbed a handful of oatmeal cookies made with extra chocolate chips the way that Old Finn liked. Once the rain was gone, I'd bring a little tin over to Miss Addie's—do something right to make up for all the wrong.

"We can save the hail for Old Finn," I said. Everything felt better under Old Finn's afghan. "Store it in the freezer." We couldn't tell him most of the things that happened these last days, but at least we could tell about the storm. Old Finn loved a storm.

"Or sell some hail slushies," Baby said. "A nickel each. We have the grape Kool-Aid!"

"Okay!" I took a bite of oatmeal cookie—a little dry and chewy the way I made them for Old Finn. "I got to save a tin to bring Old Finn. He'll like these cookies in Duluth."

"It's already been four days," Nightingale said glumly, like maybe we wouldn't see Old Finn again.

"It has." I nodded. "But we've gotten by okay."

"Sort of." Nightingale took a little nibble of her cookie; Nightingale always ate around the edge.

"We're running our own business." Baby grinned and Nightingale nodded.

"True," she said. "But we're not doing it for charity." Then suddenly she turned to look at me, a sour scowl scrunching her small face. "And Pride?" she said. "Who's Justine Matisse?"

24

REAL AND TRUE

I could've lied about Justine, but I didn't want another black blot on my conscience. Instead, I told Nightingale and Baby to sit tight while I climbed up to the loft and got the letters. Then I settled back between them with the papers in my lap.

"What's that?" Baby asked. He reached out for a letter, but I pushed his hand away. Baby's hands were always grimy; I didn't want his dirty fingers marking Old Finn's letters.

"Don't touch," I said. "These are special to Old Finn."

"Old Finn?" Nightingale asked. "You mean those letters are Old Finn's?"

"Found them in his sock drawer," I said quickly. "Yesterday, unloading his clean clothes." I knew there was a lecture up ahead.

"And you just took them, Pride?"

"I did." I swallowed hard. The cold truth was tough to

tell, but I was happy for the practice. It was easier to tell the truth to Nightingale than to Nash.

"But that's almost like my diary." Nightingale frowned.

"I know," I said. Nightingale had no idea how many times I'd stolen a quick peek inside her diary. "But I looked at these letters for Old Finn."

Nightingale crossed her arms like she didn't trust me.

"Old Finn might need some help," I said. Help wasn't really why I read them, but it sounded true enough. "And this Justine, maybe she could help."

"That's Justine Matisse?" Nightingale pointed at the stack of tissue-paper letters. "Help him how?" she asked. "Help him with his brain?"

"Maybe," I said. "I know she used to love him."

"Eeewww." Baby put his hands over his ears. "Not love."

"It's love," I said. "It's right here in the letters. So if you don't like love, you probably shouldn't listen. Why don't you get your box of soldiers and play in Old Finn's room?" Army was a game Baby always played alone; none of us would help him play at war.

"You mean you're going to read them?" Nightingale said. "Out loud?"

I hardly ever volunteered to read out loud, but Justine's letters felt almost like my own. Like a little secret key I wanted in my pocket. If I was going to share her letters, I felt safest with them held between my hands.

"I don't know that we should listen," Nightingale said. "Those are Old Finn's private things."

"Up to you," I said. "I can read them to myself. But you asked about Justine Matisse. The Matisse part I made up. Her name is Justine Ryan. But she really lived in France. And she paints fields like I said. That's how I got the lie."

Nightingale gnawed her lower lip. I could tell she was curious about the letters, whether reading them was doing wrong or not.

"The painting just sounds boring," Baby moaned. He kicked free of the afghan. He was never going to sit still for the letters.

"Why don't you go play army," I said. "And then I'll fix you lunch."

"No," he said. "I don't want to play alone."

"Okay," I said, "then listen."

October 12, 1972

"'*Dear Mick*,'" I started.

"Mick?" Baby interrupted. "Old Finn isn't Mick."

"Ssshhh!" I scolded. "That's what Justine calls him."

"Sometimes I like to dream that you'll come here to surprise me. That I'll look down the dusty road that leads up to my cottage and there you'll be, just as you

*were when I'd watch you stroll across the fields of Eden.
Happy. Handsome. At home in Eden's silence. I know that's
sentimental, but it's those little things I think of often, love."*

"Love?" Baby groaned. "She called Old Finn *love*?"

"Where is she?" Nightingale wound one braid around
her fingers.

"France," I said. "I think she's teaching painting. And she
loved Old Finn before she left."

"France?" Nightingale said. "Is that why we never met
her?"

"I don't know," I said. "I've only read a few."

"Maybe she's dead," Baby said, matter-of-fact. "Like
Daddy and Mama. Maybe Justine died."

A little shiver tingled up my spine. I didn't want Justine
dead.

"And that's why Old Finn hid them in his drawer."
Nightingale pulled the afghan to her chin. "Because he
loved her and he lost her."

I looked down at the letters; the answer might be there.
"That's why I want to read," I said. "Because maybe if she's
living, she could help Old Finn get well. Love heals," I said.
"Like Mama always said."

"She did?" Baby asked.

"Yep," I said. "She said it all the time."

• • •

We sat there in the rain, reading letter after letter, long enough that Baby crawled down from the sofa, curled up on the floor, and fell asleep on Woody Guthrie's fur. Most of the letters were talk of love and France, but in one she'd sent a snapshot of herself. A woman painting at an easel. Neat white hair flipped under at her shoulders. A big straw hat tilted on her head. Justine. The woman Old Finn loved.

Justine's letters were better than a book, because every word she wrote felt real and true and loving—her train trips to the city; fancy chocolate pastries; children skipping down the street; an artist on a farm who killed a chicken, then cooked it for Justine. She even wrote about the sheep, how she wished Old Finn had his own at Eden, because she loved the calm in their black eyes. "Like mine," Nightingale peeped, but it barely broke the spell. Both of us were far away in France with tiny cups of coffee, strong cheese, and warm baked bread, the stone cottage near the sea. The white-capped waves crashing on the rocks.

25

HARD TIMES

We were reading of an Irish doctor Justine met near the sea, when suddenly Nightingale bolted from the couch. "Baby's stitches! Miss Addie's medicine! She has to have it, Pride!"

"It's only one o'clock," I said, "don't worry. If we leave now we'll make it there on time." Outside, the rain had died to a light drizzle. Still, I wasn't in a hurry to go all the way to town. "You get down the money."

She climbed up to the counter, pulled down the coffee tin, put all we'd earned into my cupped hands, all in coins except Nash's dollar bills. "Four dollars, twenty-five cents," she said. We were lucky we'd sold so much to Nash.

"Don't read ahead," I warned. I didn't want Nightingale to think those were her letters. I'd found Justine; she was mostly mine.

"I won't," Nightingale said.

"You promise?" I drew a cross over my chest, stood solid until Nightingale gave me that same sign.

"You sure you don't want to ride on Scout?" I asked, but I already knew the answer. Nightingale wouldn't put on clothes to go to town; one trip this week to Goodwell was enough for Nightingale. I picked up the letters, put them back in Old Finn's drawer. They could wait there in the dark until I got done with all our business—Baby's stitches, Wagner Drug, our tickets to Duluth.

"I'll stay," Nightingale said. "Spend time with Miss Addie. Let her know her pills are on the way."

"Bring her down some cookies," I said. "She can have them with her tea." Miss Addie liked to *take a tea* at two.

"We better hang the Closed sign," Baby mumbled, half asleep. He rubbed his eyes, stretched out on Woody Guthrie. "We won't be here to help."

"The Closed sign?" I groaned. "We haven't made it yet."

"I will," Nightingale said. "I'll get it painted, then I'll hang it on the tree."

"You're sure?" I said. "But what if someone comes?"

"If someone comes, I'll hide out at Miss Addie's."

"Okay," I said. "You wait there for me." It was exactly what Old Finn had said to us when he sent us to Miss Addie. *Wait there.* Only I was coming home.

Baby begged to ride alone on Scout, but instead I made him share a saddle on Atticus with me. I didn't want him playing cowboy when we had to get to town. All the way to Goodwell, a steamy silver rain fog floated off the fields and small puddles pocked the road. It felt like we were traveling through Camelot—King Arthur's once-enchanted kingdom—with the silver mist I pictured when Old Finn read the book. And here I was a Round Table knight with the special gift of courage, heading off to win another war. Or at least get my little brother to the doctor; Old Finn would say that took courage, too.

"Not a day for riding," Thor said when we rode up to his place. He'd stepped out on his front porch the minute we'd come into his yard. He must have had an ear for horses' hooves. "Better day for staying home."

"Sky's clear now; I think the rain is finished. We got to see a doctor at the clinic."

"Someone sick?" Thor asked, concerned.

"I got stitches." Baby pointed at his chin. "Twelve from trying to fly. And today I get them out."

"Fly, huh." Thor laughed. "I think that's for the birds. Airplanes maybe. You gotta grow some wings."

"I just use my arms." Baby grinned. "Like Superman." He shot his arms over his head. "I fly off the swing."

Thor laughed again. "I bet you keep your grandpa busy."

"He does." I nudged my elbow into Baby's back; I didn't want him to say one word to Thor about Old Finn. "We got to hurry into town."

"I'm heading to the bank," Thor said. "Let me take you

young ones into town. I don't much like to see you walking on that highway. Especially with rain."

"We keep to the ditch," I said, but I was ready for a ride. I didn't want to walk down that wet highway with cars and trucks splashing puddles as they passed. One trip to town in Thor's truck wasn't going to hurt.

Thor hoisted Baby off the saddle. "Wouldn't be much of a neighbor if I didn't lend a hand."

We weren't long in Thor's truck before he asked about Old Finn. I reached down low and gave Baby's leg a little pinch. "Haven't seen him much these days," Thor said. "His truck still on the fritz?"

"Fritz?" Baby laughed.

"I think it means it's broken," I said. I'd rather talk about a word than tell Thor another lie.

"Does indeed." Thor nodded. "So everything all right out at your place?" He'd asked the same already, yesterday, when I talked about the Greyhound to Duluth. He might have asked the day I bought the eggs. I could tell he didn't believe the part about the truck.

"Old Finn likes it out at Eden," Baby blurted. "He stays there all day."

Thor made a little snort. "I sure do get a kick out of that name. Pretty fancy name for forty acres."

"Eden's where the world began," Baby said. "Before the trouble all got started."

"I've heard that myself." Thor gave a little chuckle. "And I don't know who'd want Duluth when you have Eden. Duluth's a busy place—has its share of riffraff."

"Duluth?" Baby said, surprised. I pinched again.

"We just like that great big lake," I said. "Superior."

"Ain't you got a pond out at your place?" Thor asked like I hadn't told the truth. "And we got Lake Louise right here in Goodwell. Three more fish holes down the road. Ten thousand lakes in Minnesota, don't take a bus ride to Duluth to look at water."

I sat there for a minute in the silence hoping Thor would find another subject; I didn't have a better reason for going to Duluth.

"So your grandpa couldn't take you to the clinic?" Thor kept his eyes steady on the road, his bony hands against the wheel. I was glad he wasn't watching me for lies.

"Not today," I said. "He's been busy out at Eden."

"Tending to that pony?" Thor asked.

"Scout?" Baby said, surprised.

"I saw the signs," Thor said. "Followed all those bright red arrows, saw they pointed to your place. 'Pony rides and popcorn.'" He wheezed a little laugh.

"And souvenirs," Baby said. "We're selling ours just like they do at Deerland. And we got cookies for a nickel each. Pride can make you coffee if you want."

"Pride?" Thor asked.

"Oops!" Baby slapped his hand over his mouth. "I mean

Kathleen. Kathleen. Her name isn't Pride. Kathleen makes the coffee." Baby better not be blabbing at the clinic, otherwise I'd have to take him home and leave the stitches in until Old Finn could handle it himself. "And today we sold two bowls of Sugar Smacks."

"That sweet cereal you just bought at the Need-More?" Thor gave a glance at me. It had only been a couple of days since Thor had packed it in our seed sack.

"Your grandpa got you selling off your groceries?" Thor asked. None of this made sense for Old Finn. A terrible blush burned over my face. My cheeks itched. I wanted Baby to be quiet.

"He doesn't mind," I said.

"Thought he preferred his privacy. Never knew he'd let those strangers on his place."

"It's just for a few days," I said. I knew Thor wouldn't believe me if I said Old Finn had changed.

"Just so you know." Thor nodded. "Hard times can hit us all."

26

SOMEONE HERE TO HELP

We'd never seen the doctor who took out Baby's stitches; every visit to the clinic we'd seen grumpy Dr. Clark. The brand-new Dr. Madden was young and tall and happy— making jokes with Baby, and asking me what I liked to learn in school. Through it all, Baby sat brave on the table, and I watched Dr. Madden work his tools the way I watched Old Finn carve. I'd never have Old Finn's patience with a chisel, but I could see myself using tweezers to coax out some stubborn stitches or pressing that cold stethoscope against a person's heart. Strong and sure at work like Dr. Madden. Maybe I could start out as a candy striper, grow up to be a doctor, get my own white coat.

"So your grandpa couldn't be here?" Dr. Madden opened Baby's chart, wrote something on the paper, same thing the nurse did when I visited St. John's. "And he's your legal guardian?" he asked, like Old Finn wasn't quite fit for that job. Old Finn always said folks were suspicious of a man his age all alone with kids; it's why the county school woman asked so many questions and why people nosed into our business when we were shopping in a store. Old Finn said if he had been a woman less people would have asked.

"He is," I said. "It's all cleared through the courts." I'd heard Old Finn say the same.

"But he's not here today?" Dr. Madden asked.

"He's out on a delivery," I said.

He nodded, wrote another couple words. "Are you often left alone?"

"No," Baby said. "Old Finn's mostly with us."

"Old Finn?" Dr. Madden grinned at Baby. "That your grandpa's name?"

"No," I said. "Not really." I didn't want Baby speaking for himself. "Michael Finnegan." I knew that much was already in the chart. "Baxter says Old Finn."

"Not just me," Baby insisted.

"Do we have to pay today?" I asked. I only had $4.25, and I still had Miss Addie's medicine to buy.

"I'm sure we'll send a bill." Dr. Madden spun his rolling stool to face me. "So how old are you, Kathleen?"

"Fourteen," I said. Maybe I could be a candy striper in his office; I was tall enough to look fourteen.

"Thirteen," Baby said.

"Thirteen, then I'm fourteen."

"Thirteen, fourteen." Dr. Madden shrugged. "Still, a girl your age shouldn't be worried about paying doctor bills."

He opened up his drawer and pulled out a jar of suckers. "Take your pick," he said to Baby, then he held it out to me. "Thirteen's not too old to eat a sucker?"

"No," I said. I chose a pink one, watermelon, my favorite sucker flavor, but I didn't get it much. Except for holidays and birthdays, Old Finn didn't buy candy for the cabin.

"Well, Baxter . . ." He started to hoist Baby from the table, but Baby mostly jumped, landed hard on the heels of his boots. "So, you're sure you got hurt flying?" I didn't know why he asked about the flying; there wasn't any other way Baby would get stitches on his chin.

"Yep," Baby said.

"Must be a big job for your grandpa, taking care of kids. Three kids." He said it like Baby's stitches were really Old Finn's fault. He gave another glance at Baby's chart. "It's a big job for my wife and me, and we've only got our daughter."

"Old Finn's a good guardian," I said. Dr. Madden made it sound like Old Finn wasn't fit to do the job. Old Finn kept us closer than Mama ever did. Sometimes at Serenity we didn't see Mama before bedtime; at Eden, Old Finn was always near.

"But Baxter's sure been hurt a lot. An ankle sprain. A broken arm. A deep cut on his finger. And twice, he's had stitches from a fall?" Every one of those was Baby's being reckless: Baby jumping off the fence; Baby flying; Baby racing down the path and tripping on a rock; Baby leaping off a tree branch. There wasn't much Old Finn could do to slow him down. "Are you left in charge a lot?"

"Me?" I said. I didn't like the way he asked it. Was Dr. Madden blaming me for Baby's wild streak? Old Dr. Clark didn't ask us all these questions; he just stuck the needle in my arm, or made me open up my mouth and give an "aaahhh."

"No," I said.

"Just today?" Dr. Madden stared at me.

"Just today," I answered back as best I could. There wasn't much for me to say these days but lies.

He ran his thumb along the red scar on Baby's chin. "You know we're here to help," he said to Baby. "If you're not feeling safe. Or bad things start to happen."

"He's safe," I said. Nothing bad was happening to Baby; nothing ever would. No one kept us safer than Old Finn. Old Finn teaching us our lessons at the table, making sure every meal was on time. Old Finn, who never lost his temper with our messes. Old Finn, who read to us before we went to sleep—a thing Mama quit back when we were small.

"But you kids don't go to school?" he asked. "I read that in your chart."

"Old Finn teaches us at home," Baby said. "I'm on my letters now."

"At any rate, a home visit might be helpful, considering the circumstances. Someone from social services could assess your situation. Sometimes when kids are too far out of a system—"

"We're not out of a system," I said. "Old Finn has a system for our school. And we're learning every day. Old Finn's already got us doing fractions. And ancient Greece. Nouns and verbs and adverbs. Poetry and spelling. Plus we have to read a book a week. Write long compositions Old Finn corrects with his red pen. And this summer we've been studying the plants. Photosynthesis and stamens." Big words I had to memorize although I didn't understand a lick of either one. I wished Nightingale were here to tell how much Old Finn taught.

"Still," he said, "someone should stop by."

Old Finn would never want these social people at our cabin. And they couldn't come with Old Finn sick in Duluth.

"We're going on vacation," I said. "We'll be gone three weeks." It was another lie that popped out of my mouth. Maybe that was how things went wrong for Richard Nixon, lie after lie, because it was easier than telling folks the truth.

"I'll let them know," he said, like he didn't trust me. When I got to be a doctor, I wouldn't pester kids with stupid questions. "In the meantime . . ." He pulled a little card out of his drawer. "Here's the number to the clinic. You kids run into trouble, you just give a call." He turned it over, wrote a second number on the back. "After hours, you just dial me directly. Anytime you need it, there's someone here to help."

27

HOW BROKEN MY HEART

I didn't tell Nightingale about Dr. Madden and his number or that he made me buy a tube of Neosporin that cost ninety-seven cents or that I'd found out the Greyhound bus left the Lucky Strike every morning at 7:20, but the tickets to Duluth were $1.80 each. Instead, I put Miss Addie's brand-new pills into her little plastic holder, two in each compartment, fourteen for the week, and tried not to think of Dr. Madden sending someone to our house.

"Bless you, Pride," Miss Addie said. She gave my hand a little pat. "At my age, I can't keep track of what I've taken."

"You just take today," I said. "Tuesday. Tomorrow you take Wednesday."

"When is Old Finn coming home?" she said. Miss Addie looked like she needed more than pills, more than bologna and Velveeta. "Did they tell you at St. John's?"

"He's in Duluth now," I said, but Miss Addie should know that.

"Oh yes," she said. "In Duluth. But why'd he go so far away?"

"His brain," I said, but I wasn't quite so sure. I'd find out more when we saw him at St. Mary's. But I couldn't tell that last part to Miss Addie; she'd never let us take the Greyhound to Duluth. "Here." I put one little pill into her palm. The pharmacist had told me Miss Addie ought to skip the morning dose she missed, take one pill today instead of two. I hoped one missing pill wouldn't make her sick. "You want me to bring you supper?"

"Is it SpaghettiOs again?" Baby moaned.

"I can fry up some potatoes," I said. "Scramble eggs with onion. Add a little cheese."

Baby wrinkled up his nose. "Pancakes?" he asked. "Can you make me pancakes, Pride? With chocolate chips?"

"Fried potatoes would be lovely," Miss Addie said. "I don't know where we'd be without you, Pride."

"The tickets are a dollar and eighty cents each," I told Nightingale on our way home along the wood path. Baby had already raced ahead; Baby never walked if he could run.

"That means we'd need five dollars and forty cents for the three of us to go into Duluth," Nightingale said, but I'd already done the numbers in the dirt. Come up with the answer on my own. "And we only have four dollars, twenty-five cents left."

"Had," I said. "We're down a dollar. I had to buy a tube

of Neosporin to help Baby's stitches heal." I didn't bother adding in the three pennies back in change. "But I didn't have to pay for the doctor or Miss Addie's pills. They'll bill the house for both. And by then Old Finn will be well to pay those bills."

"Three dollars, twenty-five cents," Nightingale said. "That's not enough for tickets."

"We can make that up tomorrow." We had the pony rides and popcorn, the souvenirs, a batch of oatmeal cookies, a few more bowls of Sugar Smacks to sell. Maybe someone new would ask for coffee.

"I don't know." Nightingale sighed. "What if we can't make it on our own? Or never make it to Duluth to see Old Finn? What if we're just left here for the winter when the tourists don't come?"

"It doesn't help to think the worst." I didn't want Nightingale to worry over winter. It was August; sweat was sliding down my skin. "He'll be well by winter."

I was already worn out from Nash and Sage, the visit to the doctor, Thor's ride into town. "Right now," I said, "let's just get our supper fixed."

Nightingale peeled potatoes; Baby beat the eggs and milk. I mixed up the pancakes, fried them on the griddle until both sides toasted golden brown. I melted down brown sugar for our syrup, stacked the steaming pancakes on a plate. While we ate, Miss Addie's supper stayed warm in our oven, the fried potatoes turning soft as oatmeal from the oil. When we'd finally finished eating, Nightingale and Baby took Miss Addie her warm supper while I stayed behind to get the dishes washed.

It wasn't just the dishes that kept me at the cabin, it was Justine's letters waiting in the drawer. When I was lost in news of France and painters, bread and chocolate, I didn't have to think of Thor or Nash or Dr. Madden or a social-someone visit or earning money or what we'd do another week from now. For some strange reason, the letters made me picture Old Finn safe. Safe and loved. Handsome in his plaid shirt and his jeans. Happy here at Eden. Not far off with a fever, gone to some strange hospital for trouble with his brain.

When I'd finished drying the last plate, I sat down on the sofa, let Woody Guthrie rest his speckled snout against my feet.

November 3, 1972

Dear Mick,

Outside Nightingale's and Baby's footsteps drummed closer in the dirt; in seconds they'd burst through the back door, drop down here beside me, listen while I read whatever words came next. Same way we listened while Old Finn read us *Treasure Island*. At least Nightingale would.

Maybe Baby would take his soldiers into Old Finn's room, plug his ears and shriek when he heard a word like *love*.

I glanced down at the paper.

Dear Mick,

How broken my heart is this morning, darling.

The kitchen screen whined open, then slammed shut. The two of them rushed in, flushed from running. Baby was always looking for a race.

"You already reading?" Nightingale panted.

"Not yet," I lied. I didn't know how to tell them Justine just broke her heart.

28

THE MISSING LIST

November 3, 1972

Dear Mick,

*How broken my heart is this morning, darling. Broken
for you. I have hardly slept since I got your call last night,
and I can't forgive myself for being off in Spain all the days
you tried to reach me. It seems impossible you've lost your
daughter, Bridget. So senselessly. But I suppose all accidents
are senseless. I keep going over everything you told me.
That image with the semi. It's a scene I keep replaying in
my mind. I know it must be the same for you. And her
three helpless children.*

"That's us," Baby whispered. I stopped reading; my heart
was in my throat. I never imagined Mama's death went all
the way to France. That someone there thought of what we

lost. I read the date again. November 3, 1972. Five days after Mama died.

I wish that I could be there with you now. I know you understand I can't leave my students, but if I could, I would. I absolutely would. Would fly home in a heartbeat to be there at your side. How wrong that you should face this loss alone.

There are no words. Of course. It's not enough to say I'm sorry. Or to send you all my love.

I shall say a prayer that all goes well in New Mexico. That the courts proceed with common sense. That you get those poor, dear children with very little trouble because it's the only right thing that can be done for now. I am glad you've hired a good lawyer, although I doubt the courts would award them to that commune. And of course they won't leave them in a shelter when they have a man like you to give them all a home.

I wouldn't worry about that old trouble with the war—surely the U.S. government has forgotten you by now. There must be enough unraveling in Washington to occupy their time, and now so many know the war is wrong.

What can I do from here but send my love? And hold you in my heart?

Please don't punish yourself for the trouble you had

with Bridget. It's the way of children and their parents to have these falling-outs. To disagree about choices made in life. And you were sadly right about Serenity, and that leader, Daniel Walker; maybe if she had left she'd be alive today. But being right can't console you now. The best that you can do is save the children.

I am here. Please call day or night. Write. I am waiting on your word.

I love you,
Justine

When I finished with the letter we all just sat there silent. Nearly two full years had passed, two years come October, but it felt like Mama's dying was happening just now. Nightingale wiped a tear off her cheek; Baby dropped his head into my lap.

"All the way in France," Nightingale said.

Baby tucked his hands under his cheek and sighed. "That letter made me sad."

"Me, too," I said. It made me think of Mama gone.

We didn't read on after that letter; instead we walked out to our peak, the highest hill in Eden, where you could see far into the fields. When we first came to Old Finn's we used to stand there in the winter, with nothing but the snow, and take turns listing off what Mama was missing up in heaven.

Every list started off with us. Then we moved on to Mama's favorite foods, the songs she liked to sing, *Charlotte's Web*, the Beatles, sunflower seeds with raisins, fuzzy socks, our drawings. Anything we did. The more we listed, the more we got to love her. Somehow Mama's list of missed things kept her there with us.

It had been a long time since we thought of Mama's list. Like every lost thing, we gradually got used to Mama gone.

"Let's make a Miss List for Old Finn," I said.

"Us," Nightingale started. "I know that he must miss us in Duluth."

"Fishing," Baby added. "Carving. Picking ticks from Woody Guthrie's fur." Old Finn loved to dote on Woody Guthrie.

We dropped down in the grass, stared up at the sky. A shadowed moon glowed white against the pink.

"Your oatmeal cookies," Nightingale said to me. "Shakespeare and Thoreau. Mozart and Beethoven. The globe."

"Who?" Baby asked. "Is *Throw*—?"

"Thoreau." Nightingale laughed. "He wrote that book about living all alone. *Walden*."

"Oh," I said. *Walden* sat on the nightstand next to Old Finn's bed. "My coffee in the morning. Atticus and Scout. Justine." I closed my eyes and wondered about love. How long it could last. If Justine loved Old Finn once, why wouldn't she love him now?

"Justine?" Nightingale stroked her long black braid. "You think he'd miss Justine?"

"Well, I'm sure he doesn't see her or we'd know her," I said. "So I guess he must still miss her."

"But she didn't help Old Finn when Mama died," Baby said. "She just stayed in France eating bread and chocolate." Sometimes Baby picked up bits and pieces I never would expect.

"She couldn't leave her students," I said. "Not all the way in France."

"But she knew Old Finn was sad," Nightingale added. "And he was here at Eden all alone."

"Not for long," I said. "It wasn't long before we came."

29

SHELTER

We were sad and scared and heartsick living in that shelter, and every day I'd wake up hoping Mama was alive, sure she'd show up at the main door any minute, scoop us up into her arms, tell us that the sheriff had made some bad mistake. I'd wake up and wait, and then it never happened.

The best that I could do was tend to Nightingale and Baby, watch over them the way I'd done when Mama was alive. It's why I'd argued with Miss Hawkins over Nightingale's braids, and fought hard with Mrs. Traynor when she made Nightingale go without her gowns. It's why I held that bully Curtis facedown in the dirt for ripping Baby's blanket and why the tutor, Mrs. Stern, said I had trouble with authority. I had trouble because I had to scrap to keep us safe, to take care of the Stars the way that Mama would.

It seemed longer than three weeks before Old Finn took us from that shelter, drove us to Serenity, and helped us pack the last of what little we had left. Our clothes and toys and crafts and Mama's things. Her photographs of Daddy. All the pictures she'd taken of us kids. Looking through her album, I wished she'd spent more time on our side of the camera; I wanted a whole book full of Mama.

While we packed up at Serenity, Old Finn stood beside us as our grandpa, but he was mostly just a stranger, a quiet, burly man Nightingale and I had only met when we were young. And there he was folding Mama's shirts and socks and undies, lining her clothes up in a box while our commune family at Serenity streamed in with their good-byes. To tell us they were sorry. To let us know that with Daniel Walker gone Serenity might end.

"I hope so," Old Finn growled at Skye. "You people need to make decisions for yourselves, not worship at the altar of some half-baked hippie leader. Daniel Walker wasn't any kind of god. What was there to follow in that man? Or any man? Bridget should have known better."

"Daniel Walker is now dead." Skye pursed her narrow lips. "Don't speak ill of the dead."

Baby pressed his cheek against my hip and Nightingale flinched the way she did when fights broke out at the shelter. Those three weeks had worn our nerves raw. Any minute an argument could go from words to fists.

"And my daughter's dead," Old Finn said, a raspy choke breaking in his throat. "These children lost their mother. Maybe in the future, when someone asks for loyalty, you'll make certain they deserve it. Few do. Daniel Walker didn't."

"He didn't," Nightingale echoed. She was crouched down in the corner, one long braid closed tight in each small hand. "Or Mama wouldn't be dead."

"You got that right, sweetheart," Old Finn said. Then he lifted Nightingale up into his arms, even though she was years past being held, and Nightingale roped her legs around his stomach, wrapped her pale arms around his neck, and sobbed into his shirt. And just like that Old Finn was Nightingale's grandpa, not just some strange man who came to save the Stars.

"I'm glad to go," I added to show Old Finn I was on his side. I didn't want Nightingale to have someone I didn't. I was too alone with Mama gone. "I really am," I said to Skye. I said it, but I didn't feel it in my heart. Serenity was the only true home I'd ever known—I didn't want to leave the mountains or the ponies, the shanty that we built off in the woods, my mornings in the big stone kitchen learning to bake bread. I didn't want to leave the last place Mama lived, but Old Finn was the only hope we had. I walked over to Old Finn and leaned a little toward his massive body; he was strong enough to take care of us all. Then I felt the weight of his big hand land steady on my head. Baby nudged his little body in between us, his arms wrapped tight around Old Finn's solid leg. "There's nothing for us here with Mama gone."

. . .

I didn't like to think much of those days, the shelter, my last time at Serenity, or how it was when we first moved to Eden—but lying in that field, remembering Mama's Miss List, made me think of how we left angel after angel in the snow like some kind of secret message we hoped Mama saw from heaven. We were always trying to find a way to talk to Mama.

"Remember how it was?" I asked Nightingale and Baby. I didn't want to have these memories alone. "Those days when we first came?"

"You didn't like Old Finn," Nightingale said. She rolled up on her elbow. "But Baby and I did."

"I liked Old Finn," I said. Nightingale held on to every memory, even ones I wished that she'd let go.

"No, you didn't," she argued. "You said you wished we lived back in Serenity. You thought Old Finn was mean— especially his schooling."

"Well, I did hate the schooling." I sighed. I didn't like our schooling now; Old Finn still put too much stock in books. And I'd never been made to sit down at a table and do lessons or write sentences I didn't want to write. But worse was all that number work he gave us—multiplication and division, decimals and fractions. I'd rather spend my hours combing snarls from Scout's mane. "But that isn't what I meant, Night."

Old Finn was sick; it hurt to think of how slow I was to love him or how quick Nightingale and Baby took to Eden, while I pouted through my reading, refused to do the math. I closed my eyes and thought of those first days, the stubborn way I stood up to Old Finn, how he always laughed at Baby or praised Nightingale's brain, but there wasn't much in me that seemed to shine. Then one day out of the blue he asked me to his woodshop, a place he went to work in private, and he showed me how the steady act of carving gave his mind some peace. "Just this," he said, and slid a tiny chisel down a wing. "Making something out of nothing, working hard to find the beauty in a plain old chunk of wood." When he offered it to me, I gouged some crooked lines into a block of basswood. Old Finn said I wasn't going to carve a bird that day, or maybe ever, but I was welcome in his woodshop to work here at his side. Just me. The two of us together learning another kind of lesson.

I thought about the first thing that I made—a wood-and-nail loom for Nightingale's birthday—and the patient way Old Finn taught me how to measure so every single nail came out right. And while we worked, we talked about the horses or what it meant to be the oldest or how watching out for Nightingale and Baby would be always up to me, and in between he taught me how working with a ruler was just another way of thinking about math.

"Remember how we had to wear those horrible Sears

snow pants?" Nightingale said. "And we couldn't keep our mittens out of Woody Guthrie's mouth? And those plays we got to put on at Miss Addie's?"

Those plays didn't seem that long ago. "I liked it when he'd count those plays for reading," I said. Nightingale's scripts were better than our books.

"You think he told those stories to Justine?" Baby asked.

"You think he wrote about our plays?" Nightingale asked proudly.

"Don't know." I shrugged. "We only have her letters."

I hoped Old Finn never told her how I crumpled up my printing or how I stormed out of the cabin the time he handed me a first-grade spelling book when Nightingale had already finished fourth. I didn't care that she'd had more years of practice; I wasn't doing less than Nightingale. *Pride*, Old Finn had said when he found me in the hayloft. *I know now how your mama got your name.*

"If he did," I said, "I hope he only told the good parts."

"Me, too," Nightingale said. "I wouldn't want our bad days going all the way to France."

30

NO ONE ELSE'S STORY

We all agreed to leave the letters for the morning; news of Mama's dying was just too sad and lonely when night was coming on. Plus Baby said that letter made him think about the shelter, the fat lip he got from David Cane, and Baby's fretting on that shelter only made my worries worse.

But when we woke up the next morning, we didn't have time to read. Woody Guthrie was barking at the window; Sage and Nash were already in our yard, the big black camera there on Nash's chest.

"It's them," Nightingale groaned.

"Sage!" Baby tore out of his pajamas, pulled on his dirty jeans and T-shirt, stepped his bare feet straight into his boots.

"Wait," I called, but Baby just ignored me; he was out the cabin door before I had a chance to tell him no.

"Now what?" Nightingale said. "We have to stop that story. All those lies, they can't be in a magazine."

"They won't," I said, even though part of me still wanted our story on the newsstands. Pony rides and popcorn. Atticus and Scout.

"No more lies, Pride." Nightingale lifted up her finger. "No more talk about that charity."

"Okay," I said. "I won't bring up the charity."

"How you fixed for Sugar Smacks?" Nash asked when I stepped out onto the porch. He gave me his big smile. In just a day his whiskers were moving toward a beard; they both still wore their same old rumpled clothes. Old Finn would never let us go that long without a bath. "Sage wouldn't get out of Goodwell without another run with Baby. You know kids, they do something once and it turns into a ritual." He nuzzled Sage's hair, then set her down with Baby to run off through the yard. Nightingale was wrong; a dad as nice as Nash wasn't sent here as a spy.

"So what about the souvenirs?" he asked. He walked over to my shelves of brick and barn boards. "Looks like you already got a little shop set up for display. Your grandpa make this showcase for you kids?"

"No," I said. "I built it. Just yesterday. Before we had the storm."

"Oh wow!" He whistled. "You all by yourself? Maybe by next summer you'll have the cure for cancer." Nash laughed.

"I don't think so," I said, blushing. It was hard for me to look him in the eye with all the lies I'd told him. "Cancer isn't much like building shelves." No one had been smart enough to find a cure for Daddy.

"No, I don't suppose," he said. "But I'd love to see those souvenirs before I leave. Maybe buy a couple for the road?"

"Okay," I said. We could use whatever money Nash still had to give.

"I'm going to Miss Addie's," Nightingale called out through the window.

"Miss Addie's?" Nash asked me. He sat down on the porch step, stretched his legs as if he wasn't in a hurry to move on.

"Just a woman on our property," I said.

"Hmmm?" he hummed. "You got a big place here?"

"Forty acres," I answered. Old Finn loved his forty acres.

He took a tiny notebook from his pocket, wrote down *40 acres.*

"Why'd you write that down?" I asked. I didn't want Nightingale to be right about the file.

"Just jotting for the story," Nash said. He slid his notebook back into his pocket. "In case I decide to take this angle after all. Three bright kids and a charity—pony rides and popcorn—all off the beaten track. That's human-interest writing at its best."

"I guess," I said.

"So what about those souvenirs?" Nash asked. "I'd love to have a look."

"Okay," I nodded. Nash could buy them quick and go. I brought the basket from our cabin, lined the souvenirs up on the shelves. God's eyes, Baby's painted rocks, Nightingale's pot holders, bookmarks, her crochet crosses, the lanyard that she made. Baby's animal tattoos he was selling for a penny.

"Baby's tattoos are a penny. Every other thing is going for a quarter." Yesterday we'd decided on a dime, but that was before the Neosporin and the $2.15 we still needed for Duluth. "Except the oatmeal cookies. They're a nickel each."

"Best deal in town," Nash said. "You kids ought to work for Wall Street." He stood up from the step, lifted up his camera, and shot our souvenirs. A long, clicking string of pictures. "God's eyes," he said. "You got to love these things. *Ojos de Dios*. I remember making them at church camp."

I couldn't imagine Nash winding yarn through sticks. "I learned them at Serenity," I said. I'd never been to church camp. "Skye taught me in the craft hut."

"Serenity?"

"A place we used to live," I said. "Down in New Mexico."

"New Mexico?" Nash opened up his eyes wide, but he didn't write that down. "I did a piece once on New Mexico. Santa Fe."

"You've been to Santa Fe?" I said, surprised. We hadn't met a soul in Goodwell who'd been to Santa Fe.

"Sure," Nash said. "Great place."

"Did you see the artist market?" I said. "Mama took us

there. Or the old woman in the square who sold those cookies?"

"Powdered sugar?" Nash smiled. "I loved those things!"

"Yes, those!" I said. "With jelly in the center."

"I guess that's where you kids got your magic spirit," Nash said. "There's enchantment in New Mexico. I had a sense you came from someplace else. But I was thinking Fairyland." He laughed.

"Serenity," I said. "It was a commune in the mountains. With ponies and a stream." Mama always said hardly any-one grew up in a commune, and someday we'd see it made us special. But Serenity was something we hardly talked about at Eden, because everything about it just upset Old Finn. "And we got to go to free school." Free school was my favorite part. Not Daniel Walker. Or how Daddy's cancer didn't get cured there the way Mama hoped it would. Or Mama dying in that van. But there were good things at Serenity I'd loved.

"Free school? Now there's an oxymoron. What in the world is free school?" He took a photo of the cookie jar.

"It's where you get to study what you want. You don't have to read," I said, but maybe that's why I didn't know what oxy-something meant. "Or do number work. So I hardly ever worked at either one. I liked taking care of tod-dlers in the kids' yard or kneading bread or baking cakes. Or tending to the ponies. We had four ponies there." Tell-ing this to Nash made me proud of where I'd come from, because no one else's story was anything like ours. Now maybe he could write about Serenity; forget the charity and lies. Serenity was true.

"Terrific," he said. "I want to sign Sage up. And what was it? Serenity?" He patted at the pocket of his shirt, where he kept that tiny notebook.

"Yep," I said.

"Great name. Serenity. So why'd you leave? How'd you end up living way up north?"

"Oh." I stalled. I couldn't say Mama died because now she was a painter. "The peace," I said. "Mama liked the peace where Old Finn lived." Peace was true; it could be in the magazine.

"I get that," Nash said. "It certainly is peaceful. So your mom? Any chance that I could catch her before she heads off to paint?"

"Too late," I said. I could feel the heat climbing up my face; suddenly I'd gone from truth to lies. "She's already left."

"Then Old Finn?" he asked. "That's your grandpa, right?"

"Yep," I said. "But he's sort of like a hermit." A hermit wouldn't come out to talk to Nash. "Do you know what that is?"

"I do." Nash smiled. "He keeps off to himself."

"That's it," I said. "Exactly."

"I understand," Nash said. "But I wonder if we might just have a word."

31

NOT ANY NUMBER HERE

I told Nash Old Finn was in Duluth. I didn't say that he got sent there sick; I said he'd gone to sell his carvings to a store. It was a story Nash seemed to take as truth.

"Ah, right," Nash said. "He carves. I saw his work in Goodwell. Found it at the Northwood Nook, exactly like you said."

"You did?" I couldn't believe he looked for Old Finn's work.

"I'd have liked one of his loons, but I didn't have the cash. Got to watch my money on the road. They don't exactly pay you millions to do a freelance gig, especially this travel magazine." I felt bad for taking Nash's money; he didn't seem to have much more than us. "But at least the owner of the Junk and Stuff let us crash out at his place, park the van out in his yard so we could sleep."

"Thor?" I said. Nash and Sage met Thor?

"Yep," he said. "Thor Jensen, that's the guy. Super-kind. But I didn't want to waste the welcome. I figured we'd get on our way before he felt obliged to offer breakfast."

"He lets us leave our horses at his place. It's the closest we can ride them into town."

"That's what he said." Nash looked out at our fields. "Said he'd seen you earlier that day. He seemed surprised about your business. Said your grandpa wasn't one to take to tourists."

A lump rose in my throat. Did Nash tell Thor about the charity? Did Thor tell Nash our parents were both dead? I didn't know how much Thor knew about our family, but I was sure he knew that we were orphans, why else would we be living with Old Finn. Same with Nosy Nellie at the Northwood Nook in town. If Nash asked her, she'd have said the same.

"Did you tell Thor about the travel magazine? The story you might write?" I tried to keep the tremble from my voice. I didn't want either of them to see me as a liar, but once they started talking they could figure that part out.

"No," he said. "No one trusts a journalist. Especially these days. Half the country blames us for destroying Richard Nixon. The other half adores us. I never know which half I've wandered into. I just said I'd brought Sage out here for a ride." He pulled his little notebook from his pocket, flipped it open to a page. "But that phone number you gave me? That's not any number here."

"It's not?" I said. "I guess I was confused. We haven't lived here all that long."

"No?" Nash squinted.

"And I guess I don't call home."

Nash rubbed his hand along his whiskered chin like he was thinking. "You know," he said. "I'm just writing freelance for a travel magazine. It's not like I'm cracking Watergate." I rearranged the items on the shelf. I wished something huge would happen, something big that would stop the conversation. Baby dropping from the swing. Another set of stitches. "And still . . ." He stopped like he was looking for the words. "Sometimes you stumble on a story. Something bigger than the one you thought you'd started."

"You want to pick your souvenirs?" I interrupted. I didn't like Nash's voice. "We've got to start our school."

"Right now? School in the summer?"

"We learn at the table," I said. "Year-round. And we have to get our lessons done." We hadn't had a minute for our lessons since Old Finn went in sick, but I'd be happy to start now if it meant that Nash would leave. We could give them up once he was gone. "Baby!" I shouted. "Come in for your reading."

"Mind if I just wait?" he asked. "For your grandpa or your mom?"

"You should come back later. Someone ought to be here."

"Like when?"

But before I had an answer, a station wagon pulled into our yard. That mean woman and her dreadful boys were back.

32

CABIN FEVER

This is it." The woman stepped out of the car, waved her cigarette in my direction. She was dressed in an old housecoat, and today her hair was twisted tight into a halo of bobby pins and big pink plastic rollers.

"Jeanette." Her husband shook his head. He looked like most of the tourist men we saw in Goodwell—pale legs, black socks with fishing shorts, a sporty shirt with a penguin stitched into the pocket, his face and arms burned red from too much sun.

Nash flipped to a blank page. "You know these folks?" he asked me.

"No," I said. "Not really."

The bratty boys scrambled from the car. "That's her," Tommy shouted. "She's the girl who yanked me off the horse."

"When was that?" Nash asked. He was writing down each word.

"I didn't," I said. I wanted something big to happen, but this big wasn't it. "I dropped him when he kicked me in the stomach."

"And then she had the nerve to ask for money," the woman said to Nash. She took a long suck on her cigarette. "Show him how you limp." She reached down and shoved Tommy forward a few steps. At first he made a little hobble, then he walked like anybody else. "His ankle's sprained."

"Jeanette," the husband snapped so she'd shut up. He looked around the yard. "Is this operation licensed and insured?" he asked Nash.

"I'm just a customer," Nash said. He took the lid off the rooster jar. "A nickel each," he tried to joke. "And they're really, really good." He held the jar out to the man in the black socks.

"So who's in charge?" The father stared at me.

"I am," I said. "I'm in charge this morning."

"Are you versed in liability?" he asked me.

"She's a kid," Nash said. "She hasn't studied law." I could see he didn't like these people either. Not even the husband.

"Have you?" he barked at Nash.

"Not a drop," Nash said. Compared to all the tourists, Nash really looked like a hippie—his curls too long, his bare feet tan and dirty in strappy leather sandals, his clothes gray and wrinkled from living on the road.

"We need to speak to the person who's responsible. You can't operate a business without being insured."

"It's not a business," Nash said. "They raise money for a charity. Three sweet kids have set this up. They're not going to have insurance."

"Regardless," the father said. "If my son's injury is serious, someone here will pay."

"How much?" I said. We still needed money for our tickets to Duluth. "You can take some souvenirs. For free." I was glad Nightingale wasn't here to see this family take her crosses.

"That crap?" the woman scoffed. "Is that supposed to pay our bills?"

"Jeanette," the husband said again. "Why don't you and the boys get in the car? Let me handle business."

"I want popcorn," one boy whined. "I don't want those cookies."

"There isn't any popcorn," I said. I wanted everyone to leave. I wanted to go back to being just the Stars. Three kids in the cabin by ourselves. As soon as they were gone I'd take the signs down from the highway. Find another way to make the money for the bus. It'd been nothing but big trouble to let strangers come to Eden. Old Finn was right—everything was easier alone.

"We want to see your mother," the woman ordered. She grabbed one boy by the arm and shoved him into the car. "The rest of you get in," she said. "There isn't any popcorn."

"She's dead," Nightingale said. I glanced over at the cabin. Nightingale was at the door watching this whole scene. Then she stepped out in her nightgown, her long black hair woven in fresh braids. Maybe she hadn't gone to Miss Addie's after all. "Our parents are both dead." Her face was serious and solid; her dark sheep eyes didn't blink.

"Is that true?" the man asked Nash.

"I would assume—" Nash said, but I couldn't look in his direction.

"I thought your brother said your dad was dead. *Your dad*," the woman said.

"He did," I said. "But both of them are gone."

"You know," Nash said a little softer, "if your son's not badly hurt, why don't you let it be?"

"Well, someone still should pay," the woman urged her husband. She ground her cigarette into the grass. "Dead or not, these kids don't live out here all alone. Someone's making money off this business. Selling rides and harming helpless victims like poor Tommy."

"Let's goooooooo." A high-pitched whine came from the back window. "I want to go to Deerland." Up in the front seat, Tommy leaned hard on the horn, so loud and long, Sage and Baby came running from the woods.

"I want to talk to somebody," the woman said. "If you can't produce a parent, we'll talk to the police. Some adult will answer for your actions."

"Now, Jeanette," the husband said. He reached into his pocket and jangled his loose coins. "If these children are real orphans, why not let it rest."

"It's the principle!" She climbed into the car and slammed the door. "You just go back to fishing, Henry," she shouted at her husband. "Go back on your boat! I'll take care of this."

"Oh, for heaven's sake." He snatched a couple cookies from the jar, put a quarter in my hand. "The wife's got cabin fever." He rolled his eyes at Nash. "Next year, I'm coming fishing all alone."

33

COULD BE THIS AFTERNOON

Are they calling the police, Pride?" Baby wrapped his arms around my waist, pressed his sticky cheek against my shirt. "Why'd that horrible woman come back to our cabin?"

"I don't know," I said. I hoped this wasn't going in our story. This, or Mama's death. I didn't want either one in Nash's magazine. "She was mad her son got hurt."

"But he kicked you in the stomach," Baby said. "And they didn't pay."

Sage crawled into Nash's lap, laid her head against his chest, stuck two fingers in her mouth like she was scared. "You kids have fun?" Nash asked. He didn't say a word about Mama's being dead; he just kissed Sage on the head the way Daddy did to me. I wished I were still small enough to sit on someone's lap. "So your mother isn't painting in the fields?" Nash said finally. He asked the question kind enough, but I could tell he wasn't happy.

"No," I mumbled.

"And is she really dead?" He looked at Nightingale.

"She is," I said. I wanted some little piece of truth to come from me.

"And is your last name really Matisse?"

"No." I hung my head. "Our last name is . . ." I wanted to say Guthrie, but I just told him Star.

"Star?" he questioned as if he thought our last name was just another lie. "With two *r*s?"

"One. But will you put that in your story?"

"The part about your mother?" he said gently.

"Mama or our names," I said. "You can't call us the Stars." I couldn't tell Nash about the county or the file the government once kept on Old Finn's life, but I also couldn't let him say we were the Stars. "If you don't like Matisse, Guthrie would work fine."

"Like the dog?" He stared at me. "Why don't we just go back to the facts? Start with those and get them straight?"

I could have told the whole truth at that minute, but I'd already said Old Finn was in Duluth; I'd only left out the part that he was sick. I pressed my fingers into Baby's neck so he'd stay quiet. Gave Nightingale a glance so she wouldn't interrupt.

"We live here with Old Finn," I said. "But we don't like to tell the world we're orphans. And we always keep our last name to ourselves."

"Okay," Nash said slowly, like he didn't trust my explanation. "And where's Old Finn today? And yesterday? Who's watching you right now?"

"Old Finn's off in Duluth just like I said. He really is. And we're watched over by Miss Addie until Old Finn gets back. Which will probably be soon. Her trailer's on the wood path, so we're not out here at Eden all alone."

"Soon?" Nash asked. "Like when?"

"Could be this afternoon," I said. It could. I didn't know when he'd be home.

Nash ran his hand over Sage's curls. "Any chance that I could have a conversation with Miss Addie? Or is she a hermit, too?"

"She sort of is," I said.

"I just need to know you have someone on this place. Substantiate this story."

"Substantiate?" I asked.

"Make sure it's true before it's in a magazine."

"It's still in the magazine?" Nightingale complained. "We don't want it printed, not a word."

"Well, let's just wait and see," Nash said. "Let's start off with Miss Addie. I'd like to ask a couple questions."

"Okay," I finally said. We needed Nash to go. "But first I have to ask her because she's not much used to guests."

"And I'll give Sage some Sugar Smacks," Baby blurted. "We didn't eat our breakfast yet."

"We're all out of Sugar Smacks," I lied. I didn't want them staying long enough to eat.

"No," Baby said. "We still have half the box."

I led Nash down the wood path to the trailer while Nightingale stayed behind to keep an eye on Sage and Baby; I knew she didn't want to listen to more lies. "You wait outside," I said. "I ought to have a word first with Miss Addie."

"Right." Nash pulled his notebook from his pocket. "I'll just jot some notes down while I wait."

I wished he wouldn't keep writing; I didn't want every bad part of this story in some travel magazine. Especially the part about that woman and her husband. Or Mama's being dead. Or the lies I told this morning.

"Hey, Miss Addie." I walked to her TV to turn the volume down. She was dozing in her rocker, a movie magazine spread open in her lap. I gave her a quick shake. "Someone's here to meet you."

"Here?" She opened up her eyes, straightened out her wig. "Someone's at *my* trailer?"

"A man," I said. "He's from a magazine."

"A magazine!" Miss Addie fluttered. "Pride dear, get my mirror!" She pointed toward her vanity. "And my powder and my rouge. Lipstick, too."

I did just as she said, set it on the metal tray where she kept her *TV Guide*. I didn't need a mirror to know how bad

I looked this morning—my thick straw hair in tangles, my dirty clothes lifted off the floor. I probably looked as road-worn and uncombed as Nash and Sage.

"What does he want here, dear?"

I leaned closer to her chair, talked into her ear so he couldn't hear us from outside. "He wants to know if some-one's watching, to make sure we're not alone up at the cabin. So you just need to tell him that we aren't. And that Old Finn should be home this afternoon. And we have a shop for charity."

"Charity?" Miss Addie blinked. "I'm not sure what you mean."

"We have a little shop where we sell stuff."

"Did you open that in Goodwell?"

"Sort of," I said. It was strange to think Miss Addie didn't know what went on at the cabin.

"Are we in a magazine?" Miss Addie asked. She looked into the mirror, drew two wavy bright-red lines over her lips, patted puffs of powder on her cheeks, then she fol-lowed that with two pink smears of rouge. "Earrings now." She straightened out her ringlet wig.

I ran and grabbed the emeralds from her dresser, waited while she clipped them on her lobes.

"Okay?" I said. Makeup changed Miss Addie, but I knew it couldn't help me. Emerald earrings either. I'd just be a hoot like Suzy said. "Can I let him in now?"

"Yes." Miss Addie ran her hands along her muumuu; her

slippered feet were propped up on a stool. All that fussing with her face, and still she looked eighty-three years old. "If you think I look presentable."

"You're fine," I said. "And remember that you're watching over us. Not a word about Old Finn being sick."

"Not a word." She put her finger to her lips. "I remember: He'll be home this afternoon."

34

ANOTHER KIND OF STAR

Nash spoke sweetly to Miss Addie, and right away Miss Addie said she was watching out for us. "I always keep my eyes on these dear children," she said. "And you can see they've never come to harm."

"I'm sure," Nash said. He looked around the trailer at the stacks of magazines, the old phonograph, the ancient record albums lined up on the shelves. "Mind if I take a couple pictures here?"

"Heavens no!" Miss Addie gave a wave. "Will you need them for your story?"

"Could," Nash said. "I still haven't settled on a story yet. This one changes by the minute, that's for sure. It's turned out to be a little like an onion. I keep peeling back fresh layers trying to find the truth."

I wrinkled up my nose; I didn't want to be an onion. I hoped he wouldn't say onion in our story: *The Stars were like an onion.*

"Maybe an apple would be better," I said. "Something folks would eat."

"Pride's right," Miss Addie said. "No one wants to be an onion."

Nash kept his eye against his camera, took photos of the inside of the trailer—the mismatched china cups hanging from the hooks, Miss Addie's old-time playbills taped to the kitchen wall, the dusty framed collection of her clippings.

"Is that enough?" I said. I didn't want Miss Addie's messy trailer in our story, just like I didn't want that mean woman and her kids. I wanted free school and Serenity, souvenirs and cookies, me and Nightingale and Baby, the business we invented by ourselves. A shot or two of Woody Guthrie. Atticus and Scout. Summertime in Eden.

"Those are all my stories." Miss Addie pointed to the wall. "I've been in magazines before. I used to be an actress."

"I surmised that from the playbills," Nash said. "Apparently, you're another kind of star." He moved his lens to focus on Miss Addie, kept it steady while he snapped another string of shots. "Thing is," he said as he kept on snapping pictures, picture after picture of Miss Addie's powdered face, "I'm having some concerns about these children."

"You are?" Miss Addie said, surprised. "But Pride is self-sufficient. Always has been. Her grandpa made sure all the children were. It's how he lives his life. Independent. Pride just got my medicine for me. Put my pills into the right compartments. Days all run together when you're old."

"Oh, I see she's self-sufficient," Nash agreed. "But I've been out here twice, and I can't find a grown-up to sign a simple consent form. And now they've got a crabby customer threatening to sue. Asking about insurance. A license for the business. I need to know there's a grown-up who takes care of these kids, so I know they're not surviving on their own. Selling coffee to buy groceries."

"Selling coffee?" Miss Addie blinked.

"No," I said. "It's nothing. But maybe you could sign the consent form for Old Finn?" If Miss Addie signed, Nash could go back to Chicago with his story, leave us all alone.

"Consent?" Miss Addie asked. "For what?"

"Permission for the story," he said. I knew that he was watching Miss Addie through that lens. Looking for a lie. "I can't run a piece on children without some grown-up saying yes. Their guardian to be exact, but he doesn't seem to be here."

"He isn't sick," Miss Addie said. "He definitely isn't."

Nash took the camera from his face. "Who isn't sick?" he asked.

"Old Finn," Miss Addie blurted. "He isn't sick. And he'll be home today."

A wave of fresh confusion washed over Nash's face.

"Okay." I clapped my hands. "I need to get back to our

schooling. Close the business down until our daily lessons are all done."

"Ma'am." Nash gave a little nod in the direction of Miss Addie. "If you're in some kind of trouble here," he said, "this may have started as a story, but I put people first. So if you or these three children need some kind of help?"

"We don't." I forced a smile. "We just need to do our lessons now."

When we got back to the cabin, Nightingale was walking Scout around the small corral. Sage and Baby sat tandem in the saddle. "Will you look at that?" Nash said. "Sage rode a real-live pony after all." He stopped and snapped another string of pictures.

"We've got to close the business now for schooling," I announced. "Open up this afternoon."

"Close?" Baby frowned. "But we still need more money for the—"

"Not now," I said before Baby had a chance to blurt another thing. I pulled Sage from the saddle, led her out the gate. "You, too," I ordered Baby. Baby hated help if anyone was watching.

"Schooling?" Baby fussed. "Is this from Nightingale's list? 'Cause I don't like the schooling or the prayers."

"Baby!" Nightingale scolded.

"What prayers?" Nash asked.

"A hundred for Old Finn," Baby complained. "Twenty-five apiece. Every day."

"That's a lot of prayers." Nash gave Baby his sweet smile.

"We like to pray," I said before Nash could ask another question.

"I don't," Baby said. "I want to play with Sage. I don't want to do our schooling now."

"I could stay," Nash said. "Watch the little ones if you girls want to study. Wait here for your grandpa to get home. I could hang out on the porch and do a little writing. I'd just as soon wait here until I get this paper signed. Make sure things are okay."

"No," I said. "The three of us always do our work as one. Right at the kitchen table. Sage will just keep Baby from his work."

"She won't!" Baby argued.

"You go and come back later." I pointed toward the road, pushed Baby a couple small steps toward the cabin.

"Okay." Nash shrugged. "We'll try back this afternoon."

"But if you start to write that story—" I said quickly. I kept one hand on Baby's collar so he wouldn't suddenly squirm free. "Don't say the part about Matisse. Or Mama as a painter." My skin was hot; I meant *don't tell my lies*. "Or that woman who came back to complain. Just tell about the souvenirs . . ."

"You'll have to leave that up to me," Nash said firmly. "In the end, I'll have to decide."

35

CHASED

As soon as Nash's van pulled out of the driveway, I hung our Closed sign on the low branch of the apple tree that stood near Eden's entrance, then went into the cabin and locked up both the doors.

"We'll stay inside today," I said. "Do our lessons like Nightingale wants. Maybe read the letters." We'd left off with Mama dying; I still wondered what happened after that. Were Old Finn and Justine still secretly in love? Once a week, Old Finn picked up his mail from a postage box in Goodwell; maybe Justine's letters waited for him there?

"Not those," Baby moaned. "And all day inside the cabin? Old Finn never keeps us in all day."

"Old Finn isn't here," I said. I closed the drapes, pulled the shades, darkened every room like it was night. I didn't want another stranger at our cabin, another person asking questions, another woman calling the police.

"Did something happen at Miss Addie's?" Nightingale asked, worried. "Something bad with Nash?"

"No," I lied. "Not really." If Nash came back with his form, asking questions, or trying to find Old Finn, we'd hide inside the cabin, pretend no one was home. "I just want a day alone," I said. The sudden darkness in the cabin felt almost like a cave, a cool dim place away from all the lies.

"Are you scared about that woman?" Nightingale peeked out from our curtain.

"But if she goes to the police," Baby said, "they'll take us far away, same as the sheriff did when Mama died. Put us in another terrible shelter until Old Finn comes home. Or worse, split us up and put us into fosters." Once we saw four brothers taken off to different fosters, and after that we feared it would be us. Bad as the shelter was, at least we saw it through together.

"She won't go to the police," I said, even if I worried same as Baby. Everything inside me felt unsettled. I kept thinking of Nash's magazine, and that mean woman in our driveway, and Baby's doctor saying he'd send someone to our house.

"But we still need a dollar and ninety cents to buy our tickets." Nightingale opened up her notebook. "Nash didn't pay us for the Sugar Smacks or souvenirs. Or Sage's ride on Scout. And if we're closed, we can't get any customers."

"But Nash and Sage are coming back," Baby said. "Nash even said."

"Back to see Old Finn," I said. "So next time when they come, we need to hide inside, wait in Old Finn's closet so they won't know that we're home."

"Hide from Sage?" Baby sulked. "But she's coming back to play. I'm going to teach her how to fish down at the pond."

"Not today," I said.

Just then, Woody Guthrie barked a loud alarm, and we all froze. Held our breath while tires ground against the gravel. "Nash?" Nightingale whispered.

I shrugged. It seemed too soon for Nash to be back for Old Finn. We crouched down on the floor, crawled behind the couch, sat there still as stones until we heard the engine disappear off in the distance.

"Our Closed sign must have worked," Nightingale said softly.

"But that could've been a customer," Baby argued. "I want to sell tattoos so I can fill my tobacco tin with pennies. We can't make money hiding in the house."

"We can't," Nightingale echoed. She gave me a dark glance. "And we don't have the money for Duluth."

"We'll get it someplace else," I said. "Baby has his pennies. Miss Addie has her JFKs."

"What?" Nightingale said. "You can't take Miss Addie's JFKs!"

It hurt to ask Miss Addie for her keepsakes, but there wasn't any other way for us to get the money by the morning. Not with our business closed. And I didn't want to wait another day to see Old Finn and ask him for help. "We don't have a choice," I said. "We need the money now."

I left Nightingale and Baby to do their lessons in the loft, raced to Miss Addie's trailer without stopping for a breath. I couldn't shake the sense of being chased down by a stranger, but every time I looked back I was on the path alone.

"That man from the magazine," I told Miss Addie. "Nash. If he comes back, don't open up your door." I didn't want Miss Addie to say another word.

"Why ever not?" Miss Addie asked, concerned. "He certainly seemed friendly."

"I just don't want him asking any questions, or finding out we're out here all alone, because we can't know for certain who he'd tell."

"Oh no!" Miss Addie said. "He's with a magazine. Reporters all ask questions."

"Still," I said. I knew Miss Addie couldn't tell a lie for long. And Nash was good at getting information; somehow his friendly manner made folks tell more than they should. I sat down on the sofa, stared into my hands. I hadn't really come here about Nash.

"We're all out of cereal and milk," I said. We were, but we couldn't buy that now. All the money that we had we'd need for tickets. "And you have those fifty-cent pieces?"

"My JFKs?" Miss Addie said. I could see she was alarmed.

"Well, you told us our first day. You said it's all the money that you had."

"Oh dear," Miss Addie fussed. "Do you need to take them now?"

"We do," I said. "I'm sorry."

"But the magazine? Won't they give us money for that story? Or maybe we'll be famous after that. Rich like all the movie stars."

"Could be," I said to keep Miss Addie's hopes high. I didn't think we'd be rich with our story in Chicago. And we sure wouldn't look too rich standing in our home clothes by a horse, Nightingale's gown down to her knees, her small bare feet black from dirt, me in frayed-hem blue jeans and my favorite faded T-shirt with the rainbow decal peeled away in patches. A plain, lanky girl too tall for thirteen. Suddenly, I didn't know why I'd imagined us as stars. "And if we are, you'll have a hundred JFKs. But for now, Baby can't go hungry. And he won't eat SpaghettiOs again."

"No," Miss Addie said. "But I have canned corn in my cupboard. Maybe peas. We could split a Campbell's soup. Nose around, see what you can find, Pride."

"It's not enough," I said as sternly as I could. I couldn't bear to be too strict with Miss Addie; she was never strict with me. "We have to have the money."

"It's all I have of JFK." Miss Addie shook her head. "Two small keepsakes of a bright life ended early. No one wants a coin of Richard Nixon. No one ever will. Not after all the terrible things he's done."

36

A DOLLAR OUGHT TO DO IT

I was almost to the cabin when Thor stepped out of the barn. "Thor!" I yelped, but it came out like a scream.

"Kathleen?" he said, embarrassed, as if he'd been as startled as I was. He pulled the red bandana from his pocket, lifted the seed cap from his head, and wiped the ring of sweat from his bald scalp. Suddenly, the pale space under his cap struck me as a spooky, hidden thing, something private that hardly saw the light. I knew Thor wouldn't hurt me, but I couldn't have him prowling Eden like Lady Jane out on a hunt. "I was just looking for your grandpa. I gave a couple knocks but no one answered. Thought I'd look around for signs of life. The cabin's all closed up."

"It is?" I stuttered. "I guess everybody's gone." I looked over at the cabin where every window but the kitchen had been covered. Probably Nightingale and Baby were hiding in the loft, waiting for the knocks to disappear. I hadn't even heard Thor's truck pull into our driveway. I slipped the

JFKs into my pocket, took a steady breath so Thor wouldn't see me flustered.

"Everybody? Your grandpa take the other young ones with him? He leave you here alone?"

"I've been visiting Miss Addie," I said. "I'm just coming from her trailer now."

"Ah." Thor nodded. He gave a little whistle through his horse teeth. "That old gal staying healthy?"

"Uh-huh," I said. "Fine." What was Thor doing at our house?

"So your grandpa got his truck fixed?" He glanced over at the driveway, the empty space where Old Finn's truck ought to be parked.

"I guess," I said.

"I've kept my eye out, but I haven't seen his truck drive past my place."

"Probably drove by while you were busy, maybe earlier this morning while you were inside eating breakfast." I had to stop by Thor's on horseback to leave Atticus, but unless he stood guard in his yard he couldn't track every driver who went past. He might have missed Old Finn in his truck. "I bet lots of folks drive by that you don't see."

"Could be," Thor said. "So what about your pony rides? Saw you had a Closed sign on the tree. No cake today? No coffee? I came to give some business, but I'm too darn big to ride that pony."

"No cake," I said. I had cookies in the jar but I didn't want to offer. I just wanted Thor to leave our land.

"Well, I see you're competing with the Junk and Stuff. Got your own what-nots for sale on the porch."

"Souvenirs," I said.

"Ah yes." He laughed. "Like Deerland." He tugged down on his cap rim, hoisted up his overalls like they'd slid down from his hips. "I could take a couple souvenirs. I like a homemade thing. Plus I got this money just burning a hole right through my pocket. You know how it is." He headed toward the front yard, climbed the steps up to our cabin porch. "Can't break the bank, but I'm happy to help out." He pulled a crumpled dollar from his pocket. "So your grandpa's off in . . . ?"

I let the question float away unanswered. I wasn't going to say where Old Finn was. I just stood there quiet while Thor dawdled through our things. He wasn't in a hurry to get home. "Pot holders are nice," he said. "You think that yarn will hold up to the heat?"

"I use them myself," I said. "But what about a crochet cross you can slip into a book?"

"Not too much for reading, but the stitching sure is fine." Thor picked up Nightingale's sewing. "Someone here is handy." He smiled. "That you, Kathleen?"

"No," I said. "Night— I mean Elise does crafts. Mostly I just bake."

"Ah yes, that chocolate cake. You ought to sell some slices at the Junk and Stuff. Cake and lemonade. Flea market days we could use a few refreshments."

"I will," I said. I hoped we'd last out here that long. "See a thing you like?" I said. Thor moved so slow shopping souvenirs, I was sure Nash would drive in any minute, with his form, and start in about Old Finn again. Where he was. How soon he'd be home. Finally, Thor settled on my God's eye, a bookmark, and one of Baby's painted rocks. He handed me the dollar, said to keep the change.

"Thanks." I blushed. Thor's dollar almost felt as wrong as Miss Addie's JFKs. He'd already been too nice and all I'd given him was lies.

"Say," Thor said before he walked down the last step. "You know that long-hair and his daughter who came here from Chicago?"

I knew right away he was talking about Nash. Nash and Sage. *Long-hair* was the Goodwell name for hippie. Nash's hair wasn't all that long, but Goodwell men kept their hair cut short.

"I think," I said. There wasn't any sense lying about that; Nash already said he'd mentioned us to Thor.

"Well, he sure has curiosity," Thor said. "He's got a lot of questions for a stranger. I'm not used to folks with so much interest in our lives."

I could feel the blood burning in my cheeks.

"He certainly seems taken with this business you kids

run. Just so you know, he was asking around town. Nosing some with Nellie."

"He was?" I tried to look surprised.

"And I know your grandpa wants his privacy. So I thought he ought to know there's a stranger sniffing where he shouldn't."

"Thanks," I said. "I'll tell him."

"Where'd you say he was?" Thor glanced back toward the barn like Old Finn might be hiding on the land.

I shoved Thor's dollar into my pocket, pressed it up against Miss Addie's silver coins. If we could make it to Duluth, Old Finn would have the answers. He'd tell me how to keep the family safe. How to steer clear of the county. Stay out of a shelter. What to do about the people Dr. Madden was sending to our house. I'd leave out the part about the magazine and how dumb I was to tell so much to Nash. And that mean woman and her husband; I could never tell Old Finn I'd let strangers on his land.

Thor made a little snort like he was thinking. "You know," he said. "I let that long-hair and his daughter park out at my place, spend the night in that old hippie wreck he's driving. Space is free, figured it was best to keep a stranger close, especially one that might be up to no good. And I got a feeling that long-hair is up to something here. If I were you, I wouldn't make him welcome—friendly as he seems—not with your grandpa gone. You follow me, Kathleen?"

"I do," I said.

"Not even for the money. You got enough today." He nodded toward my pocket, rubbed his wrinkled hand over his big nose. "That dollar ought to do it?"

"It does," I said. Thor's dollar would get us to Duluth.

"Okay," Thor said. "Keep that Closed sign on the tree. Take a break from strangers until your grandpa's here to help."

"I will," I said.

"And maybe you can ask him to swing by my place to see me," Thor said, pausing at the door of his old truck. He gave another glance up at our cabin, the curtains all pulled closed. "Today wouldn't be too soon. I'd like to have a word."

37

CLOSED

Thor's old truck was long gone from our driveway before I had the nerve to give our secret knock. *Row, row, row your boat.* Nightingale barely let me in, and when she did, Baby was tucked behind her, scared.

"Someone came while you were at Miss Addie's," Nightingale said. "Knocking on our door."

Baby held up his bow and arrow. "I was ready, Pride."

"It was Thor," I said. "He came to buy a piece of cake. Find out about our business." I didn't tell them that he asked about Old Finn or warned me about Nash. Thor's warning would make Nightingale worry more. "And he bought some souvenirs. Now we have another dollar on top of what Miss Addie had to give."

"So you took her JFKs?" Nightingale said sadly.

"Had to," I said, even though Miss Addie's money made me feel ashamed. "To get us to Old Finn." I pulled the money from my pocket, let Nightingale take it; I was tired of every hard job in the family, every bad thing no one else would do. "Miss Addie didn't mind," I lied. I checked the latch to make certain it was locked.

"Did you tell her we were buying tickets to Duluth?" Nightingale asked.

"No!" I said. "Miss Addie can't know that. She'd never let us take the Greyhound to Duluth."

"But she needs to know we're gone," Nightingale argued. "She'll be worried if she's left alone all day. Especially morning until night. And she'll be sleeping when we leave." Our bus left at 7:20 and we wouldn't get back to Goodwell until after eight o'clock at night.

"Okay," I said. "You can leave a note outside her trailer, tape it to her door so she'll see it when she lets out Lady Jane. Just tell her that we're—" I stopped. I didn't know where we'd go morning until night.

"At Paul Bunyan!" Baby said. "Remember when we did that with Old Finn? Paul Bunyan Land. And the statue talked. And I got my picture taken with the giant blue ox, Babe? And we left early in the morning, stayed gone for the whole day."

"We can't go to Paul Bunyan Land any more than we can go off to Duluth," Nightingale said.

"Wait!" I smiled at Baby. I was grateful this new lie belonged to him. "We could go with Nash and Sage to help with their reporting. We could say that Nash and Sage took us in their bus."

Nightingale wrinkled up her nose. "Nash already said he couldn't write about Paul Bunyan; it's why he was interested in us."

"Miss Addie doesn't know that," I said. "So just say that in your note. Your cursive is the best so you should write it." I wasn't even sure how *Bunyan* would be spelled.

"I can't lie to Miss Addie," Nightingale objected.

"Then find your own true way," I said, discouraged. "Just leave out the part about Duluth."

That whole, long day I tried to keep things happy, because all of us felt sad from the trouble of the morning—that horrible woman, Miss Addie's JFKs, Nash's finding out our name was really Star. We passed the time playing Lincoln Logs with Baby, making fancy get-well cards for Old Finn, learning at the table while Nightingale taught Alaska out of Old Finn's instructor copy of *Your World*. Eskimos and igloos, ice caps and caribou. After she'd read to us the last page of our lesson, I had to look up five words in the dictionary, while Baby only had to draw a picture of a bear. I wished I hadn't promised she could teach.

Every time we heard the grind of tires against gravel, we stopped what we were doing, snuck to Old Finn's closet, and squashed inside like three sardines. Most cars spied our

Closed sign, backed up, and drove away, but twice Nash came and pounded on the door. Called our names. Walked the grounds. Sat out on the porch jabbering with Sage while Woody Guthrie barked wild at the door.

"Why can't I see Sage?" Baby whispered.

I touched his lips, gave him a soft hush. "Not now," I said. He didn't understand reporters or how Nash could turn us all into an onion or the sick shame that I'd feel seeing my worst lies in print. And I knew Nash wasn't only waiting on his form; he wanted to be certain the three of us weren't living here at Eden all alone. He'd said so to Miss Addie. Nash could call the county like anybody else, bring in the police, but I didn't have the heart to threaten Baby with the shelter—not when that mean mother still sat heavy on his mind.

After the second time Nash left, I snuck out to the kitchen, filled Woody Guthrie's dish, then made a stack of sugar sandwiches for supper. Even though I'd heard his engine fade away, I had a horrible feeling he'd be back any minute, knocking on our door, asking for Old Finn.

I sliced the last small apple in the crisper, rinsed two soft stalks of celery, set it all into a basket for a picnic on the floor.

"We have to eat in Old Finn's closet?" Baby grumbled. "It stinks like Old Finn's shoes."

"It does!" I laughed. Shoes and dust and clothes left too

long on hangers. "We can have our picnic on the floor be-side his bed."

The three of us sat cross-legged on the rag rug, eating our sandwiches and Kool-Aid in a circle, the way I had in kindergarten the one year Mama sent me off to school. We shoved bread into our mouths, split the strips of apple. The soggy celery sat there on the plate.

"I want to play with Sage," Baby whimpered. "And I don't want her to go without good-bye."

Nightingale looked at me. Maybe Baby was thinking about Mama, how she disappeared one day without good-bye.

"She won't," I lied, so Baby wouldn't be sad. We were never going to talk to Sage again. Nash either. "But right now, let's make our morning plans." Baby loved a plan. "The bus leaves at seven twenty, so we'll need to leave here early, so early we might not see the sun. We can use Old Finn's red flashlight for the road."

"I get to hold it," Baby said.

"Okay," I said. I didn't care who held it. "And we have to walk the whole way. Leave the horses here."

"We're walking into Goodwell?" Nightingale moaned. "It's three miles just to Thor's. Another mile on the high-way into town."

"We can't leave the horses at the Junk and Stuff tomor-row," I said. I wasn't riding onto Thor's land to tell more lies, and I couldn't explain our horses left from dawn until dark. Besides, if we were lucky, he'd be asleep tomorrow morning when we passed. Or better yet, the day would be too dark to see us on the road. "We'll drag Baby in a wagon, walk the whole way in."

"Four miles?" Nightingale repeated. "We can't pull Baby that far."

"I will," I said. "And he can walk some, too."

"The whole way!" Baby said. "I don't need the wagon." Baby didn't know the meaning of four miles.

"I'll have it just in case," I said. "Best to be prepared."

38

NO ONE BUT OLD FINN

Before nightfall finally came—before Nightingale ran down to say good night to Miss Addie and left our morning note taped to her trailer, before the three of us took baths to look our best for our visit to St. Mary's, before we'd settled in for the last of Justine's letters—Nash and Sage had been back to our cabin three more times. They'd pounded on both doors, rapped against the windows, sat there on our porch, hoping we'd come home.

Now, even with the three of us tucked into Old Finn's bed, and Woody Guthrie standing guard, I still had the sinking feeling Nash wasn't gone for good. Thor either. Or that vicious, frumpy woman with her stinky cigarettes. I didn't say the same to Nightingale and Baby, but somewhere in my heart I knew my time of keeping safe the Stars was almost done. Our only hope was waiting in Duluth. If Old Finn couldn't come home this week or tell me what to do to save the family, we'd end up in the backseat of a sheriff's car headed for a shelter or foster families just like Baby feared, the three of us somebody else's children, orphans taken in by strangers who didn't care about Old Finn, just the way no one cared that we lost Mama. We'd be an onion with all our layers gone.

"Before we even read," Nightingale said, "I want to say our prayers."

"All twenty-five again?" Baby said.

In all these days, I hadn't even said ten good prayers for Old Finn.

"We can say them quiet inside ourselves," Nightingale said. "Just be certain to keep count."

I rolled over to my side, curved my back to Baby, pulled the covers to my chin, and closed my eyes.

Dear God, I said inside my mind. I didn't bother with the counting. *I just hope you're really listening.* I waited for a minute, but all I heard was Baby's breath. *Maybe I didn't do too good of a job.* Just thinking that made tears well in my eyes. *I know I lied. I guess I lied a lot. But I'm not a liar really. Or I wasn't.* I hugged my knees up to my stomach. I didn't want to be in charge of Nightingale and Baby anymore. *I don't know how to pray*, I said. *Or else my prayers can't make a good thing happen.*

I'd never get to twenty-five if I couldn't finish with the first.

Please make Old Finn be well. So tomorrow when I see him,

he can tell us what to do. Maybe come home with us on the bus. Old Finn would have the money for an extra ticket home. Money for our dinner if we asked.

"I don't want to pray to twenty-five." Baby yawned.

"Me either," I said into my pillow. Trying to pray made my heart hurt worse. "Let's just read the letters before we go to sleep."

"You read," Nightingale said. "I'm going to say my prayers."

Nightingale let me read aloud while she was praying, so maybe she was listening instead of talking straight to God. The first letters after Mama's death were mostly Justine saying she was sorry—Justine sorry about us and Mama gone and Old Finn raising three children on his own. The long days, the exhaustion. I could tell by Justine's letters he'd told her about our chore chart in the kitchen, Nightingale's gowns, how he'd cleared the frozen pond so we could skate and let us choose our Christmas tree. Justine even knew about the miles of paper chain we'd strung for decorations, the ornaments we'd baked from gingerbread, and how it was a thing we'd done with Mama every Christmas. *They must cherish that tradition,* Justine wrote.

Later she said she liked to picture Old Finn as a teacher with his pack of brand-new crayons, tablet of lined paper, the giant chalkboard he'd nailed to the wall. Justine's letters were more about us living with Old Finn than how much she loved France.

"He told all this to Justine?" I said. "All the days that we were living?"

"Hmmm?" Nightingale sighed like she was praying.

"Haven't you been listening?" I knew Baby was asleep, but I didn't think Nightingale would want to miss Justine.

"Some," she murmured, which really meant she was. Maybe even Nightingale couldn't say twenty-five prayers.

It wasn't until the letter that started out just *Mick*, instead of Justine's normal *Dear Mick*, that the two of us found out what happened to their love. Why Justine went away. Why we'd never met her all this time.

March 24, 1973

Mick,

I have read your recent letter many times. Read it and reread it thinking there must be some mistake, hoping somehow I'd misinterpreted your words. Your intention. But I'm afraid you've made your meaning clear.

I understand how much time the children take, and it's true, I've never had the practice. And you're right; I've enjoyed my life alone. But that doesn't mean that I can't change. Or learn to be with children late in life.

But apparently you've made that choice for me.

What hurts me most is that you can't see a place for me in this picture. I had hoped we'd still have our life together when I returned from France, that the two of us would share the burden of the children, the joys as well, at least for that first summer. I had hoped to live at Eden and offer all the help I could. Of course I can't give up my teaching job just yet, but weekends I could visit from Duluth. I see now that arrangement isn't what you want.

Maybe what you claim is true, maybe the four of you have to form a brand-new family, a thing that can't involve me or anybody else. I know how hard you've worked to earn their trust and to create a tiny haven there at Eden, a place far from the world where the children will feel safe. Perhaps another person would be too much of a disruption, but I don't believe I would have done them harm. I know I'm not a mother, but I could have been a friend to all the children. Nightingale and Pride will need a woman they can call on; in a year or two you'll see that for yourself. I'm glad that Pride has found a home beside you in your woodshop, that the two of you have made your peace over carpentry and wood. And I have no doubt she's as determined as you say—full of will and independence—with a bright mind of her own.

But Pride may not stay a tomboy through her teens,

she may want more than your woodshop, and Nightingale might find there's more to life than books. I was a girl; you'll have your hands full, Mick.

"A tomboy?" I said to Nightingale. "Old Finn said I was a tomboy?" He'd never ever said that word to me. And Justine was right—I didn't really want to be a tomboy anymore.

"Just read," Nightingale said. "It doesn't matter, Pride."

I looked down at the letter, found the place I'd last left off.

Perhaps the children aren't really the reason? Perhaps your love has faded while I've been here in France? I always feared the distance would be difficult for us. Of course, I hadn't counted on your daughter's death or you suddenly a parent or starting up a school at the age of sixty-one. I left you as a hermit; clearly you're not a hermit anymore.

I wish you all the best. You, Kathleen, Elise, and little Baxter. (Or Pride and Nightingale and Baby as you call them now.) I've enjoyed the details of their days. Your lively tales of what it's like to have a cabin filled with children. I had so looked forward to knowing them myself, and I'm sad to see that day will never come.

Life takes us by surprise, doesn't it, Mick?

So this will be my last. Come May, I'll be back in

Duluth, same place I've always been—but I won't be
a guest at Eden anymore.

Be well, my friend. You know where I am if things
should change.

I wish you well,
Justine

"So Justine's in Duluth?" Nightingale whispered.

March 24, 1973. If she went home that May, she'd have been back in Duluth more than a year.

I pictured us knocking on her door, saying we were Kathleen, Elise, and Baxter. Bridget's kids she'd said that she would help. And there she'd be with her paintbrush and her pictures, her bread and chocolate, her wide straw hat, her true love for Old Finn. "Maybe we should find her."

"Find her, Pride? But how would we do that?"

39

HISTORIC

The moon still lit the sky when we set off for Goodwell. Miss Addie was asleep out in her trailer; Woody Guthrie watched us woeful from the yard. I'd left him extra food and water in the shade—enough to get him through his dinner—still he didn't want us disappearing down the road.

All of us had dressed for the night chill: sweatshirts, nylon windbreakers, and jeans. Even Nightingale, except she kept my old tennis shoes in hand. Every pair of shoes gave Nightingale blisters; she swore she wouldn't wear them until we had to board the bus. It was enough for her to go without her gown.

It wasn't long before Baby jumped into the wagon, and my right arm ached from my shoulder to my elbow from dragging all his weight. Pulling Baby over gravel was nothing like the wagon rides I used to give at home and Nightingale wasn't strong enough to tug much beyond a minute.

"You're going to have to walk," I said to Baby when we reached the True Believer Church. True Believer was always our first-mile marker in the road. "At least until I get the strength back in my arms."

Baby barely made it another half a mile before I had to stoop low and let him leap up on my back. When we finally reached the top of our last hill, I set him on the ground and we looked down the long stretch of gravel road out to the highway where the Junk & Stuff sat off in the distance and the early morning semis rolled silent on the road. Over in the east, a strip of sunrise pink was brightening the world.

"Look!" Baby shouted. Nash's van was parked in Thor's dry field. I couldn't believe Thor had let Nash spend another night parked on his land. Wasn't he the one who said not to make Nash welcome? "Sage is still in Goodwell after all!"

"They're probably still asleep," I said, which really meant I hoped hard that they were. Except for one old farmer we saw walking toward his barn, and the semi drivers passing in the distance, most people seemed to be in bed. And all the windows were still dark in Thor's small house.

I wished there was a secret path to get out to the highway, some way into Goodwell without walking past Thor's land. But all around, the pine trees grew so thick we'd never find our way out of the forest. Last summer we'd lost Baby in a game of hide-and-seek out in those woods.

"But what if they're not here when we come home?" Baby said. "We should stop by now, so I can say good-bye. I want Sage to know I get to take the Greyhound to Duluth."

"No," I said. "It's too early in the morning. Plus, Duluth is a secret." No matter how I tried, I couldn't get Baby to keep a secret quiet. For all his worries of the shelter, he'd never understand that Sage and Nash might land us there.

"Can I tell her after we get home? Will it be a secret later?"

"I don't know." I crossed my fingers and made a silent wish Sage would be gone.

Nightingale glanced at me. "But I thought that we were hiding from—"

"Watch out," I screamed. Suddenly, a bright-red Mustang roared toward us from behind. I grabbed Baby by the hand and yanked him to the ditch. Nightingale jumped into the weeds. We watched the Mustang zoom halfway down the hill, but then it stopped. Suddenly. And just as suddenly the driver made a sharp U-turn and drove straight back toward us.

"I wish I had my bow and arrow." Baby squeezed my fingers. "I should've brought a weapon."

"Yoo-hoo! Girls!" a woman shouted from the window. She opened up her door. "Girls, it's me. Bernice!" It *was* Bernice, with her frosty blond hair poof high up on her head, her nurse's dress, the little white cap she wore the day we met her at St. John's.

"She's safe," I said to Baby. "She was Old Finn's nurse."

"She was?" Baby scrunched his face, confused. "But why's she stopping now?"

"I don't know," I whispered. Bernice crossed the gravel road. Maybe she was stopping to get her ice-cream quarters back.

"You remember me?" she said, smiling. She looked beautiful this morning with her perfect hair sprayed stiff, her lipstick glitter pink, her eyelids pale blue. It made me wish Mama was Bernice, a woman standing on a highway dressed in white for work. But Mama was too down-to-earth to wear her hair up in a poof. "What are you children doing out so early in the morning? It's barely six o'clock."

"We're going to buy groceries," I said. "Cereal and milk."

"Groceries?" Bernice asked, amazed. "You mean all the way in Goodwell at the Need-More?"

I gave a nod; I didn't want to say too much.

"You're walking into town?" She shook her head.

"It's not so far," I said.

She looked down at Baby. "It's far for him. And you kids can't walk on that highway by yourselves."

"Most of the way Pride pulled me in the wagon." Baby grinned. *Pride* again. I rolled my eyes. I hoped he wouldn't say Pride to the people at St. Mary's.

"We'll keep to the ditch," I said. "Walk along the weeds."

"Heavens no." Bernice looked at Nightingale's feet, my ratty tennis shoes hanging in her hands. "I've got room in my backseat. I'll just stick that wagon in my trunk."

"Okay." Nightingale's sudden yes surprised me. We both knew we weren't allowed to go with strangers, but her poor bare feet must have been worn from the walk.

"That's great," I added quickly. Thor would never see us in the backseat of the Mustang. "We'd be happy for the ride."

It wasn't until we crossed the road to reach the Mustang that I saw a second person in the front seat of the car. The candy striper Suzy. Suzy, who had said I was a hoot. Suzy, who knew that I was crying in the bathroom of St. John's.

"This is my youngest, Suzy," Bernice said when we were all tucked in the backseat. "I take her with me in the summers. Working as a candy striper keeps her out of trouble." Bernice snuck a little wink to us through the rearview mirror.

"Mom," Suzy moaned. She snapped her gum and kept her face set forward. I was glad she didn't say a word about the costume or the wheelbarrow or how she'd leaned against the sink and told me not to tell. Glad, too, she didn't even turn to look at us, not once.

"Couldn't your mother get the groceries?" Bernice asked.

"Not today," I said. "Today she was too sick. And Baxter needed cereal and milk."

"Was she sick the day I saw you at the hospital?" Bernice said, like she was worried. "I remember you two girls came all alone."

"I guess," I lied. "I think she probably was." I pressed my hand down hard on Baby's leg—*not a word, not a single word.*

"That's a shame," Bernice said. "I hope it isn't serious."

My head throbbed from the sweet perfume and hairspray, women smells we didn't have in our cabin. I wished so hard that Mama was just sick, that she'd wake up tomorrow morning and take us into town. Slap my leg when I put my dusty shoes up on the dash, give a wink, tease a little bit, all the mother things Bernice did on our drive to town with Suzy.

"So?" Bernice asked as we passed the Lucky Strike. Even the Texaco was closed this early in the morning. "Is your grandpa getting better? Didn't the doctors send him to Duluth?"

"Duluth," Baby said. "We're on—"

I sank my fingers in his skin. "They did," I interrupted. "They sent him to St. Mary's."

"Yes," Bernice said. "I was happy to hear that. At least he'll have the specialists. We can't help every case here at St. John's. Sometimes a bigger hospital is best."

"Yep," I said before Baby had a chance to blurt another word. "A bigger hospital is best." We were almost to the Need-More; another couple blocks and we'd jump out of this car. Head back to the Lucky Strike to catch our bus.

"Sad day for our country," Bernice said.

"Mom," Suzy groaned and slouched lower in her seat. I couldn't imagine acting that fed up with Mama. But maybe if she'd lived to see me grown to fourteen. A candy striper, a girl with my own job. "Not that crap about the president again."

"Suzy," Bernice scolded. "Watch your mouth, young lady."

Suzy tossed her head and let her ponytail sway.

"This day will be historic," Bernice said. "Trust me. It's a day you'll all remember fifty years from now. Like the two dark days the Kennedys were shot. Or Martin Luther King. Those days leave a deep dent in your mind."

I didn't know why today was so historic, but I knew I wouldn't forget the time we took the Greyhound to Duluth all by ourselves, with money *we* had made, and how we finally got to see Old Finn. And maybe we could meet Justine if we were lucky. All things more important than Nixon and his news.

40

SOME DUMB THING

The Need-More was still dark when Bernice pulled up in front. "It doesn't open up until eight," she said. She stretched one arm across the seat, turned halfway in our direction and took a good long look. This time Suzy did it, too. All the staring made me feel like some strange specimen, a creepy insect scientists would study under a magnifying glass.

"You kids intend to sit here by yourselves?" Bernice glanced down the empty street. "The Donut Hole's the only business open at this hour."

"I love the Donut Hole," Baby said. "Let's go buy a bear claw, Pride."

"Not now," I said to Baby. We didn't have extra money for a bear claw.

"Bear claws are my favorite." Bernice gave Baby a sweet smile. "Suzy's, too."

"They were." Suzy rolled her eyes like Bernice was dumb to say Suzy once liked bear claws.

"Oh, this one"—Bernice lifted Suzy's chin—"she detests the morning. And you know when you're fifteen—everything your mother says is wrong."

"Yeah, right," Suzy huffed.

It didn't seem fair that Suzy had Bernice to bicker with this morning; Mama and I would never get to bicker over bear claws. I opened up the car door, eager to move on. "I better get the wagon from the trunk," I said, once everyone but Suzy was standing on the sidewalk.

"Oh, right!" Bernice smiled. "But I hate to think you'll walk those miles home. Where do you live exactly?"

"Just down the road from True Believer Church," Baby said. "The one with the white steeple."

"On Crest," I lied. I didn't want Bernice snooping at our cabin like everybody else.

"And we might be walking home at dark so I got Old Finn's flashlight." Baby stuck his arm into his canvas sack.

"At dark?" Bernice said.

"Baby's just confused," I said.

"Crest?" Bernice asked me. "I don't know that street."

"Not Crest," Baby said.

"He doesn't know his address," I said quickly. I pulled the wagon from the trunk, set it on the sidewalk. "Get in," I ordered Baby. He sat down in the box, crossed his stubby legs.

"I know my address," he said.

Suzy stuck her head out the open window. "So what

happened to the wheelbarrow?" she asked suddenly. I wished she hadn't kept it in her mind.

"What?" Bernice asked. "What wheelbarrow, Suzy?"

"Some dumb thing." Suzy tossed her ponytail so it made a perfect bounce against her seat. When I got to be a candy striper, I wouldn't be anything like Suzy, even if I could be as pretty as she was. "I guess it's just a joke."

"Well, it doesn't strike me funny," Bernice said. She opened up her purse and handed Baby money. I didn't see how much, but I knew that it was money she put into his hand. "You go get your bear claws," she said. "And wait inside the Donut Hole until the Need-More opens up at eight o'clock."

We didn't buy the bear claws or go into the Donut Hole; instead we walked over to the Lucky Strike once Bernice's car was gone, parked Baby's wagon, and spent the fifty cents she gave him on our tickets to Duluth. With Bernice's fifty cents, we only had to give up one of Miss Addie's JFKs. The other one we'd return when we got home.

"Crest?" Baby asked while we were waiting for the Greyhound. "Isn't that a toothpaste, Pride?"

"It is," I said. "But it sounded like a street."

Nightingale sighed and shook her head; all my lies were more than she could stand. "She'll never know our street," I said.

"But everything is lies," Nightingale complained. "Every

single thing. And I don't want a bad example set for Baby. Lie, lie, lie."

"Then think of them as stories," I said. "A story like those books you like to read. *Toby Tyler? Harriet the Spy? Daddy-Long-Legs?*"

"When you write them in a book," Nightingale lectured, "they aren't lies, they're fiction."

"Okay." I tried to toss my hair like Suzy. But I didn't have a golden ponytail bouncing on my back, I had thick brown hair dull as Scout's old mane. Barely brushed and only to my shoulders with a secret nest of tangles hidden near my neck. "When all of this is over, I'll write my stories down. Then they'll just be fiction. And Old Finn can correct them with his pen."

Nightingale gave me a dark glare. "Old Finn will do more than correct them. He'll be mad you even told them, Pride."

41

ALL I NEED TO KNOW

We were the only ones to board the bus in Goodwell, but the seats inside were already filled with every kind of folk. Frail women like Miss Addie, army men, tired moms with kids, sleeping hippies stretched across two seats. I sat alone behind Nightingale and Baby, watched out the dirty window while Goodwell disappeared.

Mile after mile, my heart raced faster from my fears. What if Old Finn was angry that we came? What if Baby blabbed about the pony rides and popcorn? Or Nash? The travel magazine? The terrible, scary mother? Or what if Old Finn asked about the tickets? And I had to say we took Miss Addie's keepsakes? Spent them on our tickets to see him. What if he'd changed his mind about our having independence and we had to go to fosters or a shelter until he came home well?

"Hey." I reached between the seats and tapped Nightingale's shoulder. I didn't want to sit alone with a worry fire burning through my brain. "Is there room for me if I put Baby on my lap?"

Baby got up on his knees, looked over his seat, flashed me his happy, toothless grin. Already, I'd forgotten to put the Neosporin on his scar. And Dr. Madden said to do it every day. Dr. Madden and his questions made my head hurt worse. Now I'd have to tell Old Finn someone from social-something was coming to our house. Nightingale was right; Old Finn might be really mad. Or disappointed in me the way he was with Mama the years before she died. I didn't want to lose Old Finn's great pride. It was all the love I had left in the world.

"Come into our seat!" Baby sang. His happy eyes glistened with excitement; he didn't have a single worry on his mind. An expedition to Duluth was the perfect Baby journey; he only saw adventure up ahead. "Did you see the real-live army men?"

"I did," I said. I moved up a seat and let Baby have my lap. It was good to have Mama's too-long, sturdy legs—legs that let me balance Baby the way I did when he was only two.

Nightingale kept her head against the window, and I could see all my same worries weighing on her face. "Duluth will be so big," she finally said. "All those streets and buildings. How will we find Old Finn?"

"We'll ask," I said, even though I wasn't sure myself. "Someone there is sure to point it out. And you can read a map. Old Finn taught it in geography." Nightingale was the only one to learn to read the map. "Remember the equator? And Ecuador?"

Nightingale smiled. "You could never keep those straight. But the equator won't be here, Pride. Or Ecuador."

"See," I said. "You'll help us find the way." I dropped my head against her shoulder, but Nightingale's bones were small and hard. I could never find a soft spot to rest my head on Night.

"I'll get us where we're going!" Baby said. "I can be the guide." He pulled his plastic compass from his pocket.

"That's all we need?" I asked. The needle wiggled in the middle but I wasn't sure it worked.

"I got this, too!" He grinned and handed me a rumpled sheet of paper. It was the number for St. Mary's, plus the word Miss Addie had written down that night we carried up her cake. *Enceph*—— I hadn't seen it since I took it from her trailer.

"Where'd you get that, Baby?" I asked.

"I found it on the floor," he said. "After you took it from Miss Addie. I've kept it for my evidence. So we could find Old Finn."

"Oh, Baby, you're just brilliant!" Nightingale cheered. Somehow Baby's plans always made her happier than mine. No one ever told me I was brilliant. She took the paper from his hand, moved her finger slowly past the letters. The word was long; I could never say it, but Nightingale had the patience to sound her way through syllables. "*In-seff-a-light-us.*"

"What's that?" Baby asked.

"I don't know." I shrugged. "It's just a word Miss Addie scribbled down."

The minute we saw the wide, black stretch of water out the dirty window, we knew that we were almost to Duluth. Baby pressed his nose against the glass. "It's Superior," he said. I thought about the first time Old Finn showed us that great lake, how he'd wanted us to memorize all five—Superior and Michigan and Huron, plus a couple others whose names just didn't stick. That first day Lake Superior made me think of California and the ocean Mama took us to once when we were small. I remembered asking Old Finn if Lake Superior went all the way to California and Old Finn saying no. Then his asking if we'd ever had geography. And afterward he bought that boring book *Your Land* and made us study colored maps of North America, and later on the world.

I still hated geography, but I knew now we were far from California. And Duluth was a city in northern Minnesota. And somewhere in this city, I would finally find Old Finn. Tell him that I loved him. Maybe I didn't know Ecuador or the equator or how to say Old Finn's infection, but I knew all I needed to get the three of us this far.

42

SOMETIMES YOU'RE JUST WRONG

It was a long walk to St. Mary's, but nothing like the miles we'd had this morning before Bernice drove us into town. And every step was easier knowing we were closer to Old Finn. People helped us out along the way, pointed out the streets. I took the job of asking for directions, Nightingale listened, and Baby led the expedition with Nightingale keeping us on track.

Even in the summer a cold lake breeze blew between the buildings, whipped my hair into a wild ball of frizz. By the time we'd made it to St. Mary's and stepped into the lobby, all my morning looking good was gone. "Michael Finnegan?" I asked at the front desk.

Compared to St. John's Hospital in Goodwell, St. Mary's Hospital was huge. No wonder they had special doctors here to help. I licked my thumb and scrubbed dried oatmeal from Baby's cheerful cheeks, made sure Nightingale's feet were still in shoes. I tried to picture the surprise on Old Finn's face, how shocked he'd be when we told him we'd made it in alone, with hardly any help. Self-reliant, just the way he taught.

"Three-oh-three." The woman pointed toward the elevator. I was glad she wasn't another pretty girl like Suzy, another model-girl to mock the mess that I looked now. "Ask at the front desk."

I wished we could just see Old Finn instead. I didn't want another desk nurse asking questions about Mama, and I couldn't tell another lie, not with Nightingale right here, standing watch. I just wanted to rush into Old Finn's room, give him a big kiss, find out what he thought should happen next. Where he kept the money for electricity and groceries. What we ought to say to stay steer clear of the county. How long before he'd be home with us again.

"Maybe I should do the talking," I said just before the elevator stopped. "You better leave it up to me."

"You?" Nightingale folded her arms over her chest, stuck her chin up in the air the way she did when she was mad. "You can't be the only one talking to Old Finn. You're not the boss here, Pride."

"I'm talking to Old Finn!" Baby firmed his hands against his hips.

"I know," I said. "I just mean I ought to be the one to answer questions. And maybe tell Old Finn the things he missed. 'Cause we shouldn't mention Nash or Sage. Or the travel magazine. Or the business that we're running. Or any of the things Old Finn wouldn't like."

"Or all your lies," Nightingale added like she saw straight into my mind.

"Or those," I said. "Not while he's getting well."

"We won't," she snapped. "We know what we shouldn't mention."

"Yes, we do!" Baby stuck out his lower lip. I didn't want them mad at me before we saw Old Finn. We'd come this far together; I didn't know why they were fighting with me now.

"No one *ever tells you*, Pride," Nightingale said, making that *ever* sound accusing. "It's always you giving out directions. Stepping in as boss. And sometimes you're just wrong."

"You get to be the teacher. You take charge of our lessons." I waited for Nightingale to soften but she wouldn't. "You do. And I let you. I just want a happy visit with Old Finn."

"Me, too." Nightingale stiffened back her shoulders. "And I'm smart enough to know what can't be said."

The desk nurse said to wait there in the lounge, just beside the elevator doors until the orderly returned Old Finn from OT. "I'll have Henri bring him in just as soon as therapy is finished." I didn't understand *OT* or *orderly*, but I couldn't wait to see Old Finn again.

In the small side lounge beside the elevator, we crowded on a bench next to a coffee cart with extra packets of Swiss Miss and Lipton tea. "You want some cocoa?" I asked Nightingale and Baby, but neither of them said a single word. I poured Old Finn a cup of steamy coffee, dumped in streams of sugar the way he liked at home. Then I pulled the cookies from my knapsack, arranged them nicely on a napkin so I could serve Old Finn a snack. There were plenty there for Nightingale and Baby, but none of us would eat without Old Finn.

Nightingale walked over to the corner, turned the television down so Old Finn wouldn't have to hear it; Old Finn could never stand the sound of a TV. It's why he never lingered long in Miss Addie's little trailer.

"I know why it's historic," Nightingale announced in her too-smart teacher voice. "Today. I know why Bernice told us today would be historic."

"Why?" I said to be polite, but I didn't care. All that I could think of was Old Finn.

"Nixon is resigning," Nightingale said. "Tonight. Which means he won't be president. And *I* want to be the one to tell Old Finn."

"Okay," I said. "You tell him that. That ought to make him happy."

"What can I tell?" Baby moped.

"I know!" I said. "Tell him that you got your stitches out!"

"That isn't hysteric." Baby kicked his cowboy boots together, back and forth just to make new noise.

"Historic," Nightingale corrected. "And it is, Baby. Historic can be anything that happened and has passed. It doesn't have to be a president resigning. Your stitches *are* historic. And our trip into Duluth."

"So would my birthday be historic?" Baby grinned. "Because that was back in March?"

"Yes." Nightingale smiled; she loved to teach a lesson. "Your birthday would be historic, too."

"But Old Finn knows about your birthday," I corrected Baby.

"I'm just teaching him historic," Nightingale said. "It means more than what we're telling to Old Finn."

The two of them kept up with their list—Baby asking if this or that could be historic, Nightingale mostly saying yes. I didn't join in or take my place as Nightingale's student. It was one thing to do her lesson on Alaska, but I was tired of Nightingale trying to tell me how every little thing worked in the world.

43

SLOW, BUT SURE

All three of us were staring at the elevator the second those doors opened and Old Finn was wheeled out. Old Finn slumped sideways in a wheelchair, his strong head drooped low to his shoulder, his mouth half hanging open so we all could see inside. His thick pink tongue draped over his dry lip as if Old Finn were just too lazy to close his mouth up proper. It was Old Finn in that chair and still it wasn't. His bleary eyes just stared like he wasn't even certain who we were. He tried to lift one hand in a weak wave, but the other rested like a dead fish in his lap.

"Old Finn," I creaked, if any words made it out my mouth.

"Old Finn!" Baby shouted like that strange tongue didn't matter. He rushed across the lounge to offer the first hug. Nightingale followed stiffly, but she didn't say a word. I looked up at the ceiling, blinked my tears back quickly before they made it to my cheeks. I'd learned in the shelter to keep my tears inside. A couple hot tears fell, but I knew Old Finn didn't see them. I walked over toward his chair, pinched my cheeks, swallowed down my sadness. "It's Pride," I whispered near his ear in case he wasn't sure. I waited for an answer, but he didn't even give a nod.

The three of us stood there in a huddle with Old Finn slouched down in the middle, too weak to wrap his big arms around his kids.

"Someone sure is loved!" the orderly said kindly. Henri. He had a giant Afro and an accent that made me think of Grace, the best bread baker at Serenity, who'd grown up in Jamaica. Henri set his hand on Old Finn's shoulder like the two of them were friends. "These must be your grandkids."

Old Finn lifted up his hand again, moved it back and forth like he was trying to write. "Hold on," Henri said. "I'll get your pad and paper." He reached behind his chair, pulled a clipboard from a bag with a fat blue pencil connected by a string. The kind of learner pencil Old Finn used to teach Baby how to print. "Until he gets his speech," Henri said, "Michael first will write. Whatever sounds he can. Right now, he only has a couple letters, but he tries. We like to see him try."

"A couple letters?" Baby said, confused.

Old Finn reached for the pencil, made a fist around it the way a child would, drew a line down on the paper, then let the pencil drop.

"We brought a snack," I said slowly to Old Finn. My

heart sank to my stomach. Old Finn couldn't hold a pencil, couldn't walk or talk; he wasn't going to tell me what to do, how to take care of our family, get more money to buy groceries. He wasn't the great bear who saved us from the shelter; he couldn't save us from a shelter now. "I baked your favorite cookies. Oatmeal with extra chocolate chips." I pointed toward the napkin on the table. "And there's coffee with all those heaps of sugar like you like."

"I'm sure you want those cookies," Henri said, like he was cheering up Old Finn. "You're a lucky man, Michael. You got some real nice children here." Henri didn't even ask us about Mama; he just rolled Old Finn up to the table, locked two metal brakes so the wheels would stay put. "You help your grandpa with the cookie," he said to me like I was old enough to do his job. "Most everything's a lesson for him now. And be careful with that coffee so he doesn't get a hot splash in his lap. Everything for him is slow, but sure."

Old Finn gave a weary nod. I could tell Henri's lessons weren't the kind Old Finn wanted to learn. Same way I felt about geometry. And fractions. And decimals and adverbs. And Old Finn didn't like the sound of *slow, but sure*.

Henri crouched close to Old Finn and smiled at him warmly. It seemed strange to see a man so tender with Old Finn. Or anyone. Old Finn was always fending for himself. "You remember, Michael, slow, but sure. And don't get down with the troubles. You've got your helpers here."

Henri gave a quick pat to Old Finn's calf, straightened one loose spongy slipper.

I'd never seen Old Finn wear slippers—just baggy wool socks in the winter, boots outdoors all year round. We should have brought his flannel pajama pants from home, his hooded breakfast sweatshirt. Cabin clothes like Old Finn liked. He wouldn't get strong dressed in cotton sick clothes—like the horrible patient smocks we sometimes had to wear at Dr. Clark's.

"You'll be okay?" Henri asked him.

"I'll take care of Old Finn," Baby said, bouncing up on his boot toes.

"Good man." Henri winked. "You can help him with his ABCs. Telling time. Counting. But best of all is love. Good love goes a long way toward getting well." He put Old Finn's clipboard back into the chair pouch. "Isn't that right, Michael. We men all need good love."

"ABCs?" Nightingale said, like she was angry. "He knows his ABCs."

"Sure." Henri nodded. "But some things he's going to have to learn again."

Henri smiled at me, like he hoped I was old enough to understand Old Finn needed help. Old Finn's lessons would be long; I saw it in his eyes. Not just addition and subtraction, but getting Old Finn back to who he used to be. Doing ordinary things—but none of it seemed ordinary now. "Michael doesn't have much more than ten minutes; after that we're on the dance card down at Speech."

"Ten minutes?" I nearly shrieked. "Ten minutes? But we came to spend the day."

"Oh no," Henri said. "All day isn't possible. Your grandpa has his therapy. Therapy and rest. Lots and lots to learn. But you come back tomorrow; give him love again. After dinner would be better. His work is done by then."

I couldn't believe Old Finn just sat there silent. Here we were from Goodwell and Henri was making us head home. Old Finn hadn't seen us once since he'd been sick. If he could speak, he wouldn't let Henri be the boss. But all his words were trapped inside his brain. In all my worries of today, I'd never pictured Old Finn so beaten down or small, weaker than Miss Addie.

"Is this *in-seff-*?" Nightingale started. "*In-seff-a-* . . . ?"

Baby took the paper from his pocket and handed it to Henri.

"Encephalitis." Henri nodded. It sounded like an insect or a disease an elephant would have. He showed it to Old Finn. "I believe that's right. And he's just fresh from the fever. So Michael's starting new."

Old Finn drooped a tired nod like encephalitis was correct.

"But what exactly does that mean?" Nightingale said. "What's encephalitis? And when will he come home?"

"Ah, well." Henri gave the slip of paper back to Baby.

"I'm just here as an orderly. But I can tell you your grandpa's going to need a lot of help to get back home."

"But we can teach him all those things," I said. "How to walk and talk and read. Tell time. Nightingale can do his lessons. I'll help him carve his birds." I said it clear and strong like I believed it, but deep down it wasn't in my heart. I didn't know how I'd help a giant like Old Finn learn how to walk. Or how I'd make a word come out of his mouth. Or teach him how to tuck his tongue back behind his teeth where it belonged. All this time of learning self-reliance and I didn't have the gifts to save Old Finn.

"So, ten minutes then," Henri said as if he hadn't heard me. I hoped he wasn't counting the time we'd wasted talking. "Ten minutes. Then I come back for Michael."

Old Finn didn't want the coffee or the cookies; he didn't even seem to wonder how we made it to Duluth all by ourselves. Or what we did for money. Or if the county had come to put us in a shelter or farm us out to fosters. He just sat there staring, shaking his droopy hangdog head like he was sad, lifting the fingers on one hand like it was his only way to talk.

Finally Baby laid his head on Old Finn's leg, close enough for Old Finn to rub his one good hand on Baby's bristles. "I got my stitches out." Baby lifted up his face and pointed to the pink path on his chin. "And now Pride has to smear cream on me so I don't get a scar."

"Neosporin," I said, but I didn't add the part about Dr.

Madden's questions or the social-someone coming to our house.

"Nixon is resigning," Nightingale said. Old Finn snorted out a sniff of air, nodded. He knew what she was saying; I could see it in his face. He blinked a sad, slow blink. Then he finally moved his lips to form a word. "G . . . ," he moaned, the *g* sound hard and slow. "G—d."

"Good?" Nightingale guessed.

"Good," he said again and it was clear. And then he added, "Rid."

"Good riddance!" Nightingale clapped like she'd just won another round of Twenty Questions. "Good riddance, Richard Nixon!" she said proudly. I wished it had been me to make that guess.

Old Finn tried to force a smile, but the right side of his upper lip just barely lifted. Still, it was the first I thought he could be Old Finn again. *Good riddance* was exactly what he'd say if he were well.

I put a straw into his coffee and held it to his lips, waited patient while he took a couple sucks. Then I held the cookie to his mouth and let him nibble bit by bit. "We've done fine," I said so Old Finn wouldn't have to struggle through another sound. It was too hard for me to wait for his couple words to come—all that wondering what he'd say, when he could only make a moan. "Miss Addie, too. We're all right there at Eden where you left us, waiting like you said, and everything is good. Woody Guthrie's standing guard. I'm taking care of Atticus and Scout. Nightingale's teaching lessons."

"Good," Old Finn moaned again. A look of sad confusion washed over his lost face, like maybe he'd forgotten he sent us to the trailer or told us to stay put until he came home from St. John's.

"We'll be okay," I said. "We're self-reliant."

"Independent," Baby said.

"Self-sufficient," Nightingale added.

Maybe once we all were, but I didn't feel so certain anymore.

44

ALL THE MONEY IN THE WORLD

We didn't even get the chance to tell Old Finn we loved him, or give him the get-well cards we made, before Henri came to take him down to Speech.

"Are you sure that was ten minutes?" I complained. I held tight to Old Finn's big bear arm. We'd worked so hard to get here, rode all the way from Goodwell—ten minutes with Old Finn just wasn't fair. It could be weeks before we had the money to come back.

"You come again," Henri said. He brushed the oatmeal crumbs off Old Finn's robe; I should have put a napkin in his lap. Next time I'd know better. "Right now he works on words."

"But why can't he talk now?" Baby asked. "He only has a fever."

"The infection got the brain." Henri set a gentle hand on Old Finn's skull. "But with work it will come back."

Hearing Henri say that gave me hope; nobody worked harder than Old Finn.

Old Finn patted Baby's cheek, then nodded toward the hallway. I had the sudden, heartsick feeling he wanted us to go. He didn't even try to move his mouth to argue, he just closed his heavy lids as if he was ready for a rest. A long, long rest without us.

"Then can we come back later?" I said. "Later on today? After he does all the work you want?"

"Maybe after supper if your grandpa's not asleep." Henri yanked up on the brakes, grabbed hold of Old Finn's chair. "Today he will be busy. Tomorrow might be better. Every day is better."

"Wait!" I said. I reached into my knapsack, grabbed our stack of cards. "We made these for you." I pushed them toward Old Finn. "Nightingale's is prettiest." The front of Nightingale's card was a vase of tissue-paper flowers with green pipe cleaners for stems. Baby's card was cute—a drawing of spotted Woody Guthrie dressed in Old Finn's cowboy boots and hat. Mine was black construction paper chalked with stars, but most of them had smeared. Inside I'd written *When You Wish Upon a Star Your Dreams Come True*—from a song Mama used to sing.

I tried to close his hand around the cards, but instead they all just fluttered to the floor.

"Here," Henri said. "For now, I'll put them in his pouch.

Later on we'll set them in his room. Give him something happy for his eyes." He tucked the cards in with Old Finn's clipboard and fat pencil, the single sheet of paper where he'd squiggled one faint line.

Nightingale stuck the nub end of her braid into her mouth, gnawed the way she did when she was trying not to cry. Baby scrambled into Old Finn's lap, roped his arms around his neck. "Careful there," Henri scolded kindly. He reached down and lifted Baby to the floor. "Michael isn't ready for that yet," he said. "But someday soon." He kneaded Old Finn's shoulder. "Lots of love here, man. And all this love, it's good."

Tears swelled up in my eyes, but I didn't care. I couldn't come back tomorrow. Or the next day. Not unless someone gave us all the money in the world. I pressed my cheek against his chest, hugged hard so Old Finn would know that he was loved. He didn't smell like dirt or sawdust or Woody Guthrie; he smelled old and sickly like St. Mary's. I turned away, let Nightingale have the last good-bye. "I brought *Walden*," she said, but most of it came out as a hiccup through her tears. "I thought that we could read."

"Next time," Henri told her softly. "Next time you read. There's lots of time ahead."

"Next time for ten minutes?" Nightingale wiped her hand across her cheek. I knew what she was saying—we couldn't come all the way from Goodwell for ten minutes with Old Finn.

• • •

"I wish I'd seen that slip of paper sooner," Nightingale said. We were outside the busy front doors of St. Mary's, people streaming in and out, the bright sun glaring on our faces all swollen tearful pink. It was the first thing anyone had said since Old Finn left the lounge.

"What paper?" I asked Nightingale. After all that sadness her mind was on a paper?

"The one that Baby showed us on the bus. The one Miss Addie wrote." She wiped her nose dry with her sleeve, bit her lip to stop the flow of tears. "The one that had Old Finn's infection. *Encephalitis.* If I'd seen it, Pride, at least we could have known."

"Known what?" I shook my head. "What was there to know before this minute? And we couldn't even read that word Miss Addie wrote."

"I could read it," Nightingale insisted. I didn't know why she was mad at me right now; all day I'd been standing on her dark side. No matter what I did she called it wrong. "And you could read it if you tried. You never try to read; you just set out thinking that you already know the answer when you don't. That's why books matter, Pride. You have to read for information. Like when you got so sick with scarlet fever, Old Finn looked it right up in his book. And he knew to get you medicine. Maybe Old Finn's fever was there, too. And all this time we would have known he couldn't walk or talk. That maybe he was never coming home. Instead of sitting there at Eden thinking that he was." She didn't even try to swallow down her sobs.

"I'm sorry." I shrugged, but if that's what some book said, I was glad I hadn't read it before now. Today was soon enough for me.

"We need to find the library." Nightingale looked down the busy street. "Read about this infection Old Finn has. Same as scarlet fever or polio." This year, Old Finn had taught us both the Dewey decimal system at the library in Goodwell; he made us use the card catalog, do research for reports. I wrote two pages on Appaloosas. Nightingale wrote eight long, boring pages about polio and vaccinations. She even included illustrations of an iron lung and crutches. I didn't want Old Finn's infection to be as bad as polio.

"Nothing in a library can tell us what we need," I said. It wasn't my fault Nightingale had never seen the paper; it was Baby who found it on the floor, tucked the thing away.

"Old Finn would read." Nightingale crossed her arms over her tiny stomach; she stood there stubborn on the street, her black braids shining near blue in the sun. "Old Finn would want to know."

45

CLOSER TO A GROWN-UP

It was easier to let Nightingale hunt down the public library than to stand there at St. Mary's thinking of Old Finn. Old Finn in those strange slippers, Old Finn without his words, Old Finn with that dark cave of open mouth, Old Finn wanting us to leave after ten short, measly minutes.

When we got inside the library, I took Baby to the picture books the way I did in Goodwell while Nightingale headed off to Reference to read the big encyclopedias alone. She could write up her report on Old Finn's fever, teach us all a lesson, but it was up to me to figure out how we'd find our help. *Help*. The kind of help that wouldn't send us to a shelter or farm us off to fosters. Help for the time ahead we'd be left at Eden all alone. I could tell by Henri's face Old Finn wasn't coming home tomorrow or the next day. He wasn't coming home until he learned to walk and talk. And, worse, I had a horrible fear he wouldn't.

I opened *Curious George* because that's the book Baby begged for first. He always liked that monkey's mischief and the way George's owner tried to keep him out of trouble, same way I tried to keep Baby from leaping off swings. I wished life were as easy as keeping safe a monkey, especially one who always found his own way out of a jam. Usually *Curious George* made Baby happy, but today he sucked his knuckles, curled up close against my arm without a single laugh.

"Old Finn didn't even look down at my card," Baby finally said. "He didn't even see how I drew Woody Guthrie in his cowboy boots and hat. He just let them fall down to the floor."

"He's sick," I said.

"We don't have a grown-up left now, Pride." Baby nudged his nose into my sleeve. "No one but Miss Addie, and Miss Addie's just too old."

"I know," I said. I couldn't lie to Baby; he'd seen Old Finn himself. "But you have me." Day by day I felt closer to a grown-up than to a girl just turned thirteen.

I don't know how long we sat there, but it was longer than the ten quick minutes they gave us with Old Finn. When we finished *Curious George*, Baby picked out *Corduroy*, then *Make Way for Ducklings*, and finally a book about a bunny that had to learn to ask for help to find his way back home. Maybe Nightingale was right; maybe a book could hold the answer after all.

"Let's go find Nightingale," I said. Whatever information Nightingale needed, she must have read by now. I didn't know why she liked big books with all those pages; *Curious George* was long enough for me.

"There she is!" Baby said. Nightingale was standing at a counter, talking to a thin-faced man with heavy black-rimmed glasses and a patch of gray goatee hanging from his chin. A thick, red book was opened up between them. Someday it would be Nightingale working the counter at the library in Goodwell, her long black braids falling on the book.

"So these must be your siblings?" the thin man said. Nightingale nodded. *Sibling* was a word the shelter people used. I didn't like the way it sounded—slippery like lizards or something that could slink. I was happiest with *family*.

"We've been researching your grandpa's medical condition," the librarian continued. "Encephalitis." Miss Addie's note was there beside the book. "It can certainly be serious," he said. "No question. But, his prognosis may be better than you think. Even if there isn't much he can do now. It says right here . . ." He turned the book to me, but I didn't bother reading that whole page of little print. Baby was so lucky no one asked him to read much more than *cat*. "*It is possible for patients to experience full recovery. Or nearly full.*" He ran his finger underneath the sentences, then stopped. He looked at Nightingale. "If your grandpa's case is mild, there could be some hope."

"That's good," I said. I was happy to have hope, even if those words didn't strike me right. Old Finn's encephalitis wasn't mild. If it were mild, he'd be back home by now. "We should leave." I tugged on Nightingale. If it were up to her, we'd spend all day buried in these books. I reached out and took hold of her hand. I didn't want to learn another thing about the fever. We needed help. And help was what I had to get us now.

46

FIVE THIN DIMES

We're starting with Justine," I said once I'd managed to get Nightingale and Baby a few streets from the library.

"Justine?" Nightingale repeated like I'd just rattled off Chinese.

"Justine from the letters?" Baby scrunched his freckled face. "The one that loved Old Finn?"

I didn't know why Baby asked that stupid question—there wasn't any other Justine in our lives. "That's her," I said, impatient. "She said that she'd be living in Duluth. After France was finished. So she could be here now."

"But why?" Nightingale argued. "Old Finn doesn't love her anymore. If he did, we would have known her."

"But she loved him," I said. "A lot. So maybe she would help him."

"But we don't know." Nightingale slapped her shoes together like she had a pair of cymbals in her hands; she'd slipped back to bare feet the minute we walked out of the library. "And this city's just too big to find a stranger." Compared to Goodwell, the city did look big with its brick hotels and buses, department stores and restaurants, people rushing here and there. But Nightingale wasn't the only one who knew how to use a book.

"We'll look in the directory," I said. "See if Justine's listed. Same way I found St. John's the first night Old Finn was gone."

"Justine who?" Nightingale challenged. "We'd need to know her name."

"Ryan. Justine Ryan." Didn't Nightingale listen to those letters? Justine's name was on every envelope she sent. Nightingale wasn't always smarter; someday she'd see there were things I knew.

"But even so," Nightingale argued. "What exactly would we say?"

"Don't know." I shrugged because I didn't. Hard as it was, I knew it would be something about help. Help for Old Finn first and maybe us. Money for our groceries. A good grown-up to step in if the county came around. Someone kind to help us stay at Eden. Someone who knew for certain Old Finn would never want us in a shelter. Someone who knew how much he loved us, and that some-one was Justine. "First," I said, "we have to track her down."

The three of us crammed into a grimy phone booth, Baby crouched down in the corner, Nightingale and I stuck arm to shoulder, searching through the phone book until we finally found the *R*s. And at the end of *R*s the Ryans. *Ryan, J.* There was Jan and Jill and Joyce, a bunch of Jameses and Johns, but nothing for Justine.

"Oh no," I groaned. "What if she's still living off in France?"

"Maybe she's just *J*." Nightingale pointed toward the letters. "*J* for her first name."

"There's so many *J*s." I counted down the list. "Six." I didn't want to spend six dimes looking for Justine or stand much longer in this stinky, steamy phone booth with globs of old chewed gum stuck against the glass. Smashed cigarette butts scattered at our feet. "We'll have to call them all."

"Six?" Nightingale said. "That'll take all the money we have left."

"I don't know how else. We can't go to all these houses. Not before our bus leaves at six thirty. The city's just too big."

I handed Nightingale the final JFK. I wished I could have saved it for Miss Addie, but we needed sixty cents to make the calls. "You go get the change," I ordered. It already hurt my heart spending one of them on tickets. For once it could be Nightingale doing something hard. "Change it at the drugstore just across the street."

I stepped out of the glass box and took a deep breath of the lake. I wished we could all go down to the water, watch the seagulls bicker over scraps, buy three sprinkled ice-cream cones the way Old Finn did for us the time he brought us to buy books. I remembered how we scuttled over jagged rocks along the shoreline, even Baby, and how we rested on a bench when we were finished, the four of us like any ordinary family except our parents were both dead.

Did Old Finn and Justine ever sit on that same bench? Almost like a family? Did he buy her sprinkled ice cream? Maybe she could tell us that today, tell us who Old Finn was before he took us into Eden. Old Finn in love and healthy would make me happy now.

When Nightingale came back with five thin dimes, I knew for certain Miss Addie's final JFK was gone. "Here," she said, pressing the coins into my palm, but I didn't want them. "I'll read the numbers, but you should do the talking." She pulled another dime out of her pocket, dropped it into the phone.

I knew Nightingale would never call Justine, not any more than she would have called St. John's the first night Old Finn was gone. She had her books, but she didn't have my courage in the world—except maybe in the library, and no one really needed courage there. "But you just got mad when I said I'd do the talking to Old Finn."

"That's because I know him," Nightingale said. "I know him and I love him. And it can't just be you talking to Old Finn. But I don't know Justine. Or why we're even calling."

"We're calling her for help," I said, even though that last word barely made it off my tongue.

"Help?" Baby said. "But the Stars are independent. Old Finn wants us self-re-lay-ent."

"Self-reliant," Nightingale corrected.

"And we are," I said, but then I thought of Old Finn in that chair, how long it took for him to moan out that single *G*. How little we had waiting in our pantry. The bag of Woody Guthrie's kibble that wouldn't last past next week.

"We are," I promised Baby. "But today we need some help."

47

HOPING ON A STRANGER

Only four J. Ryans answered and none of them had heard of a Justine. The other two didn't pick up their phones.

"Now what?" Nightingale said. We'd spent Miss Addie's final keepsake, Old Finn could barely speak, and we were in Duluth until six thirty with nothing but our tickets home, two dimes and no place left to go.

I looked down at the phone book. Two addresses were left. "We could walk out to these houses. Knock or leave a note. If Justine is home, she might just ask us in."

"Just show up on her doorstep?" Nightingale said.

"Why not?" I shrugged. "It's what Nash did to us. And everybody else that came out to our business. Not everyone hates strangers on their land."

"But we don't know this city," Nightingale said. "Or any of these streets. Or how to find her house."

"Didn't we find St. Mary's?" Smart as she was, Nightingale's brain sometimes got stuck. "We'll go ask at your library." I gave Nightingale a grin. "Isn't that where all the answers are?"

"They'll tell us at the library!" Baby jumped up to his feet. "I've got my compass in my pocket; I can find Justine. That bearded man can tell us where she lives."

"Well, yes." The librarian cleared his throat and nudged his heavy glasses up his nose. Someday Nightingale would say things like, *Well, yes*. I could picture it already. This man liked to puzzle out a question just the way she did, make an answer harder than it was. "I can certainly help you with these addresses, but they're in two sections of the city, nowhere near to one another. Is there something specific that you need at either site?"

"Justine Ryan," Baby said. "We have to find her house."

"Justine Ryan?" The librarian pinched his patch of beard. "Do you mean the painter from the college?"

"Yes! That's her!" I said. "The one who went to France!"

"Indeed she did. You children certainly are sharp. I recently attended her lecture on Impressionists. Fascinating woman."

"So which one is her house?" I asked before he could tell us more or Nightingale got interested. I hoped Justine wouldn't give us a lecture on impressions.

"I can't tell you that for certain," he said. "But if I had to choose, I'd choose the one on Claremont. Claremont makes more sense."

"What about directions?" I said. "How long of a walk?"

"You'll walk?" he said. "In that case, I would estimate an hour. It isn't really close." He looked up at Nightingale. "Of course you understand, I can't guarantee this is her house."

"We do," she said.

"Well, then." He wrote down our directions, sketched a little map so we could follow left and right. Penciled in small arrows.

"Okay." I grabbed his little map even though the arrows looked like Old Finn's math to me. "Let's go find Justine," I said to Nightingale and Baby.

So far the house on Claremont was the only hope we had.

The house at 427 Claremont was fancy and yellow with a wooden, purple porch swing, a purple picket fence, and a garden so overgrown with wild bright flowers it covered the front yard. A little fountain bubbled in the center; tiny statues and cracked dishes were mixed in with the dirt. It looked exactly like a place where a painter would live, with bright blue flower boxes underneath the window just like Justine had loved in France.

"I bet you this is it," I said. We stood there on the sidewalk staring at the house. Even walking all this way, I still wasn't certain what to tell Justine. I didn't want to say I'd read her private letters; Nightingale was right, they were almost like a diary. Justine wouldn't be happy that I snooped.

"Maybe you should do the talking," I said to Nightingale. "You know more about impressions and lectures and things professors like—you know, like Beethoven and Thoreau."

"I don't know about impressions," Nightingale said. "You just say we came about Old Finn."

"And I'll say we like the garden," Baby said. "And her house is really pretty. And maybe she can even feed us lunch."

"Are you hungry?" I asked Baby. He'd eaten one or two of Old Finn's cookies, but I'd forgotten all about feeding Baby lunch.

"Starving," Baby said.

"But we can't ask for food," Nightingale said. "That wouldn't be good manners. If Baby's hungry we should eat before we knock."

I pulled a flattened sugar sandwich from my bag, unwrapped the waxy paper, and handed it to Baby. Then I handed a second off to Nightingale. My stomach was too nervous to take a single bite.

Help. I wasn't even sure how it would sound. Or how to say a thing like *we need help*—and hope that it would happen.

"It's been so long since we went someplace besides Goodwell," Nightingale said. Justine's house looked too fancy for the Stars—climbing vines and roses, a birdbath with an angel. Nightingale bent down and tightened the loose laces on her shoes. "She's a painter from a college,"

243

Nightingale said. "A professor like Old Finn used to be, so she'll be smart."

"Maybe that's why they were in love," I said.

"But she could tell the county," Nightingale added. "Like anybody else. And they'll put us all in fosters. Maybe by tomorrow. Or a shelter in Duluth. And Miss Addie would be left."

"I know," I said. I'd had the same dark thought exactly, walking all this way. It was possible Justine could call the sheriff, have us sent away. My heart pulsed in my throat; a bitter taste spread over my tongue. What if asking for her help would only hurt? The way Old Finn always warned us asking would. "But she knew Old Finn didn't want us in that shelter; she wrote it in her letter. And anyway, I can't figure out what else." I couldn't forget Old Finn slumped down in that chair. And we couldn't sell our pony rides unless we got insurance. And Nash might still be knocking at the cabin. And Thor still had his questions. And Dr. Madden was sending someone to our house. And Old Finn needed love to help him heal at St. Mary's. Henri even said so, and we couldn't be here every day.

"But Old Finn could get well," Nightingale said, like she'd been inside my mind.

"That man said that he would," Baby mumbled with his mouth full. "That man at the library."

I unwrapped another sandwich, tore off a chunk, and

stuck it in my mouth. I needed something to hide the taste of fear, something in my mouth to calm my nerves. I tried to pass the rest to Nightingale, but she wouldn't take it.

"He said there *might be hope*," I said. "Might be. But in the meantime . . ."

"But this might not even be the house," Nightingale said, like she hoped deep down it wasn't. "We might have walked all this way for nothing—"

"I think it is," Baby interrupted. He pointed down the sidewalk. "'Cause there she is, coming toward us now."

Justine. She looked exactly like her picture—a wide straw hat, a blouse, white linen pants rolled just above the ankles, woven sandals, her bright hair curled against her shoulders in a bob. She rode toward us on an old green bike with a bag of groceries propped up in the basket, a long loaf of French bread.

No one said a word; we just stood still. She didn't look like a woman who would send us to a shelter; she looked like someone Old Finn would have loved.

As soon as she got closer, she slowed the bike down to a stop, got off, and walked it toward her house. "Hello." She smiled, but just strolled right past us, steered her bike into her yard, and walked straight up her stone path. It wasn't until she reached the porch steps that she stopped. "Hello?" She turned and looked at us again. "Hello?" Not a greeting but a question. "May I help you children?"

Nightingale huddled in against me; I laid my hands on Baby's tiny shoulders. I didn't know if she could help or if anybody could. I only knew Old Finn had taught us not to ask, to solve things for ourselves if we were able. And here we were hoping on a stranger. A woman from some letters I stole from Old Finn's drawer.

48

I KNOW WHO YOU ARE

It's us," I barely managed to squeak out. "Kathleen, Elise, and Baxter."

Justine set her bag of groceries on the porch, took off her wide straw hat, and pressed it to her chest. "Kathleen, Elise, and Baxter?" she repeated. Maybe after all this time she'd forgotten who we were.

"Pride," I said. "And Night—"

"Oh yes." Justine kept her hat over her heart. "I know who you are." She brushed her snowy hair back from one cheek, searched up and down her street like she had hoped for someone else. "And Mick?" she finally asked, confused.

"He's sick," I said. Nightingale had inched behind me now. For once, Baby stood there silent. "They sent him to St. Mary's."

"St. Mary's Hospital? Someone sent him here? Who?" she asked, alarmed.

"The doctors at St. John's Hospital in Goodwell," I said.

"They sent him to St. Mary's to get better, but it hasn't really helped." Old Finn hadn't been that bad when he left Eden with his fever—the day he sent us to Miss Addie's he could walk and talk.

"Oh no!" she said. "Oh my. What horrible news, Mick sick." She shook her head and sat down on the step, pressed her arms close to her stomach like she had a sudden pain. "Mick sick? I'm so sorry to hear that. But how . . . ?" She stopped and stared again like she still couldn't understand what the three of us were doing waiting at her gate. The children from the tales Old Finn wrote. "But how did you find me?"

"The librarian," I said. I didn't want to say I stole Old Finn's private letters or that I'd read her love words meant for him.

"The librarian?" Justine shook her head again. "I'm afraid I'm just confused. So confused. Forgive me." She stood and spread her blousy arms open in a greeting. "I don't know where my manners are. Please come inside, dear children."

Inside Justine's house was another kind of garden—a garden full of paintings, fresh flowers on the tables, fancy hand-carved furniture, stained-glass windows, polished floors shining in the sun. The whole house smelled like summer or laundry off the line. We stood there in the entry, too shy to take a step. Justine's house looked nothing like the lodges at Serenity or Old Finn's small log cabin or Miss Addie's messy trailer.

"Come in, come in," she said, waving toward us. "Don't bother with your shoes." I looked down at my feet; I wasn't sure what Justine had meant by *bother*. "It's fine," she said. "You can leave them on."

I felt like we were tracking dirt just walking in. I grabbed hold of Baby's hand; I didn't want him rushing in, breaking some fragile crystal vase or marble statue. The three of us sat down on a settee—which looked like a small sofa—Baby on my lap, Nightingale and I glued nearly arm to arm, while Justine disappeared into the kitchen with her groceries and her bread.

"Please," Justine said and sat down in a fancy cushioned rocker. She set her hands down on her knees, painter's hands, with little specks of color on her skin. "Help me understand."

"Well." I coughed. Something dry was stuck down in my throat. I wished I had spent more time thinking of my story, what I'd tell Justine when we finally found her house.

"So Mick is sick?" she said, like she was trying to help me speak, trying to coax a sentence from my mouth. I nodded. Her eyebrows frowned down in a crease; a mix of worry and confusion washed over her blue eyes. Sea blue. Or maybe azure like the sky. Azure like the sea. Justine was as lovely as she sounded in her letters; no wonder Old Finn loved her so much once. "Sick with what?"

I bumped my knee into Nightingale's. "Explain," I said. I didn't want to say that big word wrong.

"Encephalitis," Nightingale started. "An infection of the brain."

"Oh no!" Justine's hands flew to her cheeks. "That sounds terribly serious."

"It could be mild," Nightingale said, even though I didn't believe it was. "That's what the medical encyclopedia said. But right now he isn't really better."

"But he will be," Baby added. "Once he learns the ABCs. And how to walk more steady. And how to talk."

"He can't talk?" Justine said, shocked. "Or walk?"

"Only just a little," I said.

"But he can write," Nightingale added, although we hadn't seen it. "Henri told us that he could."

"Oh no." A red flush rose up her smooth, sweet face. "I'm just so sad to hear this." She shook her head, stared down at her hands. "And now he's asked for me?"

I could see in Justine's face the story that she wanted; she wanted me to say Old Finn had sent us here for her. And I didn't have the heart to say he didn't, to tell Justine he'd never mentioned her, not once.

I coughed again; another lie was caught low in my throat. I gave a nod, then Baby nodded with me. When two of us were nodding, it made the lie seem real.

"Well, thank heavens that he did!" Justine stood up. "I'm glad he didn't let pride get in the way. Your grandpa can be stubborn."

"I know," I said. I guess I was stubborn, too. Maybe that's

why Mama named me Pride. Not for pride and joy, but stubborn pride.

"I have to go to see him!" Justine stood like she was ready now to leave.

"He's already gone to therapy," Nightingale warned. I could tell she didn't want Justine rushing to St. Mary's, finding out our first words had been lies; Old Finn hadn't asked to see her after all. "They only let us visit for ten minutes."

"Still." Justine sighed. "I can't very well sit here. Not knowing Mick is sick." It was the same have-to-see-Old-Finn way that I'd felt ever since he'd gone in with the fever. Justine felt like I did. "Is someone coming for you children?" Justine asked. "Someone from the library? Did you say Henri?" She glanced out her large front window like that man might be outside.

"No," I said. I didn't know how she'd mixed Henri and the library, but I didn't bother to explain. "We walked."

"You walked?" Justine said, surprised. "From where? Did you walk here from St. Mary's?"

"Yes," I said.

"That's miles. You must be exhausted. Do you need something to eat? Drink?"

"No," Nightingale said, before Baby had a chance to blurt out yes. "We just finished lunch."

"Oh fine," she said relieved. "Then we can hurry to St. Mary's. You'll come with me. We'll all go check on Mick."

49

OLD FINN AND JUSTINE

I didn't know what we'd say when we got there to St. Mary's, how we'd explain Justine to Old Finn or what we'd finally tell Justine. I only knew we were riding in the backseat of Justine's yellow Beetle and I had Nightingale's knobby elbow poking deep into my ribs. An urgent *what-next* message she was trying hard to send me. I didn't know *what next* so I stared out at the lake, wondered if the water really ended, if somewhere on the other side, there'd ever be a shore. Old Finn always told us that there was, but I couldn't see it. Same way I couldn't see God.

I was barely breathing by the time we got to Old Finn's floor. We had Justine, but I couldn't concoct a plan that went beyond this minute. *Love heals.* That's the best that I could think. It was better than the nothing hope that had sunk my heart this morning. And if everything went wrong we could still run. "Back again so soon?" the nurse said when we stopped at the front desk. "Your grandpa sure is popular today. But, I'm afraid he's gone down for some testing. You're welcome to wait there in the lounge or grab a bite to eat. Peach pie in the cafeteria today."

Peach pie sounded better than two bites of sugar sandwich, but we didn't have the money for peach pie.

"We're fine," Justine said politely. Baby took her hand and led her to the lounge, offered her a cup of coffee or Swiss Miss. A couple dried-out oatmeal cookies still sat there on the napkin, just the way I had arranged them when I set out Old Finn's snack. Looking at those cookies made me sad and scared to see Old Finn again, Old Finn slumped down in that chair, that horrible open mouth. But I didn't want to leave him sickly either. I just wanted him all better, wanted him to stand up and walk with us out the door.

"He can't really speak," I said again; I didn't want Justine's love for Old Finn to disappear when she saw the way he sagged. "Not much at least."

"Okay." Justine rubbed her lips together, straightened up her spine like she was nervous. "I will curb my expectations."

"And he may be confused," I added. "Because he was this morning when we came."

"Of course," Justine said.

"So don't be disappointed." I sounded just like Mama when she didn't want to see our hopes hurt.

"You children needn't worry about me," Justine said. She

kept her eyes held to the elevator. "Mick and I know each other well. We were . . ." She stopped.

In love, I thought. We knew that from the letters, but I didn't tell her that.

"Quite close," she finally said, as if she'd settled on two plain words that could work. "He knows that I will help, in any way. He knows I would do anything. . . ."

Nightingale glanced at me. "Anything?" she asked, her shy voice firm and flat. I knew what she was asking—she was asking if Justine would give us money or help us get the license for our business or stand in as our grown-up if someone came to snoop. She was asking if Justine would keep us from the shelter, if her true love for Old Finn could reach the Stars.

But before Justine had a chance to answer, the elevator bell rang, and there was Henri wheeling Old Finn once again.

"Mick!" Justine cried. "Mick!" She jumped up from the couch, ran over to his chair, and kissed him on the forehead. "Mick, my dear."

Old Finn's eyes misted up with tears; he lifted up his one good hand and touched Justine's pink cheek. A low moaning sound rose out of his mouth. "Jus—" He dropped his head, defeated.

"Yes, it's me, Justine!" She kissed his bristled hair just the way I did to Baby. I'd never kissed Old Finn on the head.

"More company today." Henri smiled. "Michael just

won't rest. And you children . . ." He made a little *tsk* sound with his tongue. "Weren't you coming after dinner?"

"I brought them here with me," Justine said, in case Henri's scolding might be serious. "And I certainly couldn't wait until tonight, not once I knew." She ran her hand over Old Finn's face, again and again, like she wasn't even bothered by his mouth or that terrible tongue just bulging at the edge. "And these children," she said to Old Finn. "They're every bit as special as you said. And smart. And obviously they have your independence! My goodness! They walked out to my house!"

Old Finn looked in our direction, tightened up his face like he couldn't quite understand. "How?" he managed to get out and everybody heard it. I didn't know if he was asking how we found Justine or how we made it to St. Mary's or how we were getting back to Goodwell—so I just sat there, silent, hoping that one word would pass.

"I don't know myself." Justine shook her head. "What was it, children? You're here with a librarian? Somebody named Henri?"

"No," I said. "That's Henri." I pointed to the orderly. "We just went into the library and asked about your address. And the man knew you from the lecture on impressions. So he helped us find the address for your house." I didn't want Old Finn's confusion to be worse.

"I apologize," Justine said to Henri. "This day has been a shock."

"Calm is best," Henri said like he meant it for us all. "Especially for Michael. A short visit now, then he must have his rest. Rest helps him to be well."

"Calm," Justine repeated. "Of course, I understand." She took the wheelchair and pushed Old Finn toward the lounge. "Mick, Mick," she said. She parked his chair and took a seat beside him, sat there on the edge, his hands inside of hers. The three of us just stared. Here they were, Old Finn and Justine. The people from those letters. The woman who loved him, the man who called her up in France when Mama died. It seemed like we should sit off someplace else, leave the two of them alone with their old love.

"You just tell me what you need," she said. "Anything. I don't teach until September."

Old Finn lifted up his hand, pointed toward us crowded in one chair. "Th- . . . ," he said.

"The?" Justine shook her head.

"Th- . . . ," he tried again.

Nightingale grabbed the clipboard from his pouch, set it on his lap. Then she put the fat pencil in his hand, helped him hold it. I could hardly read the letters, but Nightingale made them out. "T-h-," Nightingale said.

Baby leaned in close to the table. "He means us!" Baby shouted. "*Them*. I can really read it. Them. Old Finn is asking about us!"

50

OUR SHADOW

I wished Baby hadn't shouted, because suddenly the front-desk nurse was there telling Justine sternly Old Finn was ready for a rest. "It's too much for one day," she said over her shoulder as she took Old Finn away. "Come back tomorrow evening. After supper's always best."

"Okay," Justine said. "Certainly, of course." All of us leaned forward like we wanted to go with him. I didn't know when we'd get to see Old Finn again, and here he was wheeled off without our telling him good-bye. We wouldn't be back tomorrow, but maybe Justine would.

"But we came all this way." Baby's voice was close to tears.

"I'm sorry," Justine answered like Old Finn's leaving was her fault. "Why don't you children let me ask a couple questions. Wait down in the lobby and then we'll work things out. I'd like to have a quick word with Mick's nurse."

"Us, too," I said. "We want to hear about Old Finn." I didn't want the information jumbled the way it was when we heard it from Miss Addie or sweetened up the way grown-ups did with kids. I wished the whole world had the constitution of Serenity, so kids and grown-ups could all have equal rights. "We're Old Finn's next of kin."

"Of course you are." Justine smiled sadly. "But for now, let me be the one to ask."

I tried to have the good sense not to argue with Justine, not just now when we still needed money and a grown-up who could help. Instead I led us all down to the lobby, stepped off the crowded elevator, and ran straight into Thor.

Thor dressed in his normal overalls and seed cap, his dirty work boots, the red bandana peeking out of his back pocket. What was he doing at St. Mary's in Duluth? "Kathleen," he said. He gave a nod to Nightingale and Baby.

"Thor?" I couldn't keep the shock out of my voice.

"I saw you kids get on that elevator earlier," he said. "Thought I'd wait to say hello until you rode back down."

"You saw us in *this* lobby?" How long had Thor been here?

"Yep, I did. Not so long ago. With that woman in the hat."

"Oh," I said. A wave of fresh shame burned across my face.

"I've been up there myself," he said. "Paid your grandpa a short visit."

"You did?" I stared down at my feet. Thor knew. He knew that I had lied.

"Is that why she said Old Finn was popular today?" Baby asked. "'Cause you came here from Goodwell?"

"I reckon so." Thor smiled.

T-h-? Had Old Finn been writing *Thor*?

"He can't really talk yet," Baby said. "Or say his ABCs. But all of us will help."

"Shush," Nightingale said to Baby.

"Well, he can't," Baby said. "And he's in a wheelchair."

"That he is," Thor said. "I saw it. Nurse says it's some sort of infection in the brain. Started as a fever."

"Encephalitis," Nightingale said.

"Yep." Thor nodded. "Wish I would have known that there was trouble at your place. That your grandpa was so sick. I could've been a help."

"You were a help," I said. "You drove us to the doctor. Gave us bacon. Tried to give us eggs." Without us ever asking, Thor had helped us more than anybody else. And none of that had hurt.

"I see you found some shoes." Thor grinned at Nightingale's feet. "Put 'em on to come into the city?"

"Yep," Nightingale said. This was the first I'd ever seen her speak to Thor.

"So you get here on the Greyhound?" Thor asked.

"Uh-huh." I could hardly speak. I felt like Thor had been

our shadow all the way from Goodwell or he'd watched us like some god who knew our deepest secrets from the start.

"Quite a cast of characters on Greyhound," he said. "A dog from every town."

"Real army men," Baby said. "Old Finn was in the army. But he didn't like it much."

"That so?" Thor smiled at Baby. "Well, I think I'll drive you back," he said to me. "Save the money on the tickets."

"We already bought both ways," I said, confused. It'd be a crowded ride with four inside his truck. "Our bus leaves at six thirty."

"Naw," Thor said. "I don't want you on that bus."

"Kathleen?" Justine called when the elevator opened. I knew she was surprised to see us talking with a strange man in the lobby of St. Mary's. "Kathleen?" she said again like I had an explanation. I did, but it was difficult to tell. And I still didn't know how Thor had found us here.

"It's Thor," I said. "Thor Jensen."

"Ma'am." Thor nodded. He put his hands into his pocket when he should have shook Justine's. That much manners Mama taught us long ago.

"Thor?" Justine said. "From Goodwell? Don't you own the Junk and Stuff?"

"I do," Thor said.

"I've been to your flea market, several times, Saturdays

in summer, right? Once, I bought a lovely basket there. I still use it to serve bread. I'm sure you don't remember."

"Oh, I remember, ma'am," Thor said. "You were there with Michael." I'd never seen him look so shy.

Justine gave Thor a wide, kind smile. "So *you* drove the children in," she said. My heart stopped. I snuck a glance at Nightingale, but she looked at the floor. "At last, things are finally making sense! I've been slow to get these pieces all together. This day has been disorienting."

"I bet." Thor looked at me. "I got some confusion, too."

"Mick's news was such a shock," Justine continued. "I'm afraid my brain was in a panic. And meeting these sweet children on a day I didn't expect it. There they were right outside my house!" Once Thor told Justine the truth about my lies, she might not think of us as sweet. Me, at least. Nightingale and Baby were easier to love.

"They sure can be surprising." Thor reached for his bandana, wiped his tired face. "It's a shame to see a good man suffer so."

"Yes." Justine blinked exactly like I did to keep from crying. "Mick certainly is suffering."

"But he'll get well!" Baby said again.

"What'd the nurse say?" I asked. Old Finn's getting better mattered more than any trouble up ahead.

"Well, they were optimistic," Justine said. "Cautious, but optimistic."

"What's that mean exactly?" I looked at Nightingale; someday I'd understand as much as her. "Good or bad?" I asked.

"Well." Justine sighed. "It means Mick's making progress. Bit by bit. His brain's already healing."

"So he'll get well?" I said.

"It means that they have hope."

51

IN THE DARK

I was in a hurry for Justine to leave us there with Thor, even if it meant a long truck ride back to Goodwell while I owned up to every lie I told, and going home without an extra penny or Justine as our grown-up when we needed one right now. Anything was better than Thor spilling all my stories in the lobby of St. Mary's, telling Justine I was a liar when I'd only just now met her. If we left now, I could explain it all myself, later in a letter—still the sweet child she imagined, writing her for help.

"Well, okay," I said, "we should get going home."

"You're heading back to Goodwell?" Justine said to Thor.

Thor looked at me. "I'm not certain, yet," he said. "We got to work things out exactly."

"Baby!" someone screamed. "Baby!" We all turned to look; it was Sage in her too-long peasant dress running through the lobby of St. Mary's, heading straight for Baby.

What was Sage doing here? And why was Nash running right behind her?

"Sage!" Baby screamed.

Nightingale's black eyes filled with terror; she grabbed my wrist. Nash was here? With the consent form for Old Finn? He'd come to Duluth just for that magazine. No wonder he said no one liked reporters. I didn't like reporters.

"Oh good lord!" Nash panted when he finally caught up to Sage and Baby. "So the manhunt finally ends?"

"Got the suspects here." Thor gave a little laugh.

What was Nash doing here with Thor? It was Thor who warned me not to make Nash welcome. Now he'd come with Nash and Sage into Duluth? And how'd they ever find us at St. Mary's?

"Manhunt?" Justine asked.

"Or better yet—the kid hunt." Nash bent over at the waist to catch his breath, his shaggy curls fell around his face. His rusty whiskers had thickened to a beard. He looked less like a hippie miles away from Goodwell, but Nash's and Sage's rumpled road clothes still needed a good wash. "I ought to get a Pulitzer for cracking this big story. And a medal for chasing Sage down an entire city block."

"Pulitzer?" Justine said. "What story are you writing?"

"Oh wow!" Nash said. "I'm not sure where to start." A mix of sad and mad and tricked was right there on his face. It was a look I saw on Mama the times I let her down. The times I didn't deserve the special name she gave me. I knew I didn't deserve it now.

"These kids are running quite the operation," Nash said. "Nixon should have had them at the White House. You've got a mastermind and then some."

"Operation?" Justine asked.

"I don't know," Thor muttered. "They're not the likes of Nixon."

"Nixon?" Justine fanned her face. "I wish this all made better sense to me."

"Me, too," Nash said. "Although I have to say, today, it's finally coming clear. But Pride has all the answers. She's the one in charge."

"Me?" I said. I felt like I was backed into a corner, like all the bad I'd ever done was right there at St. Mary's for everyone to see. *Liar.* It's how Justine would think of me forever. Thor, too. Old Finn when he finally learned the truth. I looked over toward the door. I could run, I could outrun Justine and Thor and panting Nash, who was out of breath from Sage, disappear into Duluth. But I could never leave without Nightingale and Baby. Ever. "It started as a story," I tried to say, but all my words just broke. "Lots of stories."

"It isn't only Pride." Nightingale hooked her arm around my waist. For the first time since this morning we were back on the same side. "We're all in charge together. We all just did our best."

A fresh flood of tears washed over my cheeks. Nightingale was standing up beside me; she wasn't going to make me take the blame alone. Even though the lies belonged to me. Nearly every lie from start to finish.

"No," I gulped. "Nightingale warned me."

"Pride's not the only boss," Baby said. "I'm the one who brought the paper. And the compass." He tugged Miss Addie's note out of his pocket. "*Inseffalyntalitis*," he said, waving the paper in the air.

"Oh my." Justine rubbed her hand in circles on my back, a gentle comfort rub I hadn't felt since Mama died. "I can tell I'm really in the dark," she said. "Perhaps we'd all do better if we sat down for a talk. Could we gather at my house? I could fix a bite to eat before you all get on the road. I'd like to take some time to sort things out." She looked at Thor. "Or are you in a hurry to get back home to Goodwell?"

"Don't know." He stared at me.

"Let's eat!" Baby grabbed hold of Sage's hand and starting jumping. "Bread and chocolate!" Baby chanted.

"Bread and chocolate?" Justine asked, confused.

"That sure sounds French to me," Nash said.

"It does." Justine cocked her head. "Did your grandfather teach you children about France?"

"Oh no," I said. "Not really." I covered Baby's blabbermouth before he blurted out another word about the letters. "Baby's just so crazy about bread."

52

ALMOST FAMOUS

Justine said she couldn't *make heads or tails of our complex situation* until we'd had a bite to eat, because she was just too *famished* and *befuddled* to keep a single detail straight. I knew from those big words why Old Finn loved her. While Justine cooked I sat alone on that settee, my heart too heavy with all I had ahead. The lies I had to face, the help I needed for my family.

When we finally gathered at the table, Nightingale had us say a short prayer for Old Finn, one she led, even though we'd never said a single prayer at supper. I got the feeling from their faces that no one else did either, still Baby clenched his eyelids closed, pressed his pudgy hands into a steeple like a prayer. He looked like he'd been praying his whole life.

By the time Justine was ready for our story, it was Nash—not me—who did the talking first. He started with the travel magazine, and his freelance article on the back roads of northern Minnesota and how he'd stumbled on the Stars, the pony rides, and popcorn, like we were sudden boulders he'd tripped over in the road. Sometimes Baby interrupted and added something silly, but mostly I sat quiet, worried most about what was coming next.

The seven of us sat there at the table with Justine on her colorful back porch, with flowerpots in every corner and candles burning in green bottles when we didn't even need the light. I'd never had spaghetti like Justine's. It was white, and rich and creamy—some recipe she learned to cook in France—with ham, and cheese and broccoli, plus little peas and carrots that somehow tasted good.

The more Nash ate, the happier he seemed. He told Justine how he'd never seen a business run entirely by kids, not on a back road or a city, and how charming it first looked to him that morning—the cereal and coffee, the ancient spring horse Baby dragged out of the barn. He said if any traveler were on the search for something special, the Stars' Pony Rides and Popcorn would be the perfect place.

So far Nash had left out all my lies: He didn't mention Mama as a painter or our charity or how we said Old Finn would be home soon when he wasn't.

"It wasn't until I realized they were selling to survive that I started to get worried, started wondering where the grown-ups had gone. You know—what were three kids doing earning money all alone?"

"Alone?" Justine asked.

"Not alone," I interrupted. "We're there with Miss Addie."

"Is that all?" she said. "Miss Addie and you children?"

"I hadn't meant to scare them with the form," Nash went on. "I just had to have it signed. And after that, I was afraid they'd run away. Sage and I drove back to that cabin every couple hours, walked the grounds, pounded on the door, but we never got an answer." He shook his head. "Where did you kids go?"

"We were in Old Finn's closet," Baby said.

"His closet?" Justine and Nash asked at the same time.

"Pride said we had to hide," Baby jabbered. He never should've said the part about the closet; I didn't want Nash to know we were hiding from his knocks. "Shut down the store. In case that lady went to the police."

"The police?" Justine's bright blue eyes grew bigger.

Thor poked at his spaghetti; I could tell Nash had told him most of our story because he sure didn't seem one speck surprised.

"We didn't have a license," Baby said.

"Or insurance," Nightingale added. "In case someone got hurt."

"Hurt how?" Justine took a gulp of water.

"On our pony rides," I said. "One dumb boy said I pulled him off." Our business wasn't secret now except maybe from Old Finn. Old Finn and Miss Addie, but maybe neither one would ever know.

"And this woman." Nash waved his glass of red wine in the air. "She was absolutely horrible to these kids. The kind of tourist you never want to be."

"So you children ran a business?" Justine asked. "All by yourselves? You sold pony rides and popcorn?"

"And souvenirs," I said.

"And Sugar Smacks and coffee," Baby added. "And Pride's cookies."

"Oh yeah," Nash said. "Those cookies. I put those in my story. And Nightingale's crafts. And Baby's painted rocks. The animal tattoos. Pride's God's eyes. All of it was in there."

I thought about our pictures, how I'd imagined people seeing us standing next to Scout. Or petting Woody Guthrie. Baby with his arm around Sage's little shoulder. Our family almost famous somewhere in Chicago. Wishing to be famous made me feel ashamed.

"We'll be in a magazine!" Baby shined Justine his toothless grin. "And everyone will read about the Stars!"

"I don't know." Nash shook his head. He looked at me. "It'd be a different story from the first one that I started. I could write it, but I understand from Thor their grandpa is a very private man. I'd still need his consent to use the pictures."

"Yes." Justine stared at the candle. "A very private man. A man who only wants to be alone. He'd never want to see that story written."

"Never," Nightingale agreed. "And he wouldn't give his permission. Old Finn doesn't trust the world."

"No." Justine sighed like she was sad. She scratched a scab of dried wax from the bottle, broke it into crumbs across her plate. "He certainly does not."

"So there you have it." Nash drank down his final sip of wine. "If someone writes this story, it's not going to be me." He reached over and pulled Sage to his lap.

"Oh no!" Baby moaned. "You mean it isn't going to happen after all?" He slapped his hand against his head. No wonder he was always getting hurt. "We won't be in a magazine?"

"Not on my beat," Nash said. "But someday you just might."

Justine really did serve bread and chocolate for dessert. Hot crusty bread she warmed up in her oven, and a heavy bar of bitter chocolate she broke into little pieces and set out on a plate. She poured the grown-ups tiny china cups of thick black coffee and served the kids pink lemonade in the exact same fancy cups.

Sage and Baby chased in the backyard, but Nightingale and I were too worn out to move. We swayed together on a little canvas bench swing, a *glider*, Justine called it, listening to Nash's story of how he tracked us to Duluth.

"Well, after all that knocking," he said, "I finally went to

Thor and told him the whole tale. Came clean about being a reporter. And we put our heads together, we both had a hunch there was trouble at the house. So he went back there with me early in the morning." Thor's eyes were closed, little snores were sneaking from his lips. He must have been as worn out as us. He wasn't as ancient as Miss Addie, but I knew he was too old to chase three kids to Duluth. "When we couldn't get an answer at the cabin, we walked down to Miss Addie's, and Nightingale's note was right there on the door."

"You wrote that on your note?" I said to Nightingale. "You wrote Miss Addie we went off to Duluth? On the Greyhound bus alone?"

"I did." Nightingale pulled her bare feet up on the swing, wrapped her hands around her little toes, let her braids brush over her arms. Nightingale never budged in her beliefs; I should have known she wouldn't lie to Miss Addie. "I told the truth, Pride. It's what Old Finn would want."

53

LIKE EVERYBODY ELSE

Of course you told the truth." Justine stood and cleared a round of dishes from the table. "You kids are just like Mick. He couldn't tell a lie to save his soul."

Nash glanced at me, but I just looked away.

Nightingale told the truth and now everyone seemed happy. Justine fed us warm bread and French spaghetti in her fancy flowered house, with her fancy fragile dishes, and Nash wasn't going to print our story after all. Or tell Justine my lies. So maybe truth was better, maybe I should have told it all from the beginning that first day at St. John's when Bernice asked where Mama was. Or when Thor wondered why we had to walk for groceries. But if I had, we'd be locked up at some shelter, scared and trapped and brokenhearted the way we were when Mama died, far away from family, forced to follow all the rules, line up every morning for a lice check, and Old Finn would be alone here in Duluth, without a soul to see that he got well. At least Justine could do that now.

"We ought to get back to the cabin," I said. I dragged my feet along the grass to slow the glider to a stop. Even after telling all this truth, Justine still hadn't offered us her help or said she'd give us money or keep us from the shelter or step in as our grown-up when she knew Old Finn was gone. Our bus was leaving at six thirty, Miss Addie and Woody Guthrie would be waiting, and I felt best at Eden on our own. The three of us in charge. Self-reliant. Independent. Justine's fancy French food had given me some strength. Old Finn was right; we couldn't count on someone else to save us. In the end, folks had to save themselves.

Thor lifted up his tired head and looked at Nash. "I don't know," Thor said.

Justine stepped back on the porch and leaned against the doorway. She wrapped a crocheted shawl over her shoulders; it looked like a thing Miss Addie could've made. "Go back to the cabin?" she said. "All alone? Tonight?"

"Old Finn would never want us in a shelter," I said as grown-up as I could. "Even more than he wouldn't want us in that magazine. Never. Ever." I made those last two words sound serious and finished, like there was nothing further to discuss. *End of argument*, the way Mama used to say. "He'd want us out at Eden until he came home well."

"But—" Justine began.

"Our bus leaves at six thirty," I said. "And I still got the tickets in my pocket." We'd worked hard to get those tickets, spent Miss Addie's JFK. I didn't want to waste them by going back in Thor's old truck. And Baby's wagon was outside the Lucky Strike.

"Not that bus," Thor said.

"Oh no," Justine agreed. "You can't go on that bus."

"Folks," Nash said politely. He stood up from the table like he was about to make a speech. "I'm not just a reporter who came upon these three amazing kids and thought I'd found a story, I'm also Sage's father. And as a father, I know a couple things for sure. These kids can't be left at Eden all alone. I can't drive away from Minnesota without knowing someone has stepped in to make this situation right. The proper people should be notified. Regardless of what their grandpa wants. Come September, these kids should be in school. And living in a home with proper supervision. Miss Addie can't do that."

"School?" I looked at Nightingale. Nightingale couldn't go to school in her bare feet and her gowns; she'd be dressed like everybody else, and I'd be sitting in a dull desk every day.

"Notified? You mean call in the county?" Nightingale glared at Nash.

"I don't know about *the county*," Nash said like he was sorry. "But as resourceful as you are, you can't live at that cabin all alone."

"You can't," Thor said. He cleared his throat, put his fist

against his mouth like he was fighting back a cough. "I'm going to keep you children at my place."

"The Junk and Stuff?" I said. I was glad Baby was too busy playing to hear this horrible talk. School and proper people and us living in the run-down Junk & Stuff, right there on the highway with all that traffic rushing by.

"But I can't teach them school," Thor said shyly. "Didn't go beyond eighth grade myself. I'm no genius like their grandpa. But come September, I'll take them with me on the school bus. Drop them off at Goodwell school with everybody else. When their grandpa's back in the saddle, he can do the studies like he wants."

"Well, that's generous," Nash said. It probably was, but somehow it didn't sound generous to me. It sounded like pure torture. "But even so, I think someone should be called. I don't know if a man alone can take someone else's children."

"Yes," Justine said. "That was Mick's great worry. A man alone. He didn't think the courts would ever let him have them. He isn't going to want to lose them now."

"We're fine there with Miss Addie," I insisted. "Nightingale does our studies. She's smart just like Old Finn. We'll call Thor if we run into trouble. The only thing we need . . ." I knew Old Finn wouldn't want me asking anyone for money, for help of any kind, but still we had to have it. "The only thing we really need is food. Not a lot. And maybe someone to help us make sense of the bills. And that license and insurance. Or else we'll stop the pony rides and just sell the souvenirs. And if the teacher from the county comes or those folks from social-something or the sheriff, Thor can be our grown-up so we're not living there alone. And Justine can help Old Finn heal at St. Mary's. And we'll come back on the bus the minute that we can."

"Well, there you have it." Thor laughed like he thought my plan was funny. It wasn't funny; all of it would work. "You got the stubborn Irish. These kids might as well be Michael Finnegan himself."

Justine laughed, too. "I was thinking the same thing. No wonder Mick didn't send you off to school. He's got another generation of freethinkers—three fellow nonconformists—on his hands."

"Nonconformists?" I asked Nightingale.

"Like Thoreau," she said. "Or Old Finn off in Eden. People who won't follow. People who don't live like every-body else."

"Don't or won't," Justine added.

"You kids read Thoreau?" Nash said, amazed.

"Not me," I said. "But Nightingale reads it with Old Finn. So she can teach us school, and we'll stay alone at Eden with Miss Addie, just the way that Old Finn said he wanted when he left us for St. John's."

54

LOVED

I don't think we can be sure he wants that now," Justine said straight to me. "I know he wanted to keep you out of school, raise you by himself." She said that last part sadly like she was just remembering how Old Finn said she couldn't be in our lives. "But all of his ambitions can't quite happen now. Other people have to enter your small world. Perhaps we ought to talk to Mick."

"But I know what he wants," I said. "He wants us independent." I wasn't sure Old Finn could print out a word that big or say it when he couldn't spit out *Justine*.

"Of course," Justine said. "But there's lots of ways of being independent."

I reached into my pocket, felt our tickets; I was ready to take off for that bus.

"How's this?" Justine suggested. She sat down at the table, swept a trace of bread crumbs to the floor, and then rubbed her thumbs together like she had some notion on her mind. "Tomorrow Mick and I will have a conversation. Best as we can, and he can tell me what he thinks. What he believes would be the best. In the meantime, everybody stays here for the night. Nash and Sage, you're welcome if you'd like. I can't very well take Sage away from Baxter. I mean Baby." Justine smiled.

"I don't know," Thor said. I couldn't picture Thor in his faded overalls and seed cap spending the night in Justine's fancy house. He'd have to cover her clean pillow with that red bandana full of sweat.

"But what about Miss Addie?" Nightingale said.

"She has to have her pills," I said. "And Woody Guthrie needs his breakfast." Last night, I'd hosed the trough full of fresh water, but still the horses couldn't be left alone for long.

"You may phone Miss Addie," Justine said. "Remind her of her pills. Let her know you're safe and sound here in Duluth. I'm sure she has some scraps she can feed to Woody Guthrie. Or a can of Lady Jane's food. If my memory serves me right, that dog would eat a tree if he were hungry. He'll make it through one night. And when you're finished speaking, I'd like to speak to her as well."

"Well . . ." Nash laughed. "I admit I could use a shower. And Sage is a good week past a bath." *Clean clothes, too,* I thought, but I didn't say it. "And we'd both love a bed. Plus tonight Nixon's due to announce his resignation. After five long, horrible years of Nixon, I don't want to miss that on TV. If we left now, we'd still be in the van."

"Nixon's resignation!" Justine threw her arms up in the air. "I'd almost forgotten! I hope your grandpa gets to see it; he's wanted Nixon gone from the beginning."

"Maybe we could all go in." Another visit to St. Mary's would give me one more chance to see Old Finn before we left. To tell him that I loved him. "Maybe they'd let us watch it with him at St. Mary's. Henri said we could come back after supper."

"And there's a TV in the lounge," Nightingale said.

"Yes!" Justine clapped her hands. "That's absolutely brilliant! We'll watch it at St. Mary's. You kids," she said with a smile. "You're really something else."

After I got done giving medicine directions to Miss Addie and making sure she'd feed Woody Guthrie her bologna, Justine phoned St. Mary's, got permission to watch the resignation with Old Finn. When seven thirty came, Baby, Nightingale, and I climbed into Justine's Beetle, while Thor and Nash and Sage rode in Thor's old truck. Justine promised Old Finn's nurse we wouldn't stay beyond eight thirty, because the president was speaking at exactly eight o'clock.

It wasn't any easier to see Old Finn slumped sideways in his chair, but this time I was certain I saw a glint of joy in his green eyes. Maybe it was Nixon's resignation or Justine snuggled close beside him or Nightingale holding on to his hand or Baby's arms wrapped around his neck or Thor's hand on his shoulder, but Old Finn definitely looked happy we were here. All of us together. Even Nash and Sage, who sat off to the side.

I turned up the TV, sat down on the floor at Old Finn's feet, laid my head against his leg the way I sometimes did at home when he was reading *Treasure Island* and Woody Guthrie's head was in my lap. Only here his cotton patient pants smelled like chlorine bleach—I'd be glad when Old Finn smelled like wood again.

"Is that Nixon?" Baby blurted just as the show got started. Old Finn gave a nod, reached up, and patted Baby's hand.

"Good evening," Nixon started. I stared at the TV. He didn't look like a liar or a criminal or someone who ought to be in prison, like Old Finn had insisted. He looked just like a man. "This is the thirty-seventh time I've spoken to you from this office . . . ," he said. Thirty-seven times and I'd only heard him once? Then he talked about decisions and the nation and public life, but the first I understood was when he said, "I have always tried to do what was best for the nation," because it made me think about the lies I'd told to try to help my family. I'd say the same: I tried to do the best.

While we all sat there watching, other people wandered into the lounge. Workers from the hospital in uniforms and late visitors who'd just left patients' rooms. People gathered, but no one said a word. Everyone just listened. Bernice was right, this moment was historic, if that meant everything came to a sudden stop.

"I have never been a quitter," Nixon said, and part of me felt sorry that he had to give up now, even if he was a liar and a cheat. Maybe because I didn't want to quit myself. Not tonight or ever. And it seemed sad to have so many people hate you, to say bad things about you, and then to have to face them on TV. But maybe being on TV was easier than sitting in a room with the people you had lied to, knowing all the secrets and mistakes you kept hidden in your heart. Maybe it was easier than facing Thor and Nash. Or fearing what Justine would think if she knew I'd read her letters. Or how Old Finn would feel if he found out I took them from his drawer. Or let those strangers come to Eden. Or nearly ruined our family privacy in some travel magazine.

I couldn't follow most of Nixon's resignation, and I'm sure Baby barely understood a word he said. Maybe Nightingale cared about Congress, China and the Middle East, and Roosevelt, who said something about dust and sweat and blood, but I sure didn't. I only cared that I was right there with my family, that Old Finn's infection was optimistic, which meant they were hoping for the good, and that tomorrow he'd tell Justine to send us home to Eden. He'd write it on his clipboard, or slowly get the words out of his mouth. *E-d-*, he'd write, and that would be enough.

I was so busy thinking of our future, I didn't know Nixon's speech was done until a couple people started clapping, and one or two gave a little cheer. But some folks stood there silent like they weren't glad to have him gone. Finally, a young nun in the corner stepped forward, put her palms together in a prayer just the way that Baby had at supper, closed her eyes, and whispered, "May God forgive us all. Not only Richard Nixon."

And Old Finn moaned, "Amen."

Then I felt Old Finn's hand rest against my head, the way he sometimes did when he was reading or how he had that first time he came to see us at the shelter. The time he put his hands down on my head and said I might as well be Mama. Mama at my age. I remembered how he promised us he'd take us back to Eden, raise us as his own, keep us as a family the way that we belonged.

I reached up and laid my hand down over his. It was just as thick from hard work as it was before the fever. I didn't turn out to be half as good as Mama or as truthful as Old Finn, but I wasn't quite as bad as Richard Nixon either.

"I love you, Old Finn," I said and gave his hand a squeeze.

"You," he said, and I knew what he was saying. With just one word, Old Finn was trying to tell me I was loved.

55

THE ONE TO WATCH
YOU NOW

When I woke up the next morning, Justine was already at St. Mary's, Sage and Baby were outside running wild, Nash sat on the front porch with the paper, and Thor was in the kitchen, drinking coffee. Nightingale was curled up on the couch with some big book about Van Gogh.

"What's that?" I asked, but I wasn't really interested. I'd already seen his *Starry Night*. I hoped she wasn't going to want to talk about impressions now.

"Hey, Pride," Nash called in through the screen door. I walked out to the porch. All of Justine's street was pretty houses and nice gardens, square green lawns, dogs tied up on chains. Fancy as it was, I couldn't imagine living in Duluth, not without the woods or a place to sit and think or a pasture for Atticus and Scout, free land for Woody Guthrie, a trailer for Miss Addie. I hoped Justine wouldn't ask to keep us here; I couldn't bear to be cooped up like this for long.

Nash moved over on the swing, folded the paper closed, and set it on his lap. His shining face was shaved, his hair washed, his skin smelled clean like aftershave and soap. "I just want to say," he said. "All the *stories* that you told me. I understand." A lump rose in my throat. What he really meant was *lies*. "And I know that Thor does, too. And it doesn't mean you're not just like your grandpa, because without knowing the man, I can tell you that you are. Kids don't grow up to have your courage without someone strong to show them how it's done."

"Mama helped us, too," I said. "And Daddy." I blinked to keep the tears out of my eyes. It would have been easier if he'd said I was like Richard Nixon.

"And Nightingale and Baby, they're lucky they got you in the lead. They never would have made it this far without you."

"Thanks," I said. I wiped a quick tear from my cheek.

"If I could write that in a story, I definitely would. But your story's better than some travel magazine. It's pretty darn heroic—and you don't read those much."

"It is?" I said. I didn't feel heroic. Just worn out and old. Older than I felt the day Old Finn went in with the fever. Older than a girl just turned thirteen. Maybe St. John's would take me as a candy striper early.

"It is." He smiled. "But you're too good to see it. All you children are."

• • •

When Nash's van was finally packed to leave, we all walked them to the street to say good-bye. "Thank Justine for me," Nash said. She was still gone at St. Mary's talking to Old Finn. "And I hope you let her help you in all the ways she can. Thor, too."

"I will," I said, as long as it didn't mean staying in Duluth.

"I've got her address. Let her know I'll keep in touch."

"Old Finn gets his mail right in Goodwell," Baby said. "At the post office. Keep in touch with us. Send a postcard from Chicago!" Baby loved to look at postcards. "Or a letter on that fancy paper like Justine?"

I cupped my hand over Baby's mouth. I didn't want anyone to know about the letters. Not now. Maybe someday when I was ready for more truth.

"Hey!" Baby yanked my hand away. He ran up and gave Sage one last good-bye hug. Her mop of red curls covered Baby's face. Maybe someday they'd be like Old Finn and Justine—writing love letters from Goodwell to Chicago. "Can you come back tomorrow?" Baby asked.

"Not tomorrow." Nash laughed. "Sage's mother isn't going to part with her too soon. But we'll definitely be back." He reached out and shook Thor's hand. "Thanks for the place to crash," he said. "And helping with the kid hunt. And trusting a reporter when no one does these days."

"You're not so bad," Thor said. "But you could use a haircut."

Nash tossed the long bangs back from his forehead. "Will do," he said.

"Okay." Thor winked. "Take good care of that little girl."

"And you take care of the Stars," Nash said. "Although they're not so little."

"No," I said. "Not little. And we take care of ourselves."

"And you." Nash turned to Nightingale. She was standing back, her arms across her chest, watching from the steps with her dark eyes. "I have a hunch you still don't like me much." Nash shook his head. "Just so you know, I'm not going to write the story of the Stars."

"Or call the county?" Nightingale asked. "Or tell the proper people the way you said last night?"

"Not now." Nash made a cross over his chest to show it was a promise. He opened up the van door, buckled Sage into her seat. "I feel confident you kids are in good hands. Justine has assured me you won't be left alone."

"Okay then." Nightingale held tight to her black braids. "I guess I like you fine."

The wait seemed long until Justine drove up from St. Mary's. All of us were on the front steps waiting, even Thor.

"Well?" I said, before she'd stepped into the yard. "What did Old Finn say about the cabin? Can we go back today?"

Justine took off her hat and fanned her pretty face. "Maybe Mick was right when he said I couldn't keep up with you kids. You move faster than I've moved in fifty years."

"Did he say we could go back to Eden? Because Woody Guthrie needs his breakfast. And Miss Addie's all alone." Last night when we'd called her on the phone, I could tell she felt too worried without us. Miss Addie always worried. "And we still have our souvenirs to sell. Plus, Thor's right here to take us in his truck." I left out the part about our lessons because I wasn't in a hurry to get back home to those.

"Yes," Justine finally said. "I am certain he wants you back at Eden. So although Thor generously offered to take you to his home, I will be the one to watch you now."

"You?" Baby said. "You'll come and live at Eden?"

"For now," Justine said. "If you think that would be all right."

"But it isn't very fancy," Baby warned. "We don't have all your paintings. And Old Finn doesn't grow flowers. Just tomatoes and zucchini and carrots and potatoes, but they're not pretty like your plants."

"I've been out to Eden," Justine said.

"Oh yeah," Baby said, but I pinched his arm before he started on the letters.

"It has its charm." Justine smiled. "Rustic charm. Not unlike Old Finn." She laughed a little giggle. It was the first I'd heard her say Old Finn. "And best of all," she said, "it has you lively children. So if you'll accept me as your guardian, however temporarily, until Old Finn comes home, which may be in just weeks—"

"Just weeks!" I shrieked before Justine could finish. "You mean he'll be well in just weeks?"

"Better," Justine said. "At least that's the doctor's hope. Of course he'll still need therapy, but he can do some of that in Goodwell, once he's steady on his feet, able to communicate a little more."

"I can help him then," I said. If Old Finn could walk and talk, I could see him through the rest. The ABCs and counting. Telling time like Henri said. I could even teach him how to close his mouth, tuck his tongue inside. "I'm going to get a job candy striping at St. John's, so I'll know all the things to make him well." Maybe someday I could be like Henri, tend to patients, help them with their slippers, wheel them to Speech. Old Finn would be my first.

"That's excellent," Justine said. "And apparently some brains can heal quickly. Old Finn's brain is amazing, so let's hope for the best."

"Well, sure," Thor said. "I've never seen a brain better than his. Heart either, for that matter."

"That's true," I said.

"Yes," Justine agreed. "And both have served him well."

56

A HOPE THAT
SOMEONE HEARD

Justine stayed behind to pack her things, to put her house in order, to hire the next-door neighbor to babysit her plants. I couldn't believe you'd need a sitter just for flowers, but that's how fancy Justine's garden was. She said she'd see us all at Eden by tonight.

When Thor drove us into Goodwell, it seemed like weeks had passed since Bernice had dropped us at the Need-More and said it was a day we wouldn't forget. Baby's wagon sat against the Lucky Strike, just the place I left it, but Thor wouldn't let me put it in the truck. He made me sit inside while he stepped out to do it. "Don't need to do every last thing for yourself, Kathleen," he said. "You learn to take some help."

Through the front window of the Lucky Strike, I could see the owner sitting at the counter, the same gruff man who'd sold me our tickets to Duluth. "Wait!" I said, when Thor got back into the truck. "Could you borrow me fifty cents?" I knew Old Finn wouldn't want me asking Thor for money, but I needed it right now. We were down to two thin dimes I just couldn't spend. "I'll earn it back this week."

"Lend," Nightingale corrected. Lend or borrow, I could never keep those two words straight. "You going bowling, Pride?"

"Lend," I said to Thor.

"Lend or borrow." Thor smiled. "It's all the same to me." He reached into his pocket, pulled out a fist of change. "Here," he said. "Take how much you need."

I jumped out of the truck, went up to the counter the way I'd done the day before. The owner was still on his tall stool, still smoking a stinky, fat cigar. A stack of bowling shoes sat waiting to be polished. He rubbed his rag in circles over one.

"New day." He gave a nod toward the TV. "New president," he said. "Let's hope this one is honest."

"Yep," I said. "Honest would be good." I stepped closer to the register, wished hard Miss Addie's JFK was still inside. "Yesterday," I said with my best manners, "I paid a fifty-cent piece for our tickets. And I said it was a keepsake."

"I recall." He chewed at his cigar. "A JFK."

"That's it!" I said. "I've got the money here to buy it."

"Buy it!" His great big laugh sounded like a roar. "You can't buy your money back, girl."

"But it's a keepsake for Miss Addie. She's had it all these

years. And she borrowed it to me to buy us groceries. But I bought bus tickets instead."

He gave a little snort. "Spending someone else's money for a bus ride?"

"I know," I said, ashamed. It felt good to practice with the truth, even if I told it to a stranger. "I know that it was wrong." I laid Thor's change down on the counter and counted fifty cents. "So could I buy it back? Is it still there in your register?"

"Nope," he said. "Money changes hands."

"It's gone?" My shoulders sank, my heart felt heavy as a wood stack. I never should have given him Miss Addie's JFK.

He reached under the counter, pulled out a battered old cigar box, the kind Baby used to store his postcards and his rocks. "It's right here in my collection. You're lucky I save coins."

"I am," I said, relieved. "Really, really lucky." He plucked it from the box and handed it to me. Then he pushed Thor's change in my direction. "You keep your money, sweetie. I'm just glad to help Miss Addie out."

"You know Miss Addie?" I didn't think anyone in Goodwell knew Miss Addie. Just like hardly anyone knew Old Finn or us.

"Sure don't." He picked up his greasy rag. "But I know enough to see how much she's loved."

• • •

When we reached our signs out on the highway, Thor pulled over to the shoulder and parked his rusted truck. PONY RIDES AND POPCORN!!! with arrows up toward Eden.

"So," he said. "You want to take those down?"

I looked out at Nightingale's painting, her happy colored letters she'd worked so hard to make. The picket stakes I'd hammered by myself. Our business was just started; we still had our souvenirs to sell. And we could still make money on the coffee, the cookies in the jar. We wouldn't need insurance to sell that.

I turned to Nightingale and Baby. "You want to end the business?" Old Finn wasn't home to tell us no, and Justine wouldn't be here until tonight. We still had a few good hours to get tourists.

"No," Nightingale said, "we still need the money."

"I have pennies," Baby said.

Nightingale smiled. "You do, but that won't be enough."

"I don't like it," Thor said. "Strangers at your place. Your grandpa wouldn't want it. You ought to wait until Justine arrives."

"Okay," I said. He was right about Old Finn, but Old Finn wasn't here. "We'll ask Justine tonight." We might or we might not, but Thor didn't need to know about that now. "Right now we'll keep our signs up until Justine tells us no."

"I hope that woman's got some strength." Thor laughed. "She'll need it with you kids."

• • •

First thing I did when Thor dropped us off at Eden was get Woody Guthrie a double dose of breakfast and pour fresh water in his dish. Inside the cabin everything was just the way we left it: our souvenirs stacked up in the basket; Baby's bow and arrow; Justine's letters on the table; Nightingale's gown in a heap on Old Finn's floor. I wondered if she'd wear them with Justine or if she'd feel funny in a night-gown with a stranger in our house. But Justine wasn't quite a stranger now. I looked out the kitchen window—Atticus and Scout stood grazing in the pasture, Nightingale and Baby were already racing down the wood path to Miss Addie's. I wished I had two JFKs to give her, but for today, one would have to do.

I went into Old Finn's room, sat down on his bed, and pressed his pillow to my stomach. *Please, God, make Old Finn well*, I said inside myself. I said it once, not twenty-four more times the way Nightingale wanted, but for the first time in a long time I had a hope that someone heard. There was good out in the world—like Nash and Thor and kind Justine, Henri and Bernice, and help that wouldn't hurt—maybe all that good was somehow God. *Make him well completely*, I added, because most of all I wanted Old Finn back the way he was. Strong and smart. Carving stat-ues. Giving Baby his good-night ride around the yard. Teaching us our lessons, using his big words—not strug-gling to get through *Justine* and *the*. I'd even sit still for

Beethoven or those horrible Shakespeare sonnets that didn't make an ounce of sense. *I will*, I promised God. *Just so it's not too boring.*

Then I got up from the bed, stepped outside to see the sun. Old Finn's garden was a snarl; I had to weed, make sure that it got watered. I didn't want the vegetables all shriveled before Old Finn got home. Just weeks, Justine had said. And later, by October, Old Finn's pumpkins might be ready for a pie. And all of us would be here for Thanksgiving. Maybe even Thor. I'd cook us all a turkey packed with sausage stuffing, the way Old Finn had tried to teach me just last year. I could do it by myself, with Old Finn at the table passing on his secret recipes.

"Come on," I called to Woody Guthrie. He trotted up beside me, then the two of us set off down the wood path to Miss Addie, to sit there in her trailer, just the way Old Finn had ordered the day that he left us for St. John's.

Only this time we wouldn't cut photographs from movie magazines or wait there full of worry or wonder how much longer. This time we'd know for certain, that Old Finn was coming home.

ACKNOWLEDGMENTS

Thank you to all who helped to bring this book into the world: my husband, Tim Frederick, who read from the beginning; my children, Mikaela and Dylan, who saw it to the finish; my agent, Rosemary Stimola, who made it possible; the Sisters of Clare's Well, whose sanctuary gave this book a home; Sister Paula for her nursing expertise; Lynn and Frank James for twice lending me their paradise; the Bush Foundation for the gift of time and the beautiful little dream shed; Hamline University for allowing me to disappear for several months; my colleagues and students who share the writers' journey; Malmo Art Colony for quiet; Callie Cardamon for reading; Willie Wilcox and Kate Shuknecht, who helped me with the horses; Lenore Millibergity for answering endless legal questions; and as always Martin Case for everything from punctuation to politics—I could not write without you. Thank you to the good people at G. P. Putnam's Sons, especially my amazing editor, Stacey Barney. I will forever love you, Stacey Barney. Eternal gratitude to all my stars—past and present—your love sustains me.

TURN THE PAGE FOR A SAMPLE OF
SHEILA O'CONNOR'S AWARD-WINNING
SPARROW ROAD

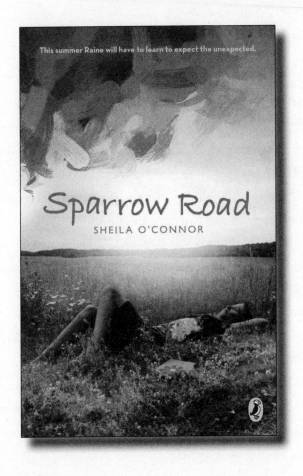

In the shadowed glow of headlights the old pink house looked huge, rambling like the mansions on Lake Michigan. A fairy-tale tower rose high above the roof. The pillared front porch sagged.

"However humble," Viktor said. He steered his truck to a slow stop. "I give you Sparrow Road."

"*You* own this place?" I gasped. Viktor's rusted truck reeked of mud and grease; his sunken face was covered in white whiskers. He looked too poor to own a country mansion, even one as worn as this was.

"Raine!" Mama jabbed her elbow in my ribs. "Viktor owns the whole estate."

"The main house," Viktor said as if he hadn't heard me, "is where the artists sleep. Your cottage is a short walk through the meadow." It was the most I'd heard him say since he met us at our train.

"Well, it's nothing like Milwaukee, that's for sure." Mama gave me a weak smile.

Just hearing Mama say *Milwaukee* made me miss it more. Already our apartment seemed another world away, a place where Grandpa Mac waited, lonesome with us gone. I thought of Grandpa Mac standing sad-eyed at the station, the secret fifty-dollar bill he stashed in my back pocket. *In case of an emergency,* he warned, like he knew one was ahead.

"I would assume"—Viktor cleared his throat as if those few words wore him out—"the four artists are asleep at this late hour." Only one small curtained window was lit up in the house. He opened up his truck door. "I shall get your bags."

"I don't want to stay," I said the second Viktor left us in the truck. Sparrow Road looked haunted-mansion creepy, the same way Viktor Berglund looked when I saw him at the train. A man so thin he looked more skeleton than human; a man with ice blue eyes and a face as cold as stone.

Mama touched my cheek. "Sweetheart, we can't leave."

"Grandpa Mac said he'd come to get me. Day or night. All I have to do is call. We can go back to the station, wait there for a train." I still had the good-bye apple muffins Grandpa baked us in my backpack. A bag of wilted grapes. Grandpa's fifty-dollar bill.

"We can't," Mama said. "And Grandpa Mac is far away. For the first time in a long time, it's only you and me." She wove her sweaty fingers between mine.

Your mother's done some crazy things, but this? Suddenly Grandpa Mac's worries were moving into mine.

"But you don't even like to clean," I said. Grandpa Mac always joked that Mama's middle name was Mess. Now I'd lose what was left of my good summer so Mama could cook and keep house for some artists in the country.

"Raine," Mama said. "We've been over this already. A hundred times at least."

We had. Still, none of Mama's reasons for this job made an ounce of sense to me. "But Sparrow Road?" I said. "You had a job back in Milwaukee."

"Sweetheart," Mama said. She opened up the truck door. "This is going to take some brave from both of us."

It took more than brave for me to follow brooding Viktor across the dew-soaked meadow. It took Mama's hand clenched around my elbow and a night so black I was too afraid to stay in Viktor's truck all by myself.

"The bats," Viktor warned. "Don't be startled by the swoops."

I pressed in close to Mama. A symphony of insects rattled in the grass. "Are there snakes?" I asked.

"Raine's used to the city," Mama said to Viktor.

Even the country air smelled strange. A mix of fresh-cut grass and lilacs, rotten apples, raspberries, and pine. Maybe fish, like a lake might be nearby.

"And to think," Mama said like she hoped to get some happy conversation started. "Just three days ago, I was serving lunch to crabby customers at Christos."

"Three days ago," I added, "I was stacking shelves at Grandpa's store." All the Popsicles and candy I could eat. Our portable TV tucked behind the counter. Brewers' games on Grandpa Mac's transistor. Chess with Grandpa's best friend, Mr. Sheehan, when the afternoons got long. The summer job I loved, and Mama made me leave it.

"Oh, Raine." Mama faked a cheery laugh. "You spend every summer in that store. Besides, we'll only be here a few weeks."

"Eight," I moaned. "If you make us stay until September."

Mama gave my arm a sharp, be-quiet squeeze. "Raine's tired," Mama said, like I was six instead of twelve. "Ten hours on a train. That long ride from the station. She needs to get some sleep."

Sleep. I wasn't going to sleep a wink at Sparrow Road. Grandpa Mac always said he couldn't get to sleep without the song of sirens, the noise of neighbors humming through our walls, the roar of city traffic on the street. It would be the same for me.

"Tomorrow," Viktor said, "I shall take you on a tour. Tomorrow is a Sunday. On Sundays we may speak."

"Speak?" I said.

4

"As I explained," he said to Mama, "every day is silent until supper. Every day but Sunday."

"What?" I said. "Silent until supper?"

"I assumed she knew the rules," Viktor said like his mouth was dry with dust.

"She does," Mama lied. She tried to nudge me forward, but I wouldn't take another step. A thick swarm of mosquitoes feasted on my skin. Tomorrow I'd be covered in red welts.

"I don't." I slapped down at my leg. "Mama never mentioned any rules."

"Just a few," Mama said. No one hated rules more than Mama. "Like there won't be any newspapers."

"Is that it?" I asked. No newspapers was nothing like silence until supper.

"Or television," Viktor said to Mama. "Or radio. Or music. Not at any time."

"What?" I said. "No TV until September? No radio? And we can't even talk?"

"Molly," Viktor said. "If it's a problem for the child?"

"It is," I answered.

"Raine's not a child," Mama said. "She'll make it through just fine."

"The artists," Viktor said, "they require quiet. They only have the summer for their work. As it is, it's already July."

I wasn't going to talk to any artists. The second I saw daylight I was calling Grandpa Mac. Collect. Just the way he taught me.

"Of course," Mama agreed. "We won't disturb the artists. We'll have enough to keep us busy, as you know."

"Let us hope," Viktor said.

"As for the rules," Mama added quickly, "we completely understand."

"I don't," I said again. "I don't understand at all."

Our cottage was a tiny Snow White house where a gardener used to sleep. Inside it smelled like dust balls and old clothes;—abandoned, like no one had lived in it for years. There was a sunken couch, a painted wooden rocker, and a little purple table just for two.

"Well, it's cute," Mama said when Viktor left.

"Cute?" The walls were butter yellow, the white lace curtains grayed. "Maybe in a rundown dollhouse kind of way." I rolled my eyes at Mama. I didn't care about the cottage. "No TV? Silence until supper? All those stupid rules you didn't tell me?"

"I was going to," Mama said. "Just not on our first day." She wiped her palm across the dusty table. "Don't worry, Raine, we'll make it our own place."

The only place I wanted was Milwaukee. I lugged my suitcase up the narrow staircase to the tiny slanted bedroom where Viktor told us we would sleep. Heat pressed down from the ceiling; a hint of breeze blew through the open window.

7

"How is it?" Mama asked, but I didn't answer.

It was daisy wallpaper peeled away in patches, two sagging beds, a broken mirror nailed to the wall. I flopped down on the musty mattress, hugged a flimsy pillow to my chest. At home, Beauty would be purring on my bed. Grandpa Mac would be watching some old western on TV.

"Love you to the moon and back," I whispered to Grandpa Mac. It's what I always said before I went to bed. A single tear trickled down my cheek. *Love you to the stars,* he said to me. *Good night, sweet girl. I'll see you in my dreams.*

The strange thing is, I slept. Long and deep, the way I sometimes did with fevers. When I woke up the next morning the spicy smell of coffee filled the cottage and Mama's bed was made.

"Mama?" I called. She never made her bed.

"Down here, sleepyhead," Mama almost sang. "Come see, Raine. I've been cleaning up our cottage. And everything looks better with the sun."

Downstairs, Mama sat at the little purple table—her long red curls still wet from washing, her denim overalls rolled up to her knees. The smell of dust had already disappeared. Warm white light poured through the open windows. "Getting ready for our week." Mama patted a stack of yellowed cookbooks. "I found these in the cupboard. The birds wouldn't let me sleep."

I slumped down in the chair and wiped the sleep out of my eyes. "I need a phone," I said. "This morning."

"There's no phone, Raine. I'm sorry." But sorry wasn't in her voice.

"No phone?" I looked around the cottage. "No phones at Sparrow Road?"

Mama shook her head. "The artists come to Sparrow Road to get away."

"Right. No talking. No TV." I dropped my head into my hands. Six days a week of silence, now I couldn't even find a phone. "But what about emergencies? A fire? Someone could get hurt." I was two when Grandpa Mac taught me how to phone for help.

"In an emergency," Mama said, "I'm sure a call can be arranged."

"Okay," I said. "It's an emergency today."

Mama stared into my eyes. "This isn't an emergency. It's change. I know that you're unhappy, but we'll get used to it. We will."

"But why?"

Mama turned the pages of her cookbook like an answer would be there. "I told you, Raine, I came to do a job."

"You had a job at Christos."

"Another job," Mama said. "A job that wasn't in Milwaukee. And I'll have my Christos job when we go home." She slapped the cookbook shut. "Raine," she sighed, "not everything's a mystery." It's what she always said when she

9

was tired of my questions or when she held a secret she wasn't going to tell.

"I know," I said. "Not everything. But this?" Our move to Sparrow Road was a mystery to me.

"But hey!" Suddenly she jumped up and an unexpected smile lit up her worried face. "If you're looking for a mystery, I've got a real one you can solve." She grabbed my wrist and pulled me toward the counter. "Look!" she cried. "Like Easter!"

Underneath a drape of emerald velvet was a lilac wicker basket filled with water-colored eggs, a jelly jar of flowers, warm banana bread, and two small tangerines. On a torn scrap of paper WELCOME had been glued in golden glitter. "I found it here this morning, at our door."

"Weird," I said. "Viktor didn't make this."

"No," Mama said. "I don't think so either." I heard a hint of wonder in her voice. Like maybe something was a mystery to her. "And this?" Mama handed me a linen napkin, white, with the towered house embroidered in the center and my initials *R.O.* stitched into the corner. "There's a second one for me," Mama said.

"So someone knows our names," I said. "Someone besides Viktor."

"Yes," Mama said. "Someone who must be happy that we're here."

Mama was right. Sparrow Road looked different in the sunlight. Outside, miles of rolling hills formed a patchwork quilt of green, wildflowers swayed graceful in the meadow, and the sky seemed to stretch forever in a perfect, deep blue sea. It was a pretty place I might have loved with Grandpa Mac and Mama. A vacation place without Viktor and his rules, and all the silent days I had ahead.

When Viktor came to take us on the tour, I let Mama walk beside him. I was happiest a few steps back, away from Viktor's stony quiet, his icy eyes, his sunken face covered in white whiskers. Plus there was something I was watching—the friendly way they talked, the way Mama seemed too sweet, too comfortable with a man as cold as Viktor. Too at home, like she and Viktor knew each other before he met us at the train.

He led us down a steep path to a lake. "Sorrow Lake," he wheezed when we'd made it to the shore. "But here, I need a rest." He sat down in the shade while Mama and I left him for the dock.

"Sorrow Lake?" I said to Mama, when I was sure Viktor was too far away to eavesdrop. "Isn't that a strange name? And how can Viktor own a lake? No one owns Lake Michigan."

Mama shook her head. "So many questions, Raine."

"Did you know Viktor before he got us at the train?"

"Know him?" Mama closed her eyes, tilted her face up toward the sun. "Viktor hired me. It's how I got the job."

"But did you know him in Milwaukee? Or some time before now?"

Mama opened up one eye and gave me a mean squint.

"You just seem to know him, like he might be your friend."

"Viktor is my boss." Too many questions got on Mama's nerves. "I'm here to work for him."

I slipped off my flip-flops and dipped my toes into the lake. A school of minnows skittered near the surface. "So can we swim after the tour?" I wanted something happy up ahead, something besides Viktor's boring tour and Mama planning out her menu for the week.

"We'll see." A flush of red washed over Mama's face. Already, her pale Irish skin burned a little pink. I didn't have Mama's coloring or beauty. I was dark-eyed, dark-skinned, with straight black hair, and skinny, where Mama was all curves. "This afternoon," Mama said, "I need to go with Viktor into Comfort."

"Comfort?"

"It's a town not far away. It's where I'll buy the groceries."

"You? You mean you're going without me?"

Mama kept her eyes closed. "Viktor's truck," she said. "There isn't really room for three."

"There were three of us last night." We were crowded knee to knee, but we still fit.

"Another time. Today you'll have to stay here by yourself."

"Alone? At Sparrow Road? Mama, there's nothing here for miles except for hills!"

"The artists," Mama said, although we hadn't seen them. "Surely one of them would be near if some emergency occurred." Sparrow Road had cast some kind of crazy spell on Mama. At home Mama worried when I walked six blocks to the library. Mama always acted like I'd be snatched off of some street. Grandpa Mac did, too. Now she was going to leave me in the country by myself?

"I want to go with you. There's room for me in Viktor's truck."

"No." Mama stood, then offered me a hand. "I'm afraid today I'll need to go with Viktor."

By the time we finally made it to the main house, I was too mad at Mama to listen to Viktor's dull descriptions. Instead I kept my eyes out for an artist, someone who'd be nearby at least while Mama was in town.

"Well, it certainly is spotless," Mama said the minute we stepped inside the house. I could tell she was relieved.

It was almost spooky clean, like a house where no one lived. The dark woodwork was all polished, floors and ceiling beams and benches. Crystal chandeliers sparkled in the sun. It smelled like Holy Trinity, our church back in Milwaukee—hot candle wax and lemon polish, a trace of sweet perfume. A wide, grand wooden staircase curved up from the front room.

Viktor cleared his throat. "The artists keep it tidy." He raised his lanky arm and pointed down a hallway. "Our poet, Lillian Hobbs, has the room off of the library."

"A poet?" Mama said, surprised. "How nice. Raine writes."

"I wrote," I said. "In fourth grade." Back when my teacher, Sister Cyril, told me to put my imagination to good use. But I didn't want Mama to tell my past to Viktor. Not a word.

"Our other summer artists—Josie, Eleanor, Diego— all reside upstairs. And each one has a shed where they create. Although Lillian and Eleanor often work here in their rooms." He'd already pointed out the little sheds as we'd walked across the meadow. Two in the tall grass. Two tucked back in the woods. "Of course the artists' sheds, their rooms, all those spaces are totally off-limits. Always. Like the silence until supper; that rule must be honored. The artists came for quiet. They must be left alone."

Viktor made it sound like every rule was for me, like there was no place for a kid at Sparrow Road.

"We understand," Mama said. I could tell she wanted to get Viktor off the rules.

"And here"—Viktor led us to a gleaming tiled kitchen where copper pots hung from silver hooks—"is where you shall prepare the evening meals. As you wished."

"You *wished* to make the meals?" I asked Mama, but Mama just ignored me.

"Every day but Sunday," Viktor said. "On Sundays you are free."

The smell of peanut butter and warm toast lingered in the kitchen. Maple syrup that reminded me of home. Earlier, an artist must have eaten breakfast. I wondered where they were this morning, what they looked like, if one of them would be here when Mama went to town. Close enough to help if something happened?

And which one left that basket at our door?